Rain Dance

Rain Mystery Trilogy Book 2

David Homick

Rain Dance

Copyright © 2017 David Homick

All rights reserved

Published by Blue Knight Media

This book or any portion thereof may not be reproduced or used in any manner whatsoever without the express written permission of the publisher or author except for the use of brief quotations in a book review. Please purchase only authorized electronic editions, and do not participate in or encourage electronic piracy of copyrighted materials. Your support of the author's rights is appreciated.

The characters, incidents, and dialogs in this book are fictional and are not to be construed as real. Any resemblance to actual events or persons, living or dead, is completely coincidental.

"If you think it's going to rain, it will."
Clint Eastwood

CHAPTER ONE

My peace had always been the harbinger of a coming storm. I awoke this morning with an uneasy feeling for the first time in over a month and recognized the pattern. I told myself this time would be different, but something inside disagreed.

The snow-covered mountains in the distance were a bigger-than-life reminder that I was no longer in Texas, but the memories remained. I'm stronger now and able to keep them at bay most of the time. I believe I put enough distance in my rearview mirror when I left a month ago with Jenny Lee Myles, the woman who may have saved me from myself.

The contentment that I'd felt for the past month was not unfamiliar; however, previous encounters had been fleeting. Like two prizefighters, pleasure and pain took turns trading punches. For most of my twenty-eight years, I'd been on the ropes, taking many more punches than I could throw. Time to stop feeling sorry for myself and wasting opportunities. Time to grow up.

It had been quite a shock to find the boy here when I arrived. It bothered me that I still referred to him as *the boy*. He called me GI Joe when I rescued him from a bombed-out village in Afghanistan. Our Humvee took a hit from an RPG before I learned his name. The boy still had no name when I returned stateside and saw him in my dreams. I know him now as Alex.

Something up on the ridge interrupted my reverie. I caught a fleeting glimpse of a dark form moving quickly through the woods. I squinted my eyes against the sun to get a better look, but it was gone. My PTSD symptoms had been in check for more than a month. Too benign to be a flashback or residual battlefield memory, I wrote it off as my mind playing tricks. Then, I saw it again.

A chill traveled the length of my spine, even as I quickly dismissed the notion that I'd been witness to one of the mythical creatures that I'd read about as a child. The figure I'd just seen was too small and graceful. It darted through the trees like a deer or other nimble-footed animal, but its shape was unmistakably human. The chill returned when I realized that the odds of seeing a person in these woods were nearly as great as seeing a Sasquatch or Yeti.

I sat in the shadow of Pikes Peak, on the northern edge of a parcel known as the Red Valley Ranch. We moved here from Bradley, Texas, three weeks ago to live on the ranch with Jenn. By we, I mean me and Mama, but that's a long story. Jenn and her cousin Seth inherited the ranch when their Uncle Roy passed away six months ago.

Red Valley is a 640-acre horse ranch in eastern Teller County, approximately three miles from Redfield, Colorado. Jenn hopes to carry on the tradition of raising horses, many of them rescued from abuse, neglect, or abandonment. Much like these rescues, I'd also been given a second chance.

I took a few deep breaths. An unknown intruder had violated my Fortress of Solitude, and I struggled to return to the relative safety of my thoughts. Perhaps it was time to head back to see if Jenn could shed any light on who or what might be running around in these woods.

I returned home and found Jenn in the barn brushing down one of the horses. She seemed to spend an inordinate amount of time cleaning the animals. I'd asked her why she stayed so involved with the mundane, day-to-day activities of the ranch when I'd seen a young ranch hand regularly performing other chores. She told me that her cleaning rituals helped her to relax and strengthened the bond with her horses. I wondered if it might work that way with people, and I made a mental note to remind her of that the next time I needed a shower.

I watched for a few minutes before I announced my presence.

"You know," I said, "I get a little jealous when I see you like this."

She turned and smiled. "You'll get your turn."

Good answer.

"Where have you been?"

"Remember the place on the ridge about a half mile north of here? You took me there the day I arrived."

"Sure. What were you doing up there?"

"I've gone there a few times. It's become my Fortress of Solitude."

"Don't get me wrong..." She grinned. "You're a great guy, Dillon, but you're no Superman."

I raised an eyebrow. "You know about the Fortress?"

"I grew up with three brothers, remember?"

"I saw something strange up there."

She stopped her brushing. "What do you mean?"

"Someone or something ran through the woods up on the ridge."

"Which was it?"

"I don't know."

"We've been known to have a bear or two up there."

"No, this was quicker and more sure-footed." I paused. "Does anyone live on the land north of the ranch?"

"Y'all think it was a person?"

"I said I don't know."

"I doubt anyone lives there. It's mostly wilderness." She resumed her brushing. "There's a small tribe of Cheyenne that live on the east side of the property, but that's quite a hike to where you were."

I considered the possibility.

"Could it have been..." She hesitated. "Another flashback, or some kind of—"

"No." I cut her off. "I saw something up there. I haven't had any problems for over a month. I'd like to think that's all behind me."

"It's just that I worry about you, Dillon." She took a deep breath. "But you're right. I won't bring it up again."

I met her gaze, and my eyes thanked her.

"Looks like y'all might have another mystery to solve."

That was the last thing I needed right now. "We don't want to go through something like that again."

"You're right. So, whatever you may or may not have seen... forget about it."

That wasn't going to happen.

***

I returned the following day, not to relax and be alone with my thoughts, but to scout for the creature that had eluded identification the day before. After two hours, I abandoned my watch. I told Jenn later that I'd been out exploring, but conveniently forgot to mention my trip back to the ridge.

On the third day, I saw it again. This time, I jumped up and ran toward the spot where I'd last seen the mysterious creature. I arrived a few minutes later, out of breath and too late for another glimpse. Convinced that I was alone, I turned to leave and noticed a small clearing fifty yards east of my position.

I traversed the ridge until I stood at the edge of the opening. My eyes were drawn to a group of stones arranged in a circle with a diameter of approximately twenty feet. Four spokes of slightly smaller stones met at right angles in the center. Judging by the position of the sun, the spokes represented the four compass points. Not a natural formation. Perhaps it represented the remains of Native American rituals or even an ancient alien civilization.

I stepped inside the circle, half expecting to be beamed up to the mother ship. Nothing happened. I made an educated guess that I stood at the highest point on the entire property. I turned slowly, soaking in the impressive panorama. The snow-covered summit of Pikes Peak reflected the morning sun like a sparkling gem reflects a museum exhibit's spotlight.

When I reached three o'clock, or due east, I noticed a small cemetery approximately forty feet away. I walked across the patchy tundra grass that covered the windswept plateau. Because we were well below the tree line, someone would have had to clear this plot by hand.

A two-foot wooden cross had been planted in the ground at the end of a recently disturbed patch of dirt. A second grave, similarly marked, appeared older and more settled. Unlike the unadorned first grave, a strand of beads and feathers hung over the second cross's horizontal member, while a spattering of colorful ornaments and trinkets lay at the base.

I scanned the immediate area and found no additional markers. What appeared to be a smaller, unmarked grave lay barely visible a few yards from the others, its edges giving way to the scrubby vegetation.

I removed my hat and held it against my chest as I dropped to one knee. I examined the beads, Native American perhaps, then picked up a shiny crystal gemstone and turned it between the fingers of my free hand.

Something attacked me from behind and the stone fell to the ground. I silently berated myself for letting my guard down as my attacker wrapped its legs around my chest and tightened its grip around my neck.

Whatever I'd seen earlier was back, and I'd fallen into its trap.

Chapter Two

A thick braid of black hair slapped the side of my face as the force of our collision nearly knocked me to the ground. I gained my feet quickly and pulled at the arm that had tightened around my neck. I dropped to one knee again, grabbed the arm with one hand and a fistful of hair with the other, and flipped my attacker over my head. She landed on her back with no time to recover before I pinned her arms with my knees and her neck with my right forearm.

I shook my head as I studied her face, thankful for my combat training. Her hunting skills were stellar. I never heard her coming.

She appeared to be maybe ten years older than me—attractive, in excellent shape, and probably Cheyenne. "I moved out here to get away from this shit." I glared down at the fire in her ebony eyes. "Who are you, and what are you doing up here?"

She struggled beneath my weight, but I was twice her size and outweighed her by a hundred pounds.

"I'm not going to hurt you," I said. "But that has to work both ways." I glanced around to make sure she was alone. "If I release you, we're going to talk. That's all. Got it?"

I loosened the pressure on her neck enough for her to nod. I straightened up, keeping her body pinned beneath my knees.

"So? Who are you?" I said as I checked her for weapons.

"My name is Cassidy."

"Now we're getting somewhere." I relaxed a bit. "What are you doing here?"

"I could ask you the same thing," she replied with a heavy dose of attitude.

"I'll ask the questions."

"Last time I checked, it was a free country. Unless you don't think Native Americans should enjoy the same freedoms as white folk."

"I didn't say that." I was a little insulted that she'd assumed such a thing without knowing anything about me. However, with such a big chip on her shoulder, one could easily assume that most of her conversations began that way.

"You're hurting me," she said, her voice losing some of its defiance.

"I'm sorry. I just want to talk."

"Okay. We'll talk."

I stood and offered my hand. She ignored it and made it to her feet on her own. She rubbed her arms where I'd knelt on them.

I picked up my hat and knocked the dust off against my thigh before placing it back on my head. "What's a beautiful woman like you doing running around the woods in the middle of nowhere?"

She tripped over her words before offering an honest answer. "I... I... come here to visit my sister."

I glanced at the crosses, then back to Cassidy. "You're the one who decorated her grave."

She nodded. "Mostly, I come here to talk to her."

"Do you live around here?"

"There's a small village east of here."

It made sense to me now. Jenn had mentioned that Roy had allowed a small tribe of Cheyenne to settle on the eastern edge of the property. "It's a long walk."

"I don't mind."

"So, why did you jump me?"

"I thought you were here to rob her grave."

"That's some welcome to the neighborhood, ain't it?"

"I'm sorry."

"I'm Dillon Bishop." I held out my hand. "I live down at the main house."

Her muscles tightened and her eyes darted back and forth like she was about to bolt. "I have to go."

"Wait."

"If you value your life, you'll go back to where you came from. This ranch is a dangerous place. People die here."

I glanced at the graves. "What happened to your sister?"

"My sister is stuck here, buried next to the man who killed her."

"The other grave." I stared at the wooden cross planted at the head of the unadorned grave. "Who's buried there?"

She hesitated, like she couldn't bring herself to say the name. "Roy McDonald."

"Roy?" My head snapped in her direction, and I met her gaze. "Roy McDonald killed your sister?"

"In the end, he got what he deserved."

"What do you mean?"

"Live by the sword, die by the sword. Isn't that what they say?"

"You think someone killed Roy?"

"I have to go."

"Wait. There's another grave over there. A smaller one. Do you know anything about it?"

"It was already there when my sister died. I don't know who it belongs to."

I bent over to brush the dirt from my jeans. I straightened up and she was gone.

***

I returned to the ranch and found Jenn and Alex together in the main corral with Apollo, one of the smaller, gentler horses. She'd taught the boy how to ride a few days ago, and he seemed to get the hang of it. Alex smiled in the saddle while Jen called out encouragement from against the perimeter fence.

I folded my arms on the top rail, a couple of feet from Jenn, and offered some encouraging words.

"Y'all are next," Jenn said with a smile.

I shook my head. "Not today."

"When?"

I gave her a *let's-not-do-this-right-now* look.

She took a step closer and turned around to face me. "Is everything all right?"

"Sure." I lied. "I'm just not ready to ride."

"Not ready? You've been here for three weeks."

"Mama, look," Alex called.

I raised an eyebrow. "Mama?"

"Don't look at me like that. We're just trying it out." Her eyes grew wide. "Sounds nice, doesn't it?"

"Sounds like you've made your decision."

"Sounds like you're having second thoughts." She turned and waved to Alex. "Great job."

"What did you tell him to call *me*?"

"I haven't said anything yet, but 'Pop' would be nice."

The truth is, I was less ready to be anyone's 'Pop' than I was to ride a horse. The boy needed a male role model as much as he needed a mother. But role models typically possess a great deal of wisdom and a sense of who they are. In other words, they had their shit together. I'd like to think that, one by one, I'd picked up the pieces of my shattered life, carefully shuffling them around, looking for the right fit. But my shit wasn't together yet. Not by a long shot.

I used to think that this whole thing was Jenn's fault. After all, she'd been the one who befriended the boy while stationed in Germany. She's the one who sought him out after returning stateside. And she's the one who initiated the adoption proceedings without my knowledge. However, she's quick to point out that if it hadn't been for me, the boy would never have made it out of Afghanistan.

I'd found him sitting in the rubble next to his dead mother, his father's lifeless eyes staring out from under a jagged slab of concrete. He wouldn't have lasted more than a few days. If not for me, he'd probably be in heaven right now, surrounded by seventy-two virgins or something. But instinct took over and I just couldn't leave him.

"*Pop*? Jeezus, Jenn."

"What's the matter with that? I'm not gonna let him continue to call you Mr. Dillon or GI Joe."

"Whatever," I said, then turned and walked toward the house.

"We need to talk about this," she called after me.

I threw my hands in the air. "Fine, we'll talk."

I wasn't looking forward to *that* conversation.

CHAPTER THREE

I made two ham sandwiches and grabbed a couple of beers from the fridge. The keys were in the Bronco, so I started her up and drove toward my Fortress of Solitude. I needed some time to sort things out.

I felt bad for the poor orphan boy as I parked the Bronco and made my way through the trees to my clearing. Admittedly, he'd been dealt a worse hand than mine, but I wouldn't let him come between Jenn and me. I didn't come out here to raise a family, at least not yet. *Pop?* I sure as hell wasn't ready for that.

The sound of an approaching vehicle interrupted my thoughts. I retraced my steps back to the trail and found Seth sitting on an all-terrain vehicle next to the Bronco. I approached, and he turned off the engine.

"I saw the Bronco and thought it was Jenn."

"Just me."

"What are you doing up here?"

"Jenn showed me a great spot. I come out here sometimes when I need to be alone."

"Sorry."

"What did you need Jenn for?"

He looked at me like I had no business asking such a question. "It's nothing. I'll catch up with her later." He reached for the ignition switch.

"Wait."

Seth paused.

"I've got sandwiches and beer. You want some lunch?"

He looked as surprised as I was by the invitation and hesitated before climbing down off the vehicle.

"Pull up a rock," I said when we reached the clearing. I handed him a sandwich and a bottle of beer.

"I've spent some time here, myself," he said.

We both ate in silence for a few moments before I took a long drag on my beer. "So, what can you tell me about Roy's death?"

I got the look again, like it was none of my business. Probably not the best way to start a conversation.

"He had a heart attack. Right here on the ranch."

"I heard he didn't die of natural causes."

His eyes narrowed. "Where'd you hear that?"

"I'd rather not say."

"Coroner's report confirmed it." He took a drink while he held my gaze.

"I see." I did not see. Back in Bradley, the crooked police chief doctored Pop's autopsy report to make it look like Mama killed him. Did the same with the security tapes at the hospital.

There was more I wanted to know, but his steely eyes told me the subject was closed. "So, what's there to do around here for fun?"

He shrugged. "I ride a lot. Don't leave the ranch much unless there's a rodeo."

"Mama used to take me when I was a kid." I took a bite of my sandwich and washed it down. "Alex seems to be gettin' the hang of riding."

"This ranch is no place for that boy."

"Appears Jenn's taken a shine to him."

"What about you?"

"I think I did a good thing when I pulled him out of that hell-hole. Bringing him here to live with us is a horse of a different color."

He nodded. "I was as surprised as you."

"Jenn didn't tell you?"

He shook his head.

I finished my sandwich and washed it down with the rest of the beer. We finally had something in common.

Seth stood. "Thanks for lunch."

***

After dinner that night, I strolled through the main stable. The first time I'd done that, I caused quite a ruckus. By now, most of the horses knew me and went about their business. I had to admit that I enjoyed their company.

The one named *Chance* was chatty that evening, and I lingered outside his stall. He appeared to be getting on in years and moved a little slower than the younger animals. I'd watched him in the paddock or grazing in the pasture, but this was the first time we'd been up close and personal.

I'd learned that horses come in many colors and sizes. Chance was a Paint Horse. His mostly chestnut brown coat had large, random splashes of white, like he'd been playing paintball with a bazooka. A wide white streak, or blaze, ran along the bridge of his nose.

I'm not sure whether it was his distinctive markings or the sadness in his big brown eyes that drew me to him. I noticed several nasty scars on his haunches and felt a twist in my stomach as I imagined the abuse this poor boy had suffered. He reached outside his stall in search of a gentle hand to scratch his forehead and stroke the side of his neck. I obliged.

We talked about all manner of things. Well, I did most of the talking. Chance responded with a snort or a head bob at what seemed like the appropriate times. I told him about my friend Coop back home and I wondered to myself how he'd been since I'd left. I realized that I still referred to Texas as home, even though, for many years, it had been the last place I'd wanted to be. Now, it was home to Bishop Oil, the company that I'd started with Mama to pull up the oil from beneath Pop's land. The land that he died for. Coop agreed to work as part-time operations manager to oversee the day-to-day activities.

"I see you've made a friend."

I turned to find Mama standing six feet behind me. She smiled as I silently berated myself for letting someone sneak up on me again. I must be losing my edge. "How long have you been there?"

"Long enough." She gestured toward Chance. "They're pretty good company."

"I reckon they are, once you get to know them."

"I heard you mention Cooper. Have you spoken to him lately?"

"Not since we left."

"Why not?"

I shrugged as I continued to stroke Chance.

"Aren't you curious about what's happening with the company?"

"Sure. It's just that..."

"Something's bothering you, Dillon. What is it?"

I stopped what I was doing. "I didn't expect it to be like this."

The look in her eyes told me to continue.

"I'm not ready to be a parent."

"Very few people are."

"You have to admit, I never had very good role models."

"I can't argue with that," she conceded.

I detected a note of remorse in her voice, and I regretted the accusation.

"What is it you want, Dillon?"

"Same thing I've always wanted."

She lowered her head. "I took that away from you the day I walked out."

That much guilt was more than anyone should have to bear. "There was more to it than that."

Mama looked up, and I saw the pain in her eyes as a smile flickered and faded.

"Moving here with Jenn felt like the right thing to do. Like I finally had a real shot at a *happily ever after*."

She nodded. "Then along came Alex."

"Jenn and I are good together. I can't believe I'm saying this, but I think she might be *the one*." I looked away. "We don't need anyone else."

"Does she feel the same?"

I caught her gaze and frowned. "Why wouldn't she?"

"Because she's a woman." Mama gently touched my forearm. "Women are designed to nurture, to take care of others."

"She can take care of *me*."

"Women have maternal instincts."

I resisted the urge to question hers. "Some women don't want children."

"Did you ask Jenn what she wants?"

"Not in so many words. But she's always been so independent."

Mama smiled. "The two aren't mutually exclusive."

A memory resurfaced. On the first day I'd seen Mama again after she'd gone AWOL for sixteen years, I let her have it good. I said some cruel things, even though most of them were true, or at least they seemed justified in my mind. The next morning, I awoke to find her fixing me breakfast.

"Children were never part of the equation. I'm not father material."

"You don't know that."

"I'm sure I won't be any better at it than Pop was. Alex has been through enough. He needs more than..." I shook my head.

"You're a good man, Dillon, despite the way your daddy and I behaved. That's a sure sign of strength and character."

She was trying to make me feel better, but I still felt the weight of my inadequacies. "I'm thinking of moving back to Texas... before it's too late."

Mama said nothing.

"The longer I wait, the tougher it's gonna be for everybody." After a few moments of silence, I raised an eyebrow. "Here's where you're supposed to throw in some motherly advice."

"I'm afraid I don't have any. I want to tell you how much I regret running away, but..."

"But what?"

"I've been trying to find a way to tell you that I can't stay here with you."

"Seriously?"

"I'll always be a Texas girl. Besides, Mort and I have been talking..."

"I knew he had a thing for you, but I didn't think you were interested."

She shrugged. "I didn't think I was either."

"Don't you see what you've done?" I lifted my hat and raked a hand back through my hair. "You've just made it a whole lot easier for me to run away."

"Don't make this about me. It's your decision. Do what's right for you."

"I love her, Mama. But it's like she's put a gun to my head."

"Don't be so dramatic," she said as she gently slapped my shoulder.

"Let's leave tonight."

"Stop it, Dillon."

"Go pack your bags. I'll pick you up in thirty minutes. We'll be back in Texas by morning."

"You can't be serious."

I hesitated. "No... I guess not."

"Talk to her."

When I didn't respond, Mama pulled me in for a hug. "I know you'll do the right thing," she whispered in my ear.

That made one of us.

CHAPTER FOUR

O n school nights, Jenn made sure that Alex was in bed by nine. She'd enrolled him in the public school in Redfield in case he made this his forever home. If for some reason that didn't work out, at least he wouldn't have missed too many classes.

There had been an elephant in the room all evening, and he wasn't going anywhere until Jenn and I talked. The social worker expected an answer in the morning.

Stubbornness had always been an inherited trait in the Bishop family. When it reached my generation, I preferred to call it *persistence*. Whatever I chose to call it, one more conversation had fallen prey to its influence. Exasperated, Jenn threw in the towel after half an hour, and I stepped out into the cool night air. Unwilling to go back inside for another round, I climbed into my truck and headed for town.

I thought I'd come from a small town until I drove through Redfield, Colorado. As I recall, Bradley had more than one stoplight. I passed a place called the Wet Whistle Saloon, then circled back around and parked next to two motorcycles near the front door.

Inside, the old-western decor gave the feeling that I'd just passed through a pair of swinging doors. I found a seat at the long wooden bar and looked around the room. I waited for the barkeep to finish filling a glass from the tap for a scantily clad young woman. She caught my gaze and smiled. I tipped my hat, thinking that she was gonna freeze her pretty little ass off on the way home in those Daisy Dukes.

A lone cowboy played an old country tune on a vintage Gretsch White Falcon from a folding chair at the far end of an empty dance floor. Two couples sipped their drinks on stools along the narrow counters that flanked the hardwood.

The patrons were mostly men, ranging in age from the pimple popper with the fake ID in his wallet to the old farmer wearing denim overalls and nursing a longneck alone in the corner booth. Beneath a stained-glass pendant lamp, the woman I'd acknowledged at the bar moments ago attracted a good deal of attention as she bent over the pool table.

By the time I'd ordered my second drink, two young bucks were getting pretty noisy on the other side of the room. I shot a sideways glance in their direction before turning my attention back to the label on my bottle, which I'd begun to tear off in little pieces. I'd just run away from a fight. The last thing I wanted to do was get involved in another.

The music stopped for a moment before a cover of "Melissa" by the Allman Brothers drifted across the room from the speakers at the edge of the stage. I watched the two couples make their way to the dance floor as the ruckus behind me intensified.

I told myself to stay out of it, but when I turned and saw the old man standing next to their table shaking his fist, all bets were off. The two younger men—who appeared to be Native American—stood and pushed him.

My heart pounded as I watched their confrontation, knowing that if it escalated much further, I'd have to step in. I didn't know who started it, but I wasn't about to sit and watch the old man get his ass kicked. I set down my bottle and walked over to see if I could prevent another Little Bighorn.

"Is there a problem here?"

"Who the hell are you?" one of the boys asked.

"Let's just say I'm a guy who doesn't want to have to hurt anyone."

"Then I got some advice for ya," he said through clenched teeth. "Mind your own damn business."

"He started it," the other one added, pointing at the old man.

I turned. "Is that true?"

The man looked to be in his seventies. Silver hair splayed out from under a worn hat that might have been about the same age. He looked at me with a pair of soft blue eyes that seemed out of place set in such a hard exterior.

"These two animals started this a long time ago," he said.

One of the animals took a step toward the farmer. "What did you call us?"

I put my hand on his chest. He slapped it away. Before the old man could answer, I positioned myself between them. We'd attracted the attention of some of the other patrons who gathered around us. I could see this little misunderstanding turning into a full-on barroom brawl if I didn't quickly diffuse the situation.

"Maybe you should move on, old man," I said.

"I didn't do nothin' wrong. Why do I have to go?"

Because I'm tryin' to save you from a major ass-kickin'. "You've had enough for one night. Now, get on home."

I held my ground until the old man cleared the front door and the crowd that had gathered began to disperse. "Problem solved," I said. "I suggest you boys sit back down and finish your drinks."

The two hesitated, presumably calculating their chances against me. They made the right decision and slid back into the booth. I walked back to my seat, finished my beer, and stepped outside. The man I'd sent home was nowhere in sight.

As I left the parking lot and started down the road, I saw him walking along the shoulder. He wasn't the sharpest tool in the shed, but at least he was smart enough not to drive home. I slowed down and lowered the passenger window. "Want a ride?"

He shook his head as he continued to stagger down the road. I pulled ahead about twenty feet and waited for him to catch up.

"You don't look so good," I said. "You sure you don't want a ride?"

He stopped. "I could have taken 'em."

"I'm sure you could, but pretty soon, every swingin' dick in that bar would've been throwin' punches. When the cops showed up, they'd haul your ass off to jail for instigatin'."

"I told you, I didn't start nothin'." He pointed a wobbly finger at me. "And furthermore, my life ain't none a yer concern."

"Last chance. You want a ride or not?"

He waved me off. "Go on, get the hell outta here."

As I drove off, I glanced in the mirror and realized that I had at least one thing in common with that sorry old soul. *Persistence.*

Chapter Five

I returned home around midnight and heard the floorboards creak upstairs. I'd hoped to find Jenn asleep and slip under the covers unnoticed. Not in the mood for another *conversation*, I grabbed a bottle from the liquor cabinet and headed for the stable.

I sat on a bale of hay across the aisle from Chance's stall, a horse blanket over my shoulders. The sweet smell of hay mixed with animal musk was soothing, and together with the whiskey, relieved some of the tension in my neck and shoulders.

I'd been avoiding the all-important conversation with Jenn for several weeks. I'd hoped that, given enough time, I could face down my fears and wrap my mind around raising a child, or perhaps she might decide that I was enough for her. Time had run out. The adoption agency needed an answer in the morning.

I knew how much Jenn wanted this, but letting her down now seemed like the kinder thing to do. If I went through with it, the fall would be much farther for both of them down the road. But somewhere inside this conflicted heart, I couldn't picture the rest of my life without Jenn in it.

Jenn walked toward me in the half-light. I swallowed another gulp of liquid courage, set the bottle down on the cement floor, and pushed it behind the bale with the heel of my boot. Chance stirred as Jenn looked his way before looking down at me.

"I saw the light on. What y'all doing out here?" she said as she hugged herself against the cold.

The wrath that I'd expected to suffer was absent from her voice. I gestured toward Chance who watched us intently, two columns of steam rising from his nostrils into the night air. "Life would be a lot easier if I was a horse."

"How's that?" She sat next to me on the hay.

"He seems content, doesn't he?"

Jenn smiled. "He sure does."

I held one side of the blanket out, and she slipped her shoulders underneath. We spent the next few moments in silence. Chance turned his head to get a better look.

"Y'all want to move out of the house and into one of the stalls?" Jenn asked.

"I doubt he thinks much beyond what he's doing at the moment," I continued. "He spends his whole life in his own little world of eating, sleeping, playing, and dropping a load whenever and wherever he feels like it."

Jenn laughed. "I had no idea that last one was something you aspired to."

"I'm sure there's no little voice in his head replaying the past, or forecasting the future, or telling him he's not good enough."

"Life wasn't all sunshine and rainbows for Chance. He was a rescue."

"Is that what I am?"

She hesitated. "Talk to me, Dillon. You haven't been yourself lately."

Maybe that was the problem. Maybe *this* was the real Dillon. The Dillon no one wants to see. The Dillon no one can love. The Dillon that doesn't belong in a family.

"Is this about Alex?"

"I guess it is."

"What did you say to Seth?" she asked.

"Why?"

"We had a little chat. Sounds like the two of you are ganging up on me."

"It's not like that."

Jenn slipped her hand in mine.

"I don't think I can do this," I said and withdrew my hand.

"Dillon, please..."

I had a feeling that the pain and disappointment that she'd been holding back was about to be unleashed. I braced myself against the inevitable attack.

"Look at me, Dillon."

I turned my head and met her gaze.

"Don't do this again. Whether or not you believe it, you're better than that."

I wasn't sure where Jenn had gotten the image of me she held on to. It was far better than anything my jaded eyes would allow. I hoped that she'd seen something in me that I was as yet unable, or perhaps unwilling, to see in myself.

"I can't deny that you had it rough growing up," she said after a few moments of silence. "But that only makes you stronger."

"I don't feel stronger."

Jenn sat up straight. "I think you're denying yourself things that might make you happy as... as some kind of penance."

"You've got me all figured out, don't you?"

"That's why y'all up and joined the Army. And why I almost lost you to Nicole back in Texas."

"You didn't lose me. I'm still here."

"Because I wouldn't let you do that to yourself." Her voice became brittle. "It's happening again with Alex, but he's just a child. He's not that strong."

I said nothing.

"I can see what's going on here, how you've been keeping your distance from him. From both of us. At first, you were shocked and happy to see him again, to know that he made it out alive and that he seemed so well-adjusted. I'm not sure what y'all are feeling now."

She had a way of *seeing* things and getting to the heart of a situation that I couldn't begin to understand.

"You're not like your mama or your daddy," she continued. "You're better than that. Stop thinking you can't do this."

"Some people don't belong in a family."

"None of that was your fault."

How could she possibly know that? She wasn't there when little Dillon Bishop became disposable. "So, you don't think Mama's leaving had anything to do with me?"

"I didn't know her back then, so I don't claim to understand why she left." Her voice softened. "But I believe you're the reason she came back."

I wanted to believe it, too. I didn't mention that Mama was thinking of leaving again.

"Talk to me, Dillon. What are you afraid of?"

I took her hand again. "When I moved my life from Texas to Colorado, I thought it would be just us."

"You brought your mama with you."

Despite the tension, I nearly laughed at the irony of my last statement. "Okay, but that's not the same as raising a child. Alex needs a role model, someone to teach him all the things my daddy never taught me."

"So, be that for him," she said a little too loudly. She lowered her voice. "Instead of always talking about what you're not, show him what you are. I think you'll be surprised."

"I don't know, Jenn."

She stood. "This adoption is going to happen with or without you. So, if y'all plan to stay on here, Alex and I are a package deal."

"So, that's it? You're going to let a stranger, someone who's been here for a month, come between us?"

"I hoped he'd bring us closer together."

"And yet, here we are."

"This is bigger than both of us. We're making the world a better place."

"For who?"

"For Alex. And whether or not you believe it, for us. And for… for countless other lives that he may touch. We're all connected. Everything we do touches everyone else."

"You believe that?"

Jenn sat next to me on the edge of the bale. "I'm a straight shooter, Dillon. You know that. I don't say anything that I don't believe."

I didn't respond.

"You once told me that all you wanted growing up was a normal life. Maybe that's all Alex is looking for, too. He won't get it if we don't do this. He might go back into the system and…"

Her words trailed off. Neither of us wanted to think about the ending to that story. An awkward silence descended upon us.

Jenn gave my thigh a couple of quick pats and stood. "Maybe you should come to bed."

"I'll be there in a little while."

She walked over to Chance and scratched his forehead. "Remind you of anyone?" she asked the horse.

Chance snorted and bobbed his head.

"I'm not surprised you chose Chance to confide in," she said over her shoulder. "He's a lot like you." She gave me one last look, then walked away.

I had the strangest feeling that I didn't choose ol' Chance. He'd chosen me.

Chapter Six

I couldn't remember how long I'd stayed in the barn, but I awoke in bed the next morning with a new perspective. I'd like to think it was Jenn's encouraging words that had made the difference rather than her ultimatum, or the reflection I'd seen in the eyes of the stubborn old man walking home alone on the side of the road. Whatever it was, I felt better than I had in weeks.

When I rolled over to tell Jenn, I found the bed empty. A glance at the clock told me I'd slept in longer than usual.

As I swung my legs over the side of the bed, Jenn walked in with a steaming cup of coffee.

"Good, you're up."

I pulled a pair of jeans on and sat on the edge of the bed.

She handed me the cup. "We need to talk."

I nodded. "I don't even remember coming to bed last night."

"It was late."

I nodded.

"I want you to know that whatever you decide is what we'll do," she offered.

I frowned as I took a sip. "Really?"

"No. I'm doing this no matter what." She flashed a hopeful smile. "But I'd much rather do it with you than without you."

"The truth is, so would I."

"You would?"

"Last night, I realized... no, it's more like I remembered... how much you mean to me. If this is what you want, then I'm in."

I steadied my cup with both hands as she threw her arms around my neck.

"You're the best," she whispered in my ear.

Unfamiliar words, but I liked the way they sounded.

"I'm going to call the social worker right now." She stopped at the door and turned. "You'd better be hungry. I'm gonna make you the best breakfast you've ever eaten."

Jenn closed the door behind herself, and I'm sure I heard her squeal as she ran down the stairs.

One weight had been lifted from my shoulders and another had taken its place. The decision had been made and the tension between us diffused. But I knew nothing about being a father, adoptive or otherwise. I reminded myself that I was not adopting the boy. Jenn was. However, our lives had become intertwined, and I had every intention of keeping them that way. Someday, when I made her my wife, it would be a package deal.

In the meantime, Alex needed a father, if not in name, at least in purpose. Someone caring and wise and patient with his inevitable missteps. The weight pressed down a little harder as I realized I'd just volunteered for the position. In a moment of strength and clarity, I pushed back.

Jenn made good on her breakfast promise. Fried eggs, bacon, biscuits and gravy, and fresh-squeezed orange juice. I watched Alex lick his plate when he finished. I nudged him with my elbow, then licked my plate with exaggerated movements and sound effects.

"You're funny, Mr. Dillon."

"From now on, you can drop the mister. It's just Dillon. After all, we're practically family." I leaned back in my chair. "That is, if you still want to live here with us."

Alex's eyes grew wide. He turned toward Jenn, well aware of the day's significance.

She nodded with a smile that nearly brought tears to everyone's eyes. "I made the call this morning."

Alex stood, threw his hands in the air, then pulled them down quickly. "Yeeessss!"

I watched him wrap his arms around Jenn's neck.

"Thank you. Thank you. Thank you." He pulled back after a tight squeeze, and their eyes met. "I love you, Mama."

Jenn pulled him in again. Tears rolled down her cheeks, and I knew I'd made the right decision.

A moment later, his arms were around my neck. "Thank you."

I tried to nod despite his chokehold.

"I love you, Mister... I mean, Dillon."

An awkward silence hung in the room before Jenn stood and cleared the table. Alex announced that he was headed for the stable to saddle up Apollo for another lesson. Jenn promised to meet him after she cleaned the kitchen. I joined her at the sink with a stack of dirty dishes.

"We're really gonna do this, aren't we?" I said as I slipped my arms around her waist from behind.

She turned as the water continued to fill the sink. "I'm proud of you, Dillon."

"You should be proud of yourself." I smiled. "I'm becoming a better person because of you."

"That's not a bad thing, is it?"

I shrugged. "It was time for a change."

"Seth seems to think otherwise." She turned her attention toward the dirty dishes.

I grabbed a towel and waited for her to continue.

"I'm not sure why he cares."

I had an idea. "Maybe he doesn't like kids."

"He's been spending a lot of time away from the ranch lately and the work's been piling up."

"Really? He told me he doesn't leave the ranch much unless there's a rodeo."

"Well, there must be a whole lot more rodeos than I remember."

"How can I help?" I asked.

She handed me a plate. "You can start with this."

"I mean it. I haven't been pulling my weight around here. I know that. I want to help."

"Does that mean you're ready to learn to ride?"

I set the dry plate on the counter and picked up another from the drainboard. "If you still want to teach me."

Jenn turned, took my towel, and dried her hands. She tossed it on the counter and locked her arms around my neck. "Are we still talking about horses?"

Her lips brushed mine, and something inside me moved. I whispered, "I hope not." I closed my eyes and pressed my lips hard against hers. My hands made their way down to the small of her back, and I pulled her in.

"Ready for your first lesson, cowboy?" she asked when we came up for air.

"Right here?"

She appeared to consider it for a moment. "Let's start upstairs and see where that takes us."

We turned to find Alex standing in the doorway, wearing a smile. "Apollo is saddled up and ready to go."

Jenn looked at me, and I gave a disappointed shrug. She smiled. "Rain check?"

"Absolutely."

She nodded her approval, then tilted her head. "Were you serious about helping with some of the chores?"

"Where do I start?"

"We need a few things at the hardware store."

"I was thinking something a little more, you know, *ranchy*."

"You could clean the stalls."

"Hardware it is. Do you have a list?"

"It's on the counter." She kissed me on the cheek before turning to Alex. "Let's get you back up in that saddle."

"You think you can get me into one of those saddles?"

Jenn turned, surprised.

I grinned. "The hardware store's not going anywhere."

"Let's see what you got, cowboy."

I shoved the list in my pocket and followed them outside.

CHAPTER SEVEN

I opened the front door to Hattie's Hardware and a bell jingled. I shuffled inside, feeling the fresh bruises that Chance's saddle had left on my backside. Jenn did an admirable job of hiding her amusement.

A woman looked up from behind the counter.

"Welcome," she said with a warm smile.

I touched the brim of my hat as I nodded in her direction.

She wore a denim apron over a red flannel shirt with the sleeves rolled up, exposing a peace sign tattooed on her left wrist. Her long gray hair had been pulled back behind her head, but a few wayward strands that had broken free framed her kind face. Eyes that still sparkled told me she'd been a force to reckon with back in her day.

"Haven't seen your face in here before."

"I'm new in town," I said.

"I figured as much." She paused as she gave me the once-over. "There's food in the back if you're hungry."

"This is a hardware store," I said as I glanced around again to see if maybe I'd missed something. "Isn't it?"

"Sure is." A playful smile crossed her lips. "What gave it away?"

"I reckon my first clue was the sign out front."

"Yeah," she wrinkled her nose. "Kinda hard to miss that one."

"Why is there food in the back of a hardware store?"

"I like to show a little hospitality while folks are gettin' settled in."

"What kind of folks?"

"Mostly Mexicans and Indians that come here to harvest crops."

"So, which one do you think I am?"

"Others come, too. We get the occasional down-on-their-luck drifters."

I smiled. "I'm flattered, but that's not why I'm here."

"Well, then, how can I help you?"

"You really thought I was a drifter?"

She hesitated. "If it's any consolation, you're about the most handsome drifter that's set foot in here in a mighty long time."

"Why, thank you, ma'am." I smiled, maybe even blushed. "My name's Dillon Bishop."

She picked up an open soda can from the counter and took a drink. "I'm Harriet Scott. Don't much like the name Harriet, so everyone 'round here calls me Hattie."

I took a few steps toward the counter. "So, tell me, Hattie, why would anyone come around looking for fieldwork this time of year? I imagine all the crops must be in by now."

"You really aren't from around here, are you?"

I held up my arms in submission.

"There's a marijuana farm down the road a piece. Greenhouses big as airplane hangars. They grow the stuff all year long." She set the can on the counter. "It's been legal here for a few years now."

"No shit."

"Good shit." She smiled a coy smile. "Or so they say."

"Who's they?"

Hattie fired off a couple rapid blinks. "So, what brings you to our humble little town, Mr. Bishop?"

"Call me Dillon. We just moved into the Red Valley Ranch."

"We?"

"My friend Jenn. It's her Uncle Roy's place."

"Little Jenny's back in town?" She placed her hand on her chest and all eight of her bracelets jangled. "I adored that child. She was cute as a button."

"Still is. She's all grown up now."

"You tell her she must come to see Miss Hattie while she's here."

"There'll be plenty of time for that," I assured her. "Jenn wants to work the ranch. Well, her and her cousin Seth."

"I've seen Seth in town plenty over the past couple years, but Jenny, why, I haven't seen her in forever."

"I'll make it a point to tell Jenn you said hey."

Hattie raised an eyebrow. "Are you sure you're not hungry?"

"I'm good," I said with a wink.

"Alrighty, then. What can I do you for?"

I smiled and handed her my list.

Hattie took the list, and I followed her around the store as she pulled items from the shelves and handed them to me. My arms filled up quickly. Hattie set a five-pound box of nails on top of the heap, then looked back at the list.

"Says here you need some fence rails. They're in the barn." She folded the list and tucked it into the front pocket of her apron. "How 'bout you get your truck and meet me 'round back?"

I nodded.

"You might want to set them things down before you do." She pointed to the counter. "Easier to drive that way."

We loaded the truck, then returned inside to settle the bill. I pulled out my wallet.

"I'll just put it on your tab," she said with a dismissive wave.

"You sure?"

"The ranch has always had an account in good standing. I don't imagine Seth and Jenny are gonna change that."

"I reckon they won't," I said and signed the charge slip. A large glass jar filled with candies in brightly colored wrappers sat on the counter in front of the register. "How can you still sell candy for a penny?"

"It's not about the money. Most of the migrants bring their families. I usually give 'em away to the kids." A warm smile spread across her face. "Go on. Take one."

I leaned over and studied the contents through the glass. I reached in, grabbed a Jolly Rancher, and held it up like a little kid. "Watermelon. My favorite."

Hattie boxed up my supplies and slid them across the counter. "You come back and see me again, and you can have another."

"Deal," I said as I picked up the box. I'd become fond of Ms. Hattie Scott. She was good people.

Back at the ranch, I set the supplies on the porch and went inside. Mama and Alex sat at the table, while Jenn pulled a pitcher of lemonade from the fridge.

"Hi, Dillon," Mama said.

Alex turned and smiled, his mouth full of peanut butter and jelly.

"Good, you're back," Jenn said. "Sit and I'll make you some lunch."

I put my hand on Alex's shoulder. "How'd you and Apollo get along after I left?"

"I did really good," he said after he swallowed.

"Really well," Jenn corrected.

"Memaw said I looked like a real cowboy."

"Memaw, huh?"

Mama flashed a playfully stern look. "That would be me, of course."

"I see. Technically, my mama's not—"

Jenn cut me off. "Alex's getting comfortable with his new family. I think it's wonderful. Don't you, Dillon?"

"Uh…" I caught another stern look from Mama. This time, not so playful. "I reckon I do."

Jenn set a grilled cheese sandwich and a cup of tomato soup on the table in front of me. She leaned over and kissed my cheek. "Now, shut up and eat," she whispered in my ear.

"You looked pretty good in that saddle this morning," Mama said.

"You saw that?" I took a bite of my sandwich and shook my head. "I felt sorry for Chance."

"Nonsense. I can see that you and Chance have a bond, that he trusts you. He'll be patient with your missteps as long as you maintain that trust."

I shifted in my seat. "I hear you, but I'm not sure my backside is feeling the love."

Mama smiled before raising her brow. "Where'd you run off to this morning?" she asked.

Jenn sat across from me with her lunch. "I put him to work."

"I drove into town to fetch a few things."

"Were you able to get everything on the list?" Jenn asked as she picked up her sandwich.

"With a little help from Hattie, who said to say hey."

Jenn stopped abruptly, the sandwich stuck in a holding pattern in front of her mouth. "Hattie Hunter?"

I frowned. "She said her name was Scott."

"She must have married Jim Scott. He was a state trooper who used to make excuses to come into the store. I knew he was sweet on her." A faraway look washed over her face like the remnant of a fond memory. "Whenever I went into that store with Uncle Roy, she'd let me take a piece of candy from the big jar on the counter. Didn't matter if I had the money to pay for it or not."

"That's her," I said with a smile and a nod.

"Next time you go into town, I'm coming with you."

"I reckon she'd like that."

"I don't suppose that town's got a place where I can rent a DVD," Mama said. "I get a little bored some evenings."

"I didn't notice, but you're welcome to borrow the truck and find out."

"I think I'll do that."

"After I unload it." I turned to Jenn. "Where do you want the fence rails?"

"Why don't you go out to the barn and see if you can find Charlie, the foreman? He can show you."

"Roger that."

"Charlie's a great guy." Jenn stifled a laugh. "I'm sure he'll be able to find something *ranchy* for you to do."

Chapter Eight

The closest thing to a mountain I'd seen in Texas was Mount Bonnell near Austin. To give you a little perspective, Mount Bonnell's 800-foot elevation was a mere pimple compared to the 14,000-foot Pikes Peak. An additional fifty-two *fourteeners,* as they were called, are located within the state of Colorado. Perhaps that's why I still felt like a tourist, walking out to the barn with my head tilted up in the air the whole time.

The barn, which stood adjacent to the stable, looked like the kind you'd see on a postcard—red paint, white trim, and a massive wooden door that traveled laterally on a thirty-foot steel rail. A black weathervane with the likeness of a rearing horse sat atop the shingled roof. I passed a half-full hay wagon parked near the open doorway.

Bales of fresh hay piled high along both walls gave the place a sweet, earthy smell that hit you as soon as you stepped inside. The back of the barn had room for a tractor and a large workshop where Jenn said I might find Charlie.

I walked through a large double door about halfway down the length of the building. A man wearing denim overalls tinkered inside the front end of a tractor. Silver hair spilled out from the back of a green ball cap. A Willie Nelson tune played through the static of an old transistor radio with a wire coat hanger where the antenna used to be.

"Hello," I called.

The man turned his head to the side, his arms still buried inside the engine compartment.

"Whatcha need?"

"I don't need anything."

"Everybody needs somethin'," he said as he set down his wrench. He straightened and turned to face me.

My eyes widened. "You're..."

"Busy. Whatcha need?" He removed a tattered John Deere cap and ran a greasy hand through his hair.

"No. You're the guy from the bar last night."

He placed the hat on his head and adjusted it like he was fixin' to get his picture taken. "So what if I am? You gonna tell me what a damn fool I was?"

"That depends."

"On what?"

"On why you were botherin' those fellas."

"I probably shouldn't say nothin'."

"Then I think you're a damn fool."

He looked at me with squinted eyes. His weathered skin reminded me of an old catcher's mitt. A bushy gray mustache hid his upper lip and quivered as the muscles in his face tightened.

I held out my hand. "Dillon Bishop."

"I know who you are."

I withdrew the hand. "I take it you're Charlie."

"Nobody 'round here calls me that."

"Jenn does."

"She ain't from around here, is she?"

This is a great guy? I wondered how Jenn might describe *me*. "What's your problem?" I asked.

"The only problem I got at the moment is you."

Clearly, I'd made a mistake. This must be the wrong barn and the wrong Charlie. "You should be thanking me for saving your hide last night." I waited. When he didn't respond, I spun on my heel and walked away.

"Buck," he called after me. "Folks call me Buck."

I stopped.

"You never told me what you was after."

I turned. "I came to see you about a job."

He nodded. "The missus makin' ya earn yer keep, huh?"

"We're not married. No one's makin' me do anything. I volunteered."

"We might get along after all." He picked up a pair of leather gloves and tossed them at me. "You're gonna need these."

"For what?"

He walked past me without a look. "Follow me."

I obliged.

Buck turned to me when we reached the back of the hay wagon. "You can help me finish unloadin'."

"Roger that." I rolled my head from side to side, loosening the muscles in my neck.

Buck watched with amusement, then looked at the gloves in my hand. "You can put those on now. I'll throw the bales off the wagon, and you stack 'em up over yonder." He pointed to a spot fifteen feet away, where he'd left off.

"Try to keep up," he hollered as he climbed up the back of the hay wagon like a monkey climbing a tree. I watched him pick up a fifty-pound bale of hay and toss it like a giant marshmallow. At the bar, I hadn't noticed his muscular frame. Hell, if he was twenty years younger, I'd think twice before gettin' up in his grille.

I picked up the bale, walked it over to the stack, and pushed it into place atop the others.

"I coulda taken them boys," he called down to me when I returned.

I smiled and picked up another bale.

We sat on the tailgate after the last bale had been stacked. Buck pulled a small metal flask from his back pocket and offered me a drink.

I held up a hand. "I'm good."

"Helps the muscles recover." He unscrewed the top and brought it to his lips. "At least, that's what I tell myself."

"So, how'd I do?"

"You're hired." He slipped the flask back into his pocket and studied me. "But I don't know much about you."

"Not much to tell."

"You and Jenny Lee?"

I laughed. "Are you asking about my intentions?"

"Maybe." He looked away. "It's just that this land is valuable, and I've seen my fair share a people try to get their hands on it."

"I assure you, I'm not after the land. I'm in love with Jenn."

"And the boy?"

"Alex? He's a good kid who had a rough life. Jenn's adopting him."

"Some folks in town been callin' him a terrorist."

"Who said that?"

He shrugged. "Folks 'round here ain't all that tolerant of foreigners."

"You tell those cowards, if they got somethin' to say, they can say it to my face."

Buck held up his hands. "Calm down, son." He shook his head. "You gonna beat up the whole town? And the next one over? And the next?"

I took a deep breath, surprised at how defensive I'd become. "Sorry."

"No need." Buck pulled out his flask and slapped it into my open hand. "They treat Indians the same way. Like *they* were the foreigners. Imagine that?"

I took a swig. "So," I said as I handed him the flask, "What happened last night? What do you got against those two Indians?"

Buck hesitated. "Them sons-a-bitches killed Roy McDonald."

I blinked back my surprise. "What?"

"You heard me."

I thought about it for a moment, then shook my head. "Let me get this straight. You think Heckle and Jeckle from the bar killed Jenn's uncle Roy?"

"It's no joke." He took another hit from the flask before slipping it into his pocket. "Them boys is nothin' but trouble."

"I thought Roy died of a heart attack."

"That's what they want you to think."

"Were they trying to steal his land?"

He shook his head. "Roy was fixin' to marry their mother."

"How do you know that?"

"There ain't a leaf that blows 'round here that I don't know about." His gaze drifted to the wide-open spaces beyond the corral. "That's just bein' a good foreman."

"Foreman? I've only seen two other hands working here. Why do we need a foreman?"

"We had plenty other hands back in the day, but things been headed south lately."

"Were you and Roy close?"

"Close enough."

"Who was the woman?"

"Asha Whitehawk. She lived in the Cheyenne village on the property."

"Lived? Where is she now?"

"Buried up on the ridge next to Roy."

Thoughts of my recent encounter with Cassidy flashed through my mind. "Did she have a sister named Cassidy?"

"That's right." Buck studied me for a moment. "How'd you know that?"

"I met her the other day," I said under the weight of his stare. I thought it best not to elaborate. "How did Asha die?"

"Them Whitehawk boys'll tell you that Roy killed her, but I believe it was an accident." Buck retrieved a can of Skoal from his pocket and put a pinch inside his cheek. "They were on their way to Grand Junction to get hitched. Only place they found a preacher willin' to marry 'em. They ran into some bad weather up in the mountains and had a terrible accident. Roy was lucky to be alive, although he didn't see it that way. Any luck Asha had, ran out on the side a that mountain."

"I'm sorry."

"Not as sorry as her boys. They was trouble from the start. Didn't take kindly to no white man sniffin' around their mama. 'Course, they blamed Roy for her death and swore revenge." He waved a hand at the barn. "Nearly burned down this here barn a few years back."

"And you think they finally got to Roy?"

"Somebody did." He fired a stream of tobacco juice from the side of his mouth. "I'd bet my left nut that it was them Whitehawk boys."

Did Jenn know any of this? If not, how might she react when she found out? I reckoned it didn't matter. I had to tell her.

Chapter Nine

The cool morning air swept inside my jacket and under my hat, chasing away all memory of the warm bed I'd left behind. A chilly forty-eight degrees on the outdoor thermometer had me second-guessing my offer to help with the chores. Ranchers worked from sunup to sundown, a fact that my enthusiasm to lighten Jenn's load had overlooked. But she needed to spend more time with Alex, and I wanted to help make that happen.

Ben and Sadie, the two remaining ranch hands that had been helping with the daily chores, had quit unexpectedly, so I stepped up. Buck said he was working on replacements, but I didn't have a lot of faith in our HR department.

The sun edged above the horizon, hidden for the moment behind the barn, where the bulb still burned in the gooseneck lamp above the main door. The pasture sparkled like a field of cut diamonds. I slid the door open enough to squeeze inside.

I called Buck's name, and he responded from somewhere in the back. Seeing his face again reminded me of his story about Roy's death, a story I had not yet shared with Jenn. I reckoned I needed a little more proof than a conspiracy theory from an old booze hound.

"I hope you came ready to work," he said as he led me out the back door and toward the stable. "There's a lot to do before breakfast."

What had I gotten myself into?

I filled water buckets and delivered them along with hay to the stalls. Then, the troughs in the turn-out pens had to be filled. After I finished, Buck sent me back to the house to get some chow. Warm air infused with the smell of hash browns and bacon greeted me at the door. I stood in the doorway and watched Alex set the table while Mama worked the stove, unaware of my presence.

Mama had really stepped up and proven that she could be part of a family again. She still talked about moving back to Texas, but I hoped it was only talk.

"Where's Jenn?"

"She's upstairs getting dressed for an appointment in the city. I offered to make breakfast." Mama turned and shooed me with a spatula. "Go get washed up. It's almost ready."

Instead of his usual jeans, Alex wore a pair of pressed khakis and new penny loafers. I'd forgotten that Jenn had asked me to drive her to Woodland Park to sign the adoption papers this morning.

"Oh, no. I'm supposed to drive her."

Mama frowned and shook her head. "You best get a move on if you know what's good for you."

I took the stairs two at a time. The bathroom door was closed, so I ducked into our bedroom and threw on the best clothes I could find. My boots were a little rough, but who looks at your feet, anyway? I nearly bumped into Jenn on the way out the door.

"I thought you forgot," she said with equal parts of approval and relief.

"Who me?" I shook my head. "I just need to wash up. Breakfast is ready."

"I'll be right down."

We ate quickly, then left, with Alex on the bench seat between us.

***

"It says here that your birthday is this Saturday," Jenn said on the ride home as she examined the paperwork. She turned to Alex. "Why didn't you mention it?"

"I didn't know."

I assumed he meant that he forgot. There'd been many years I'd wanted to forget mine.

"We need to have a party," Jenn said.

Alex looked up at her. "Why?"

I glanced at Jenn.

She frowned. "Every child should have a party on their birthday."

"With presents," I added.

"We never had parties back home... or presents."

Again, I looked at Jenn. I thought she might burst into tears. He'd said it so matter-of-factly. I reached my arm around his shoulder. "Welcome, my little friend, to the U S of A, land of the free and home of the birthday party."

"And presents, too?"

I gave him a squeeze. "It wouldn't be a party without presents."

When I pulled up in front of the house and turned off the truck, Alex climbed over Jenn and opened the passenger door. "I'm going to tell Memaw."

"Are you thinking what I'm thinking?" Jenn asked after Alex had disappeared inside the house.

I grinned. "Best. Party. Ever."

"We don't have much time."

We'd passed a Walmart on the way back from Woodland Park. I ran into the house and asked Mama to keep an eye on Alex for a couple of hours.

We spent the first hour picking out party decorations and a couple of new games for his Xbox. The real fun came when we found a place called Mitchell's Western Store. We took our time picking out the perfect cowboy hat and boots. Before we left, I convinced Jenn that Alex needed his own saddle. She asked if we could afford it, and I told her not to worry. What I didn't tell her was that I still had one more present to buy. And it was a whopper. After all, we had ten years of unacknowledged birthdays to make up for.

I knew a thing or two about unacknowledged birthdays. After Mama left us when I was Alex's age, birthday celebrations weren't high on Pop's list of priorities. In fact, he spent most of his time racing to the bottom of a whiskey bottle. Fortunately, he'd kept it together enough to put food on our table. He didn't cook it, he just put it there.

On my sixteenth birthday, right about the time I'd gotten used to the idea that my birthday was just another day on the calendar, Pop surprised me with a present. As presents go, this one was a humdinger. He bought me a car. That '69 Mustang was in pretty rough shape, but it was a classic. More than that, it was my favorite car ever built. To this day, I'm not sure how he knew.

Alex's birthday had to be special. When we returned home, Jenn kept Alex busy while I unloaded his presents and hid them in our bedroom. We had a difficult time keeping a straight face the rest of the day. I'm not sure who was more excited about the upcoming celebration, the birthday boy or his new mama and me.

I did a little covert research on the Internet after dinner. The next morning after chores, I made an excuse to disappear for a couple of hours. When I returned, I threw a tarp over the back of the truck and convinced Buck to let me park it in the back of the barn overnight.

Alex followed us around Saturday morning as we hung streamers and blew up balloons. He never sat, or even stood in one place, for more than a few seconds. His excitement was contagious. Seth showed up just after lunch with present in hand.

I nodded. "Have you seen Buck?"

"I gave him the afternoon off. He said he had something to do in town."

"Well then, I guess we're all here." I looked at Alex. "Let's get this party started."

Alex ripped into his presents, reminding me of myself before Mama left. His favorite gift so far came from Seth, a beautiful book about horses. His thoughtfulness surprised me, particularly after his comments over lunch the other day.

After the candles had been blown out and the presents opened, I reached for a second piece of cake. Before the first bite, I held my fork in the air.

"I almost forgot," I said. "There's one more present."

Alex straightened in his chair, scanned the room quickly, then turned his gaze to me. "Where is it?"

I hooked a thumb over my shoulder. "Outside. In the back of my truck."

Jenn shot a surprised look my way. Alex rose from the table, and I followed him to the door. Once outside, his feet barely touched the ground as he covered the thirty feet to my truck.

Jenn stood beside me on the porch. "Are you crazy?"

We watched him climb up onto the seat of the Kodiak 700 ATV and grab the handlebar.

"I can't take it back now," I said, unable to hold back a childish grin.

"It looks dangerous."

"If he can learn how to ride a horse, he can learn how to ride one of those."

"This is a big place. What if he gets lost?"

"No worries." I slipped my arm around her waist and whispered in her ear. "I had a GPS tracker installed. You can monitor him from an app on your phone."

Chapter Ten

S eth looked at his watch as Alex's party wound down. He stood and excused himself.

"Where you headed?" I asked.

"Barn. Gotta get back to work." He grabbed his hat and said his goodbyes.

I followed him outside. "Seth. Can we talk?"

He turned. "I don't have time."

"Who found Roy after he died?" I asked when I caught up.

"You ask a lot of questions." He slid open the barn door, and I followed him inside.

"Just curious."

"Buck found him in his office."

"He told you that?"

"He didn't have to. I heard all the commotion when the sheriff arrived."

"What were you doing at the ranch?"

"Roy asked me to help out while he was sick. Had some kind of experimental treatment that knocked him on his ass."

"I didn't know."

"I don't think he told anyone else." Seth's face tightened. "You can check with his oncologist, Dr. Richards, if you don't believe me."

"Why wouldn't I believe you?"

Seth shrugged. He walked up to a small door between two stacks of hay along the north wall. He opened the door, then pushed the green button on a control box mounted on the wall beside it. A conveyor belt moved to the sound of an electric motor.

"What's this?" I asked.

"Hay transport."

He pulled on a pair of gloves, picked up a bale of hay from a nearby stack, and dropped it on the belt. I bent down and watched it travel through a tunnel toward the stable.

"Roy installed it so he didn't have to move the hay outside. It might rain cats and dogs, but the hay arrives clean and dry on the other side."

"Pretty cool." I stepped back and watched him drop another bale on the belt.

"There isn't a lot of storage space in the stable. With this baby, we can move a few bales at a time, as needed."

"Do you know the Whitehawk brothers?" I asked.

He turned to me as he carried another bale to the conveyor. "I've got to get six more of these over to the stable. How about you climb up there and toss them down to me?"

"So, the Whitehawk brothers?" I said after I tossed him the first bale.

"I know who they are. Everybody around these parts knows those two hoodlums."

"Buck seems to think they had something to do with Roy's death."

Seth loaded the next bale in silence.

"Says it was revenge for killing their mama," I added.

"Roy had a heart attack." Seth frowned as he looked up at me. "I don't see how the Whitehawks or anyone else could have killed him."

"Don't you think we should find out?"

"I think we should spend our time making sure this ranch is profitable. I'm not sure how much Jenny has shared with you, but the place isn't doing so well."

"She didn't mention it."

"This isn't a charity, you know. You can't make any money taking in strays. They're a lot of work and don't fetch a good price when you're done. You end up keeping most of them because nobody else wants them."

"I thought you were on board with that."

"I'm on board with turning a profit." He punched the red button and the conveyor stopped. "If you're going to live here, I'd appreciate it if you help us out."

"Uh... sure."

He closed the tunnel door. "C'mon. We need to take care of the other side."

"Turn that thing back on," I grinned. "We can ride over."

"I'd never make it. Claustrophobic."

Buck stood in the doorway as we turned to leave. He leaned forward, hand on his knees, breathing heavily.

"You boys best come quick."

"What's the matter?" Seth asked.

"Pasture," he said, then took off running.

Buck was pretty fast for a man his age. We caught up to him at the pasture fence. Buck climbed through the rails while Seth and I vaulted over the top. Two of the six horses we'd put out this morning stood about fifty yards away, with Chance on the ground at their feet. I knelt next to him and stroked his neck.

"What's the matter, boy?"

He lifted his head like he wanted to stand, but it flopped back to the ground. His breathing was labored, and his powerful muscles twitched.

I looked up to see three more horses on the ground. Buck pronounced two of them dead. Seth stood over the third, which was still alive. He pulled his phone from his pocket and called the vet.

"We've got two dead horses in the pasture, and another two about to follow them. Hurry." He ended the call and turned to us. "He's on the other side of the county. It'll be a good half hour before he gets here."

"We don't have that much time," Buck said. He punched a fist into an open hand. "Roy always knew what to do."

"Roy's not here," Seth shot back.

Buck thrust his hand out toward me, palm up. "Gimme your phone. I might be able to get us some help."

I tossed my phone to him, and he dialed. He spoke quickly, not all of it was English. Buck returned my phone, then ran off toward the barn.

I looked at Seth and shrugged. He looked away, and I turned my attention back to Chance. His big horse eyes fluttered.

"Hold on, boy." I wasn't sure why Buck had run off or how much longer Chance could hang on. Whatever had happened to these horses had happened quickly. Remington, the other sick horse, didn't look any better than Chance.

A motor roared, and I turned to see Buck approaching on an ATV. He skidded to a stop a few feet away and jumped off. Buck handed me a large syringe, then knelt next to Chance. He pulled the top off a second one with his teeth and spit it to the ground.

"What's that?"

"Atropine. It'll regulate his breathing and his heart rate." He pressed a spot about two-thirds of the way down Chance's neck and held it. A large vein, running the length of his neck, appeared to rise above the skin. "There you are."

Buck slipped the needle into the vein and pushed the plunger. He released the pressure and pulled out the syringe.

"Is that it?"

He nodded. I followed him over to Remington and watched him repeat the procedure.

Buck stood. "It may be accidental, or it may not, but these horses were poisoned."

"How do you know?" I asked.

"I've seen it before. Oleander, hemlock, yew, maybe even monkshood."

"Could any of that grow wild in the pasture?"

"That's what they want you to think."

"Who's they?"

"Them Whitehawk boys. Killin' Roy wasn't enough. Them Indians want to run us all off the ranch, or maybe kill us too. Probably figure this ranch to be a fair trade for their mama's life."

Seth, who'd been quiet until now, took this opportunity to throw gasoline on the fire. "So, Buck, what are we going to do about it?"

"We can't let them get away with it, that's for sure."

Seth looked at me. "You in, Dillon?"

This just got personal, and the Whitehawks were the most likely suspects, but I had to be sure. "We don't know for a fact that they did this."

Seth sneered. "Who else could it be?"

"I think we should call the sheriff. Let him sort it out."

Buck shook his head slowly. "That's not the way we do things 'round here."

Seth nodded.

"There's no proof." Buck removed his dirty cap and ran a hand back through his hair. "It would be our word against theirs."

"They're not gonna stop 'til someone stops 'em," Seth added.

I had a feeling I wouldn't like the answer, but I asked the question anyway. "How y'all fixin' to do that?"

"The Bible says an eye for an eye. The way I see it, we got two dead horses." Buck turned to me, his eyes narrow and cold. "You do the math."

A black Ford F-350 pulled up the drive and stopped at the pasture fence. A middle-aged Native American man jumped out and ran toward us. His thick braid of gray hair trailed out the back of his suede hat, swinging from side to side like a tail. Buck met him halfway, and the two shook hands. They approached together, Buck pointing toward the horses and talking as the stranger listened.

Buck introduced the man as John Standing Bear, an old friend of Roy's and the resident horse whisperer in the village where Cassidy lived. John knelt next to Chance and stroked his neck and muzzle. He spoke in soft tones for a moment before examining the horse's mouth. He leaned in close and inhaled before he moved down to Chance's chest then his stomach, his hands on the animal the whole time. Finally, he examined the pile of fresh manure on the ground.

"Did you do as I instructed you, Buck?"

"I did."

John performed a similar examination of Remington, then moved to one of the dead horses. He pulled up on the first animal's head, opened his mouth, then let the head fall back to the ground.

"If you want my professional opinion, these horses ingested some type of poison, probably in plant form."

"What do you think it was?" I asked.

"Your guess is as good as mine. There are all kinds of poisonous plants that grow on these hills."

I'm sure my guess wasn't as good as his. Buck shook his head slowly, and the look in his eyes worried me.

"I'm afraid the survival rate in these situations is low. It depends on how much was ingested and how fast we can remove it or move it through their systems. I had Buck give them atropine to stabilize their breathing and heart rate. That will buy us some time."

"Thank you," I said.

"We've still got work to do."

John gave Buck a list of items to retrieve from the stables as I walked back toward Chance to offer some additional comfort and support.

"Dillon," Jenn called from the edge of the pasture.

I ran to stop them as they climbed over the fence.

Chapter Eleven

Jenn quickly closed the distance between us with Alex a few steps behind.

I held up my hands. "Jenn, wait."

She stopped in front of me. "What happened?"

"We're not sure yet."

"Are they okay?" She tilted her head to get a look behind me.

"Jenn. Wait."

"Get out of my way." She took a step to her right, and I moved to block her.

"Maybe you shouldn't—"

"Don't make me go through you, Dillon."

Not a battle I wanted to fight. I glanced at Alex who stood beside her. His expression alternated between curiosity and fear.

"I'll stay with Alex," I said as I stepped aside and let her pass.

"He's coming with me."

"Jenn!"

She turned, clearly losing whatever patience she might have had left.

"One of the dead ones." I lowered my voice. "It's Apollo."

Her eyes flashed, and she looked at Alex. "Come on."

I watched the two of them jog the remaining sixty feet to where Buck and Seth stood, then walked in their direction. Alex ran to Apollo and knelt at his side. He stroked the neck of his fallen friend before resting his forehead there.

Buck passed me in the ATV while I walked. As I approached the group, I overheard John explaining the treatment options to Jenn. There were two—siphoning out the stomach contents through their noses or pumping them full of laxatives to flush it out the opposite end. The siphon would be quicker, but because the end of the hose must be below the stomach, this method would only work if the animal was standing. After several unsuccessful attempts to coax Chance to his feet, we agreed to go with the second option.

John slid about six feet of plastic tube into Chance's nostril, then attached the end to a hand pump. He set the pump into a bucket of mineral oil and pumped it through the tube. Buck refilled the bucket, and John pumped it in. They moved to Remington and repeated the procedure.

"Now what?" I asked.

John turned to me. "We wait."

"How long?"

"Anywhere from a couple of hours to overnight."

John shook hands and said his goodbyes. We thanked him for his help. It occurred to me that if he hadn't arrived, we'd still be waiting for the vet and most likely be preparing to bury four horses instead of two.

Buck walked John back to his truck while Seth gathered the tube and buckets. He loaded them onto the ATV and headed back to the barn.

"I'm not leaving them," Jenn said, her voice ragged.

I put my arm around her shoulder. "I'll take Alex back to the house and have Mama look after him." I lowered my hand and stroked her back. "I'll gather up some blankets and firewood."

After I dropped Alex off, I loaded supplies onto the ATV. Inside, Alex had just finished his dinner and excused himself to go play video games. A pot of coffee brewed on the counter, an empty thermos beside it. Mama had her head in the fridge, gathering up fixins for sandwiches for Jenn and me.

Mama set everything on the counter and asked me to sit.

"I have something to tell you," she said in a voice that was as firm as it was quiet. She sat next to me.

I'm not sure what I expected, but given the way the day had gone so far, I wasn't optimistic.

"I've decided to move back to Bradley."

Unsure how to respond, I said nothing.

"I'll catch a bus on Monday."

"So soon?"

"Mort is going to meet me in Albuquerque. He has family there. We'll stay for a few days before heading back to Bradley. It'll be like a vacation."

"I can drive you to Albuquerque."

"Thank you, but that's not necessary."

"Is this really what you want?"

She put her hand on mine. "I'm sorry, Dillon, but I have to do this. You have Jenn and Alex. I need to fall in love again."

"You'll find someone here."

"Dillon..."

I shrugged. "I didn't say it would be easy."

"At my age," she smiled, "I need easy. Besides, I've already found someone."

An all-too-familiar feeling surged in my chest. "I'm going to miss you."

"It'll be different this time," she said, biting her lip against tears. "I promise."

"We can spend holidays together," I offered.

"Absolutely." She laughed through more tears before her expression grew solemn. "This time, I can't leave without your blessing."

"I'm not going to lie and say I want you to go. But I won't hold you back." I forced a smile. "You have my blessing."

Mama patted my hand before she stood. "Thank you," she said, then leaned over and kissed my forehead.

I watched her walk to the counter and pick up a knife.

"Do you want turkey or roast beef?"

"One of each."

***

Remington and Chance rested quietly under a crescent moon. The absence of any clouds made the night air brisk. Jenn sat near the fire, a wool blanket wrapped around her shoulders, while I checked on the horses. Their breathing had stabilized, and it appeared the laxative had worked. I returned to the fire and sat next to Jenn. I poured two cups of coffee from the thermos. Jenn and I had agreed to take shifts, but neither of us had slept much.

"They seem to be doing better," I said as I handed her a cup. "How are you holdin' up?"

She nodded, staring off into the night.

"Mama told me she's moving back to Texas."

"I'm sorry, Dillon. I'm sure that brings back some difficult memories." She took a sip of coffee. "This time will be different."

Before I spoke again, Jenn stood. She took a step toward the darkness that hung just beyond the reach of the firelight.

"What is it?" I scanned the area in front of her but saw nothing but black.

Chance became agitated. I went to him and stroked his neck. "What's the matter, boy?"

He let out a loud, frightened neigh and continued to thrash his head around. It appeared he wanted to stand. Remington made similar sounds and movements.

I attempted to calm them, then turned to Jenn for help. "Jenn."

Jenn had dropped her blanket and taken another few steps toward the darkness. She turned her head and put a finger to her lips.

In the spaces between the horse sounds, I heard a low, but unmistakable, sound that caused the hairs on the back of my neck to stiffen. A slow, throaty growl oozed from the darkness in front of us. I picked up the rifle as Jenn walked toward the sound.

The growl stopped, or maybe the pounding in my ears drowned it out. Jenn continued to walk. The click from the Winchester seemed amplified as I cocked it. Jenn turned, wild-eyed, her hand up to stop me.

The noise started again, closer this time. The horses resumed their agitation. Jenn squatted near the edge of the fire's glow, eyes forward, as if inviting the dangerous creature to join us. My finger twitched as I brought it closer to the trigger. I couldn't risk a shot past Jenn in the direction of the sound. A shot into the air would surely scare the intruder away, but I trusted Jenn's intuition, even as I struggled with her irrational behavior. I pointed the rifle above my head, finger hovering over the trigger, as I let the scene play out.

It took all my strength to keep my finger steady as a pair of green eyes reflected the firelight from the edge of the darkness. Jenn held her position no more than twenty feet from the biggest wolf I'd ever seen.

Chapter Twelve

The wolf took a couple of tentative steps in Jenn's direction, acting as if he might be more afraid of her than she was of him. He stopped, and they stared at each other. Every second felt like a minute. Despite the cold air, sweat beaded up on my forehead and neck.

The wolf took another step, and my finger twitched.

The horses remained silent, and I glanced at them, confused. I looked back at Jenn and saw her lips move like she whispered something to the wolf. He seemed to respond with a nod, then turned and disappeared into the blackness.

I slipped the safety on and walked over to Jenn. "Are you okay?"

She nodded.

I knelt on one knee. "What just happened?"

Jenn looked at me and smiled briefly before lowering her gaze. "He won't hurt us."

"He told you that?"

Her eyes met mine. "In a way."

"I saw you say something to him."

"I thanked him."

"I think there's still some coffee in the thermos. You should have offered him a cup and asked him to hang with us."

"Now you're just being a jackass."

"You scared the crap out of me."

"You had a rifle, and you had my back. You always do."

Her words disarmed me. I removed my hat and wiped my forehead. "Just don't do anything dangerous like that again."

Jenn retrieved her blanket and wrapped it around her shoulders. She sat near the fire and studied the ground as I sat next to her.

"Remember the night I showed you my tattoo?" she asked without looking up.

"Of course." How could I forget? I have the image of a wolf tattooed on my forearm. I'd gotten it just before I left for basic training. It represented the image I had of myself as a lone wolf, driven from the pack to wander alone. I'd been reluctant to talk about its meaning, but Jenn coaxed it out of me. Imagine my surprise when she unbuttoned her shirt and showed me a nearly identical tattoo in the middle of her back.

"Do you remember why I got it?"

"You called it your spirit animal." I scratched the side of my face. "I don't even know what that means."

She smiled. "Spirit animals carry wisdom. The spirits of different animals embody distinct qualities. We have a special connection with the animals that represent characteristics or abilities we currently have or hope to develop."

I said nothing as I tried to process her words.

"They appear from time to time to remind us," she continued. "As you deepen your connection, deeper meanings are revealed."

"What kind of meanings?"

"For example, the power of the wolf brings forth instinct, intelligence, and the importance of social connections. It can also symbolize fear of being threatened and lack of trust."

"The trust thing. I get that."

"When the wolf shows up in your life, pay attention to what your intuition is telling you."

"You mean like a gut feeling?"

She nodded. "Do you know why he was here?"

"Dinner would be my first guess."

"He was here for you as much as he was for me." She put her hand on my knee. "What did you feel when you saw him?"

"I was too scared to feel anything."

"You didn't trust—"

"I'm supposed to trust a growling wolf?"

"I did."

"Yeah, and I thought you'd just lost your mind." I felt the muscles in my face tighten. "What you did was reckless. I guess I got a little angry because I don't know what I'd do without you. I need you, Jenn."

She tilted her head and flashed a smile that I felt in my gut. "Dillon Bishop, that might be the nicest thing y'all ever said to me." She scrunched her nose. "Except for the reckless part."

"Uh... Alex needs you, too."

"I know what Alex needs." She slipped her hand into mine. "I want to hear more about what you need."

"I love you, Jenn, and I need you to stick around. For a long, long time."

"I stand corrected." She squeezed my hand. "*That* was the nicest thing y'all ever said to me."

A sliver of moonlight reflected in her eyes as she stared into mine. I leaned in and she met me halfway. Her soft lips warmed me instantly, and I pushed in closer. It would have been a perfect moment had we not been sitting thirty feet from two dead horses.

***

I awoke to the sunrise with Jenn in my arms, a heavy wool blanket pulled over our heads. The cold ground felt like a sucker punch to the kidney. I reluctantly extricated myself from Jenn to sit and rub my lower back. The heavy blankets we'd laid over Remington and Chance lay scattered on the ground. I scanned the pasture, still wet with dew, and found the two horses grazing together near the fence.

I nudged Jenn. "Hey."

Her sleepy eyes opened slowly. She looked at me, confused, and her lips formed an uncertain smile.

"You're gonna want to see this," I said, hooking my thumb over my shoulder.

Jenn pushed herself up on her elbows and turned toward the horses. She flashed a huge smile, then jumped to her feet and took off running. It happened so fast that I pictured one of those old Saturday morning cartoons where it takes a second or two for the runner's head to catch up with the body, snapping back into place like a rubber band.

She stood between the two horses, an arm around each of their necks. She turned her head, giggling like a schoolgirl as I approached. "They made it. It's a miracle."

"I hate to admit it, but I had my doubts last night."

"You boys didn't want to leave me yet, did you?" she said to the horses.

"Buck thinks they were deliberately poisoned." As soon as I'd said it, I wished I'd given her a little more time to enjoy the moment.

"What?" Jenn stopped what she was doing. "By who?"

I hesitated. "A couple of Indians—"

"Native Americans."

"What?"

"They're Native Americans."

"Whatever. They live on that little reservation Roy set up. Buck thinks they're trying to run us off."

Jenn stared at me with squinted eyes. "Why would they do that? Uncle Roy was always good to them."

"Maybe a little too good."

I told her about Roy and Asha Whitehawk and the trouble their relationship had caused. As I went over the details of Buck's theory, it seemed more plausible than the first time I'd heard it.

"Uncle Roy had a heart attack."

"That's what they want you to think." I closed my eyes and stopped for a moment. I sounded like Buck. "What I mean is that it could have been made to look like a heart attack."

"What do *you* think?"

"I wish I knew what was going on around here when he died."

Jenn grabbed my arm. "I might be able to help with that."

"How?"

"Uncle Roy liked to write things down. He kept daily journals for his practice. He wrote about all the animals he worked on, what was wrong with them, and how he fixed them. Kind of like a homemade vet encyclopedia."

"How is that going to help us?"

"He also kept a personal journal. He wrote in it every night before bed." She shrugged. "That was a long time ago, and I don't know if he kept up with it, but we should at least try to find out."

A diesel motor roared as Buck drove a backhoe through the pasture gate on his way to bury the dead horses. I positioned myself to block Jenn's view. "C'mon, let's go. I'll come back later to clean up our campsite."

Jenn heard it, too. Her bottom lip quivered as she nodded.

CHAPTER THIRTEEN

After chores and breakfast, Jenn and I slipped away to the attic to look for Roy's journals. By the time Jenn had moved in, most of Roy's things had been stored away in the attic.

The old floorboards creaked as we made our way through a lifetime of another man's memories. I ducked my head a couple of times along the way to avoid the rough-hewn wooden rafters. The summer's heat still lingered in the stale air, even as the calendar neared the end of September.

We knelt beside a dozen or more boxes with Roy's name written in black marker on the sides.

"Why didn't Seth move into the house? He got here before you."

"I'm glad he didn't," she said as she lifted the flaps on the first box. "As far as I know, Seth always kept to himself. I think he's happy where he is. Those cabins by the river are nice, and I think he likes the seclusion."

"I heard he spent a lot of time here before Roy died. Maybe he was already living in one of those cabins and didn't feel like moving."

"Who told you that?"

"Hattie." I opened one of the boxes. "Do you know what they look like?"

She stopped to look at me. "The cabins?"

"The journals."

She blinked a few times. "They were leather-bound. Seth must have boxed all this stuff up, so I don't know where they ended up."

I watched her for a few moments, deciding if I should say anything more about Seth.

"Does Seth seem different to you, or has he always been a jackass?"

"What?" She looked up from her search. "Did something happen?"

"It's more like something he said."

"Y'all gonna tell me what it is?"

"He told me not to get too comfortable here."

"Seth said that? When?"

"The night we arrived."

"That doesn't sound like Seth." She resumed her search. "I'm sure you heard him wrong."

I hesitated as I considered how to respond. "Yeah, maybe that's it." That wasn't it.

After rifling through the last box, I sat back on my heels. She hadn't seen them because they weren't there. "Where else do you suppose he might have kept them?"

"I went through the entire house before I moved in." She dragged the back of her hand across her forehead. "I guess they could be in his office, but he used to write in them before bed. Why wouldn't they be here?"

"Do you think he got rid of them?"

"Who writes in journals just to throw them away?"

"What if there was something in them he didn't want anyone to see after he died?"

"He had a heart attack. He didn't have time to ditch them before he died."

"Maybe he didn't want someone to see them while he was alive."

Jenn stood. "I guess we should check his office."

The air temperature changed quickly as I followed Jenn down the attic stairs. The cooler air chilled the beads of sweat on my forehead. When we reached the stable, I called Buck's name and then Seth's. No answer. Several of the horses that hadn't been turned out yet watched with indifference as we marched down the wide center aisle. The others went about their usual business.

Roy's veterinary office occupied a large room that he'd added on to the back of the stable next to the tack room. We found the door locked when we arrived.

"Do you have the key?" I asked.

"I don't know." She pulled the biggest ring of keys I'd ever seen from her pocket. "I found these in the house. Maybe one of them opens this door."

Jen tried the first few keys with no luck.

"Maybe I should go look for Seth or Buck," I said as she neared the end of the ring.

"There's still a few more to try." As soon as she said it, the knob turned, and we were in.

A large wooden desk that had seen better days sat in the center of the room. A credenza underneath three shelves full of books occupied the wall behind it. The rest of the room contained two file cabinets, a glass-front case filled with medical supplies, and a six-foot metal storage locker. A single wooden chair provided a place for clients to sit.

I walked around the desk and sat in Roy's worn leather chair. Jenn stood next to me, examining the books on the back wall. I nudged her leg, and she turned.

I pointed to the framed picture of an attractive Native American woman on his desk. "This must be Asha. She looks a lot like her sister."

"Roy had good taste."

Jenn handed me a leather-covered book. I opened it to find handwritten pages detailing client visits—names, dates, symptoms, diagnosis, and follow-up notes.

"These might come in handy next time someone tries to kill our horses."

She narrowed her eyes at me and shook her head. "There isn't going to be a next time."

"So, where are his personal journals?"

"I don't know." Her eyes widened. "You could try looking."

One by one, I opened the file cabinet drawers and examined their contents. Mostly business records, property records, and folders for each of the horses. The bottom drawer of the second cabinet refused to open.

"Let me see those keys," I called to Jenn.

She tossed the ring, and I tried every key. The drawer remained locked.

I returned to Roy's chair and rifled through the desk drawers, starting from the bottom. Nothing noteworthy in the first two except for a couple of pill bottles for drugs with unfamiliar names.

"What did you say Roy died from?"

"A heart attack. Why?"

I shoved them in my pocket. "Looks like his doctor's name was Richards." I was pretty sure that was the name Seth mentioned earlier.

I found a revolver in the top drawer. I held it up with two fingers, the barrel pointing at the ground. "Look what I found."

Jen turned, probably expecting to see me holding up a key. "Jeezus, Dillon. Is it loaded?"

I flicked my wrist to swing the cylinder out. All six chambers were full. I turned the gun upside down and tapped the extractor rod. The bullets dropped into the drawer.

"Not anymore," I said, then swung the cylinder back into place and set the revolver back in the drawer.

"Why do you suppose he kept a loaded gun in his desk?" she asked.

"I don't know." I shrugged and grinned. "Horse mutiny?"

Jenn frowned. "I'm serious, Dillon."

"I hope we don't have to find out." I continued my search but found no keys. We left disappointed.

Someone called out as I locked the door behind us. "Hey!"

Buck trotted down the aisle toward us. "What were you two doin' in there?"

"We were looking for Uncle Roy's journals," Jenn offered.

Buck eyed us suspiciously. "Then I reckon you didn't look hard enough. They're right up there on the shelf behind his desk."

"We found those," I said. "We were looking for his personal journals."

Buck shook his head. "I wouldn't know nothin' about that." He tested the doorknob to make sure we'd locked it. "All I know is that this door needs to stay locked."

"Why is that?" Jenn asked.

"There's some harsh chemicals in there." He shot Jenn a steely glare. "Some a that stuff will kill a horse, let alone a boy."

Jenn covered her mouth with her hand.

A few seconds passed as Buck's gaze alternated between us.

Jenn put her hands on her hips. "What's in the locked—"

I tugged on her arm. "We'll be careful," I assured Buck. "And we'll make sure Alex knows to stay away."

I felt Jenn's glare as I pulled her down the aisle. I glanced behind us to see Buck turn and walk in the opposite direction.

When I let go of her arm, Jenn put both hands on my chest and pushed. "What the hell was that about?"

I grabbed her shoulders and locked onto her eyes. "He had a loaded gun in there. Maybe Roy was protecting himself, or maybe he was protecting whatever was in that locked drawer. Either way, I think we need to get some answers first."

She shook herself loose and straightened her collar. "What if Buck has the answers?"

I folded my arms across my chest. "What if Buck was the reason for the gun?"

Chapter Fourteen

J enn and I drove Mama to the bus station on Monday morning. Our goodbyes were said with few words. On the way back, I told Jenn about the spirited conversation that took place in the pasture the day we found the poisoned horses.

"What do you think?" she asked.

"I think we need to find some proof."

I had a feeling that Buck or Seth might decide to take the Whitehawk matter into their own hands, so I kept a close eye on both of them for the next few days. Neither left the ranch or spent any time together as far as I could tell.

When I saw Buck cross the cattle guard on Wednesday evening, I told Jenn there was something I had to take care of, and I followed him into town. He parked his truck outside the Wet Whistle as I watched from the street. I didn't want it to appear that I'd followed him, so I drove around the block a couple of times to give him some space. Hopefully, it would take him longer than ten minutes to get himself in trouble.

I entered the building and noticed Buck in the corner booth, eyes fixed on one of the Whitehawk boys sitting alone at the bar. I sized up the room, careful not to let on that I'd seen Buck. Lynyrd Skynyrd sang "Free Bird" through the jukebox speaker to a handful of indifferent cowboys huddled around the far end of the bar.

I sat down at the bar next to Heckle, or maybe it was Jeckle. He glanced at me before quickly draining his beer. He picked up his money and got up to leave.

"Sit down," I said.

We locked eyes for a moment. The muscles in his neck tensed as he clenched his fists. He didn't take kindly to being ordered around. He might have been dumb enough to throw the first punch if anyone was watching, but no one paid us any mind.

"I just want to talk," I said.

"That makes one of us."

"First drink's on me."

"First and last." He kicked the empty stool a few inches to widen the space between us, then sat.

"Where's your brother?" I asked after I ordered two beers.

"Probably out poisoning more horses," Buck interjected from over my shoulder.

I turned. "Go back and finish your drink. I'll handle this."

"You know that crazy old man?"

"I reckon I do." I held out my hand. "I'm Dillon Bishop."

He stared at my hand for a moment, then picked up the bottle that the barkeep had set in front of him.

"I guess I'll just have to call you guys Heckle and Jeckle," I said when he didn't respond.

"Jacob." He took another drink.

"Now we're gettin' somewhere." I lifted my bottle in Jacob's direction before taking a long pull.

"If you've got something to say, just say it and leave me alone."

"It's more like a question." I picked at the label on my bottle. "How well did you know Roy McDonald?"

He thought for a moment. "I knew him well enough not to like him."

"Here's the thing. My crazy friend over there thinks you knew him well enough to kill him."

Again, he took his time before answering. "I had every right to. He killed my mama. I told her to stay away, but she wouldn't listen."

I nodded. "I see. So, it was justifiable homicide?"

"I didn't say that." His muscles tensed and he squeezed his bottle so hard, I thought it might shatter in his hand. "I said I had every right to kill that bastard. I didn't say that I did it."

"What about your brother?"

"Jeremiah didn't do it."

"Okay. Let's just say you boys didn't do it. Who else wanted him dead?"

He gestured toward the corner booth. "Why don't you ask that crazy old man? He and Roy weren't always the best of friends."

"Maybe I will." I picked some more at my label. "One more thing. Someone poisoned our horses last weekend. You know anything about that?"

He leaned in closer, face to face. "Look. I don't give a rat's ass about you *or* your horses. Roy is dead. He got what he deserved. I just spent a year in prison for something I didn't do. I don't need any more trouble." He picked up his bottle, drained it, then set it firmly on the bar. "You think I might be able to go take a piss now?"

I held up my hands like I wouldn't try to stop him.

A few minutes later, Jacob walked out the front door without so much as a look in my direction.

I picked up my drink and walked over to the corner booth.

Buck raised an eyebrow. "Well?"

"He said they had nothing to do with Roy's death. They've moved on."

"He's a damn liar," Buck growled, shaking his head.

"He told me he's been in prison for a year. If that's true, he couldn't have killed Roy."

Buck took a long draw on his bottle, then set it down. "I think they got out just before Roy died."

I studied him for a moment, wondering what Jacob had meant when he pointed the finger at Buck.

***

Jenn watched in amusement from the center of the round pen. Chance trotted along the perimeter fence with yours truly in the saddle. I felt like that little rubber ball at the end of a rubber band connected to a wooden paddle.

"You're doing great," Jenn shouted.

My backside disagreed.

Chance came with a five-speed transmission—walk, trot, slow lope, fast lope, and gallop. I shifted into third gear with a firm kick. Chance lowered his head and stepped on the gas. My hat blew off as he accelerated, and I grabbed the saddle horn so the rest of me didn't follow. Jenn shouted encouragement between bursts of laughter. Halfway around the pen, as I relaxed into the saddle and moved my hips to the rhythm of his stride, horse and rider became one. We circled the pen a half-dozen times, the wind in my hair and a big, goofy grin painted across my face.

Jenn shouted something, and I pulled the reins to apply the brakes. We came to a stop, and I leaned forward to give Chance a pat on the neck. "Good boy."

Jenn picked up my hat and ran to meet us. "That was great, Dillon."

The goofy grin was back as she handed me my hat.

"You looked like you were having fun."

I nodded vigorously.

Jenn giggled. "I sure had fun watching you. You looked like you were ridin' a bucking bronc instead of a tired old rescue."

I set my hat on my head and looked down at Jenn. In my best John Wayne voice, I said, "Young lady, if you're lookin' fer trouble... I'll accommodate ya."

She laughed and slapped my thigh. "If I was lookin' for trouble, you'd know it."

I had a feeling there was a good measure of truth to that statement.

"Seriously," she said. "You had a nice rhythm there at the end. You looked like a pro." Jenn took the reins after I climbed down from the saddle. "I'm going to cool him down. Walk with me."

I fell into step with her as she walked Chance along the fence.

"So," I said, "there's something I've been meaning to talk to you about."

"I'm listening."

"Apparently, Buck's not convinced that your uncle Roy died of natural causes."

"What does he think happened?" she asked, her eyes fixed on the ground in front of her.

"He's convinced that Jacob and Jeremiah Whitehawk killed him."

"Asha's boys?"

I stopped. "You know about them?"

Jenn turned her head as she continued to walk. "Seth told me."

"Did he tell you Roy was sick?"

She nodded.

I caught up to her and fell into step. "So, what do you think?"

"I think his heart attack saved him from a slow, painful death."

"Seth said he was taking some experimental drugs."

"What's done is done."

"Why do you suppose people think he was murdered?"

"People?" She raised an eyebrow. "You mean Buck?"

"Buck and Cassidy Whitehawk."

"That's right. The Native American girl who runs around up on the ridge and thinks Uncle Roy murdered her sister. The sister he was about to marry. Is that the one?"

"Don't you want to know the truth?"

She studied my face for a few moments. "You've got that look again. The same one you had just before you bailed on me in Texas."

"I didn't bail on you."

"You let me go to Colorado alone."

"I'm here now." I squeezed the back of my neck. "Don't you see? I had to stay and find out the truth. They were family."

"And Uncle Roy?"

"He's *your* family. That's close enough for me."

"That's nice, Dillon, but—"

I grabbed her arm. "Someone was willing to kill innocent horses. Buck thinks they're trying to run us off the ranch. I don't want to see you in harm's way."

"I can take care of myself." She straightened her shoulders.

"Maybe so, but I don't want to take any chances if there's a credible threat."

"I'd hardly call Buck's theories credible."

"Okay. Maybe you're not worried about yourself, but what about Alex?"

She didn't have such a quick answer this time.

CHAPTER FIFTEEN

Don't ask me why, but Alex looked up to me as a father figure. I have to admit that the idea had been growing on me, even though it scared the bejeezus out of me. Jenn threw her arms around my neck on Saturday morning when I told her it might be time for a male bonding ritual. After chores, Alex and I headed out on a day trip into the wilderness. I'd considered making the journey on horseback, but truth be told, I wasn't quite ready to go riding off into the outback unsupervised.

Indian summer had arrived with plenty of sun and a seventy-degree weather forecast for the weekend and beyond. After a Texas-sized breakfast, Alex and I saddled up the ATVs as Jenn watched from the porch. Alex ran to her for a kiss goodbye, then climbed up on his shiny new Kodiak. I promised Jenn we'd be back before dinner and waved goodbye.

I turned the throttle a couple of times and looked at Alex. "You ready, pardner?"

He nodded and flashed a smile so big, I thought the top of his head might come off. I told him to buckle his helmet, which I figured would hold it in place.

We rode for about an hour, racing across open fields, splashing through streams, and climbing into the foothills east of the homestead. I stopped for a drink of water and checked the map Jenn had given me. My suggestion that we head north to Fletcher's Pond prompted a thumbs-up from Alex.

I parked my ATV near a small waterfall that fed the half-acre pond named for the first settler of the property. "This looks like a good place to stop for lunch," I said when Alex pulled up beside me.

Alex nodded and parked his vehicle.

"But first," I said as I removed Pop's old hunting rifles from the back of my ATV, "I'm going to teach you how to shoot."

Alex approached cautiously. "What are we going to shoot?"

"We're going to start with these." I held up three tin cans that I'd rescued from the trash bin. "You wait here while I set 'em up."

I placed them on a flat rock approximately one hundred feet from where Alex stood. When I rejoined him, I gave him a lesson in gun safety. Next, I explained the finer points of taking out a stationary target. Finally, a demonstration. At this distance, I could have hit the target with my eyes closed and one hand tied behind my back, but I took my time and explained each step. My first shot hit its mark, and Alex clapped.

"If you think I'm a good shot, you should see your mama."

"Mama can shoot?"

"Better than anyone I've ever met." I held the rifle out in front of me. "Now it's your turn."

His first two shots were off the mark. Each time, we discussed the proper adjustments. The third time, as they say, was the charm. He lowered the gun barrel, and his face lit up.

"Nice shot, Alex."

"Can I try another?"

I nodded. "Take your time, then slowly *squeeze* the trigger."

Another hit. I let out a hoot, or maybe it was a holler.

Alex blushed. "You're a good teacher."

I showed him how to replace the safety before he handed me the rifle.

"The first time Pop took me out to shoot," I said as I retrieved our lunch from the saddlebag, "he loaded my gun with blanks. Naturally, I didn't hit a thing. But it made me concentrate on the fundamentals. By the time he handed me his rifle with live rounds, I couldn't miss. Of course, I was madder than a hornet when I found out, but I got over it."

"How come you didn't do that today?"

"To be honest, I thought about it." I pulled two sandwiches from the sack and handed one to Alex. "While his method seemed to work, I never trusted him after that."

"I'm glad you did it your way," he said with a mouthful of ham and cheese.

Halfway through lunch, a jackrabbit darted out from a rock near our target area. I grabbed the rifle.

"With a moving target," I said as I released the safety, "you don't aim for where it is, you aim for where it's going to be." I squeezed off a round and dropped the little critter in his tracks.

"Why did you do that?"

I looked at him, puzzled. "It's called hunting. In the old days, that was how people got their food."

"Do we have to eat it?"

"Shhh." I held up my hand. "Do you hear that?"

Alex nodded.

The sound of a truck engine came from just beyond a stand of spruce trees. Alex and I crouched behind a boulder. Through the trees, I saw a pickup truck that had just stopped in the middle of a meadow about a hundred yards away. Two men got out and grabbed some equipment from the back of the truck. I watched one of them twist what looked like a large auger into the dirt. When he pulled it out, the other man bagged the soil he'd extracted.

I'd seen geologists take core samples for oil or mineral deposits, but they were much deeper and usually required drilling equipment. These guys only seemed interested in the first twelve to eighteen inches of dirt.

I told Alex to stay down and be quiet, then I crawled back to the ATV and grabbed my rifle. Alex watched, eyes wide, as I returned. I checked the safety, aimed my rifle at the truck, and peered through the scope for a better look.

"Are you going to shoot them?"

"What?" I turned to Alex, eyes narrowed. "No. Why would you even ask that?"

"You shot the rabbit," he whispered.

I shook my head. "That's different."

"How?"

An answer that would satisfy an eleven-year-old boy eluded me. "It just is."

Alex stared.

I raised a finger to my lips to indicate the conversation was over. With my eye to the scope, I read the three letters on the side of the truck. Romeo. Mike. Alpha. It meant nothing to me. I continued to watch as they packed up and drove away. In the distance, I saw them stop and repeat the procedure. I lowered the rifle. *Who is RMA, and what the hell are they doing on our land?*

"It's clear," I said to Alex.

"Who were they?"

"I don't know."

It still bothered me that I couldn't answer his rabbit question. Perhaps Jenn could help when we got back.

"I watched them shoot my grandfather, like you shot that rabbit, when he tried to escape the Taliban."

I put my arm around his little shoulders. "I'm sorry that happened. And even more sorry that you had to see it."

Alex hung his head.

"Look. I don't have all the answers. Maybe killing animals isn't the best thing to do, but I can tell you that killing people is something no one should ever do for any reason. Right?"

He nodded as he continued to stare at the ground.

"You like to eat steak and hamburgers?"

He nodded, then added, "And bacon."

"There you go. I think God put some animals here just so we wouldn't starve to death… or maybe so we wouldn't eat each other." I pretended to take a bite out of his shoulder.

I couldn't see it, but I knew he smiled. I took another bite.

Alex pulled my forearm up to his mouth and made a chomping sound.

"C'mon, pardner," I said. "Time to move out before there's nothin' left to move."

"What about the rabbit?" Alex asked as we packed up the ATVs for the rest of the trip.

"You got any suggestions?"

"Bury it?"

"Here's what I think. If we bury it, he died for nothing. That doesn't seem fair to the rabbit, does it?"

Alex shook his head.

"But if we take him home and have Mama cook him, then his death had a purpose."

He thought about it for a moment. "Okay. Let's take him with us."

I held out my fist.

"Are you going to punch me?"

"What? No. Of course not." I realized it may be a strange gesture to someone who spent most of his life in rural Afghanistan. "Hold out your fist like mine."

He obliged, and I gently tapped his fist with mine.

He stared at me. "Why did you do that?"

I reckoned I'd always just done it and never tried to put it into words. "Uh, it means a lot of different things. I guess it could mean hello, or good job, or that's cool."

"What did that one mean?"

"It meant... I got your back, little man."

He smiled. "I have yours, too, big man."

We returned as promised a little before dinner. I let Alex explain the whole rabbit thing.

Chapter Sixteen

When I heard the shower running Sunday morning, I grabbed Jenn's laptop from the nightstand and googled RMA. Rocky Mountain Agriculture was a Denver firm, one of the largest marijuana growers in Colorado. I set the laptop on the bed and opened the bathroom door. A cloud of steam rushed out and swirled around the bedroom ceiling.

"Don't use up all the hot water," I said.

"Then stop wasting time and get your butt in here."

Steam wasn't the only thing rising as I watched Jenn through the glass. I peeled off my clothes and stepped into the shower.

She batted her big blue eyes. "I thought maybe you'd run off and left me here alone."

I watched the water drops splash on her shoulders and slide down her breasts. "Well," I said in my John Wayne voice, "there are some things a man just can't run away from."

Arms and legs untangled quickly as the water temperature dropped five minutes later. I grabbed the towel off the door.

Jenn protested. "Hey, that's my towel."

"I thought it was for guests."

"Since when are you a guest?"

"Since you invited me in." I stepped out onto the mat.

Jenn shivered. "That'll be the last time you'll get invited any-where if you don't hand me a clean towel right now."

I quickly obliged and felt another stir down there as I watched her towel off.

Jenn noticed and rolled her eyes. "You'd better holster that thing, cowboy. You've got chores to do."

I nodded reluctantly before stepping out into the bedroom. When I saw the laptop on the bed, I realized that I'd forgotten to ask her about RMA. I wouldn't get any chores done if I walked back in there, so I finished dressing and went downstairs.

I inquired about RMA at breakfast, but Jenn hadn't heard of them. She suggested I check with Seth or Buck. If someone was on our land, surely one of them would know about it.

I found Buck in his workshop.

"Sure, I herda RMA. Most folks 'round here have."

"Did you know they were here yesterday?"

"No, sir. I did not." He had a worried look in his eyes that made me wonder if he was holding back.

"You once told me you know about every leaf that blows on this ranch."

Buck spat a stream of tobacco juice onto the floor before turning a defiant eye in my direction. "I ain't God, you know?"

"Yeah, I figured that out."

"I told you I don't know nothin' about it."

I guessed I'd have to make a few phone calls and get the information straight from the horse's mouth instead of trying to get it from the other end.

I left the barn and walked toward the corral. Alex and his new horse, Romeo, were warming up for another lesson. I leaned against the rail near the gate to watch them while I waited for Jenn.

"Hey," she said and lifted the latch on the gate.

I nodded. "I still haven't met this *nice guy* Charlie of yours."

She stopped to look at me with squinted eyes. "What do you mean?"

Buck stepped out of the barn and walked toward the stable.

I tilted my head in his direction. "It couldn't be *that* guy. The one who calls himself Buck. He could start a fight in an empty room. And that's when he's sober. You don't want to see him when he's drunk."

"Really?" She lifted an eyebrow. "When have you seen him drunk?"

"I guess I didn't tell you about the night I met Buck."

"I guess you didn't."

"You remember the night we had that fight about the adoption?"

"I try not to."

"Well, when I left, I drove into town for a drink. I found a mean old drunk in the bar pickin' a fight with a couple of Indians—"

"Native Americans."

"What?"

"They're Native Americans."

"Whatever. The point is, they were half his age. If I hadn't stepped in..."

"That was nice of you, Dillon."

"I didn't know that old man from Adam, and I stuck my neck out to keep him from gettin' his plow cleaned. Did I get a thank-you? No, ma'am. I even offered to give him a ride home."

Jenn stood on her toes and kissed my cheek. "You've got a big heart, Dillon. You're always trying to help the underdog. The thing is, not everyone wants to be helped." She patted my chest. "You need to accept that."

"I guess he's not always a jackass. We've had a few good conversations, but whenever I start asking questions, he jumps on me with all four feet. I think he's hiding something."

"I'm sure an old cowboy like that has a few skeletons in his footlocker. We all do, don't we?"

"I guess." I didn't want to start diggin' up any of my old bones, so I let the conversation die right there.

"Promise me you'll give him a chance?"

"I'll think about it."

Buck seemed to be everybody's go-to guy around here, but trust had to be earned. As far as I was concerned, he hadn't done that yet.

Seth walked out of the stables with Buck a few steps behind. They stopped for a moment and exchanged words. I called to Seth and waved him over. I leaned against the fence and waited.

"Do you know why I saw an RMA truck over by Fletcher's Pond yesterday?"

Seth came to an abrupt stop about eight feet in front of me. "I do. They were taking soil samples."

Jenn turned around on the other side of the fence. "Why?"

"I'm looking for ways to increase our revenue. Leasing some of the land that we're not using makes sense."

"That may be true," Jenn said, "but next time, I'd appreciate it if you discussed it with me first."

"We didn't sign anything. They're just doing some preliminary testing."

"That's not the point."

"Do you even know anything about running a ranch?"

Jenn's back stiffened, and she put her hands on her hips. "Do *you?*"

"I know a little something about making money, which is more than I can say about you."

Jenn climbed up on the bottom fence rail and pointed a finger at Seth. "Y'all better pay me some mind. You and I are equal partners. That means we make decisions together. If you think for one minute that you—"

I held up my hands. "Let's all take a deep breath before we say something we're gonna regret."

Jenn glared. "Stay out of this, Dillon."

"At least we agree on *something*," Seth said.

More finger-pointing. "Y'all better shut your pie hole, or I'll shut it for ya."

Seth looked at me. "Buck needs a hand in the workshop. He's overhauling one of the tractors. It's a two-man job."

"When we're done here." I didn't want to leave these two wildcats alone.

"We're done."

I looked at Jenn as Seth walked away. Clearly, this was not the time for further discussion. I set off to find Buck.

Seth's wiseass remarks didn't sit well with me. And I didn't much care for the way he ordered me around like I was one of his lackeys. I stopped when I reached the barn door. Instead of going inside, I shuffled off in the direction of my truck.

CHAPTER SEVENTEEN

I drove into town, fighting the urge to turn into the Wet Whistle parking lot. Instead, I parked in front of Hattie's Hardware. When I found the front door locked, I remembered it was Sunday and drove off.

Sitting in my truck outside Hattie's house, I debated whether to turn it off or turn it around and head straight to the Wet Whistle. In our two previous meetings, Hattie Scott and I had made a connection that I couldn't quite explain. Her son had drowned when he was twelve, the same age I'd been when Mama left. Kindred spirits, she called us.

Stop by any time you feel the need to talk, she'd said when she heard about Mama moving back to Texas. I was about to take her up on her offer.

I counted sixteen wind chimes suspended from the perimeter of her porch roof. An orchestra of tubular bells translated the morning breezes into music. The flower boxes that hung from the wrought-iron railings offered every color of the rainbow. The only thing missing was a big peace sign painted on the white siding between the upstairs windows.

I knocked on the wooden screen door.

"It's open," Hattie called from inside.

I found her sitting on the edge of the sofa, hunched over the coffee table.

"Hello, Dillon," she said with a quick glance before returning her attention to her work. "How nice of you to drop in. Have a seat."

I perched on the edge of the chair across from her and watched her finish rolling a joint. She held it in front of her face with both hands and ran her tongue along the edge of the paper.

She held up a fat one. "Want to join me?"

I thought about it for a moment. "It would be rude not to," I said with a smile.

Her eyes sparkled and, if I didn't know better, I'd have thought she was hitting on me. We'd only met on two other occasions, so it was possible that I *didn't* know better. I watched as she held the joint up to her lips. She took a long drag and held it in.

I shifted in my seat. "We're just friends, right?"

Hattie blew a small stream of smoke through her nostrils. She responded with something between a laugh and a cough. Her eyes sparkled again. "If I were forty years younger, I'd be all over you like white on rice. But as far as romance, you can stick a fork in me, I'm done." Her long turquoise earrings swung playfully as she shook her head. "Fact is, I haven't had an orgasm in—"

I held up my hands. "Whoa. Too much information."

She shrugged. "How's Jenny?"

"She's great. Thanks for asking." I hesitated. "Something you said earlier bothered me."

"Honey, if I had a dollar for every time I've heard that, I'd be retired and livin' on a beach somewhere."

"You said Seth had been around here for a couple of years."

"I did. But I think it's been more like three or four."

She held the joint out in front of her, and I took a hit. I handed it back and settled into the soft cushion of the chair. I watched her inhale once more.

"I thought Seth came out here around the same time as Jenn. You know, after Roy passed."

"No. He's been coming in the store for quite a while." She offered me the joint again, and I took a big hit.

"How long you been smokin' this stuff?" I asked after three hard coughs.

She smiled, licked the thumb and forefinger of her left hand, and snuffed out the end of the joint. She set it on the edge of the table and leaned back into the sofa.

"August 1969." The faraway look of a fond memory washed over her.

"You remember the date?"

"Are you kidding me?" She blinked a few times. "I smoked my first joint at Woodstock." Her eyes drifted. "The greatest concert of all time."

I guess that shouldn't have surprised me. It fit her ex-hippie persona.

"How did you get there?" I asked.

"We drove."

"We?"

"Me and Charlie Owens."

I blinked back my surprise, probably more than once. "Buck?"

"We went with another couple." Her eyes got dreamy and I couldn't tell if it was the memory or the pot. "We took off after graduation and drove around the country. We were driving through New York, thinking about heading home, when we heard about an outdoor concert on a nearby farm." She smiled. "Synchronicity, dontcha think?"

My mind had just been blown. "You and Buck?"

She frowned. "Why is that so strange?"

I studied her scrunched-up face just before I burst out laughing. Hattie followed. When we finally stopped, she asked again.

"Why is that funny?"

My smile turned to a frown as I searched my short-term memory banks. Nothing. "I... I don't know. I guess because he's such a miserable old fart, and you're..."

"A real catch?" She wore a smile on her face, but disappointment in her eyes.

I let a few moments of silence pass before I continued. "Was it, like, a *thing*?"

"If you're asking whether I slept with him, the answer is no. Not that I didn't want to, mind you. Buck was old-fashioned. It was sweet. But I guess I liked to play a little more fast and loose in those days. I took a ride on the magic bus that weekend, but not with Buck."

I sank further back into my chair and remembered the first day I met Hattie. I'd seen a little bit of devil in those angel eyes.

"Your phone's ringing," Hattie said.

I reached into my pocket and turned the ringer off.

Hattie shook her head. "I don't know why I'm tellin' you all this. To this day, Buck doesn't know what really happened that weekend."

I promised her that her secret was safe with me. "What happened when you returned home?"

"Oh, it was pretty much business as usual for me."

"What about Buck?"

"The poor man was smitten, and I couldn't look him in the eye."

Imagining how ol' Buck felt was a bit of a buzzkill for me, as images of Nicole faded in and out. I pressed her for more. "Do you have any regrets?"

"Doesn't everybody?"

I nodded.

"It gets worse." Hattie hung her head. "Buck was like a lost puppy until he took the foreman job at the ranch."

"How's that worse?"

She glanced up, but only for a second. "I might have started up with Roy McDonald when he bought that ranch."

"You what?"

"I was young. He was new in town. He had money in his pocket... and he was handsome as hell, which is where I figured I was goin' anyway."

I watched her silently.

"Don't look at me like that. Roy was a kind man. He rescued horses, for God's sake. I probably would have married him if I hadn't lost the baby."

I choked. "You got something to drink?" I said, wheezing.

Hattie stepped into the kitchen and returned with two cold bottles of beer. "You look like you might need some alcohol."

I nodded quickly and took a long draw.

"The baby was Roy's?"

"I trust I don't need to explain how something like that happens."

I shook my head, then tipped the bottle back again. "What happened to the baby?" I asked after I swallowed.

"Stillborn. A boy." Her voice became brittle. "I don't know what happened. He just died inside me. Probably karma's way of takin' me down a notch."

"How did Roy take it?"

She hung her head. "He didn't know I was pregnant. I hid it from everyone while I decided if I wanted to be a mother."

"That decision was made for you."

She gave a quick nod without looking up. "So, I never told Roy I lost it. What would be the point?"

"Did anyone else know?"

"The only person I ever told was Buck."

"Buck?"

"I thought he was gonna kill Roy... or maybe me." She looked at me as a tear slid down her cheek. "He helped me bury my son on the ranch. We didn't mark the grave for fear that Roy might find it."

"Oh, God. That must have been awful for you."

"I reckon it was worse for Buck." She wiped her cheek. "That's when I realized he was still carryin' a torch and would do anything for me."

"It took a lot of nerve to ask him to do that," I said in a tone that I wished had been a little less judgmental.

"I never said I was a saint."

"And I'll never say it either."

"I found out later that he'd bought an engagement ring for me but didn't get around to proposin'. He never married after that. To this day, I wonder if it was because of me." She paused and swallowed hard. "Talk about regrets..."

I stood. "I should probably get going."

Hattie gave me a big hug and told me to visit anytime.

I walked to my truck, feeling much better than when I'd arrived. Between the weed and Hattie's stories, I'd forgotten why I'd driven there in the first place.

Chapter Eighteen

Whatever remnants of a buzz I'd felt on the way home were quickly pushed aside by flashing lights and a wailing siren. An ambulance blew past me in the opposite direction on the narrow road, forcing me onto the shoulder. My heart pounded and gravel flew as I stomped on the accelerator.

Fire trucks surrounded the barn. Water sprayed from the top of an extension ladder through a hole in the roof near the back of the barn. The acrid smell of burning rubber and oil filled the air. I scanned the immediate area for signs of Jenn and Alex. I held my breath.

Jenn waved from near the stable, and I ran to her and threw my arms around her neck while Seth looked on.

"Thank God," I said. "Where's Alex?"

"He's in the house."

"Are you all right?"

She nodded.

"Can't say the same for Buck," Seth added.

I turned to him. "What happened?"

"Some kind of explosion in the workshop. Hopefully, Buck can tell us more."

"How bad is he?"

"Too soon to tell."

"Where were you?" Jenn asked. "I've been calling."

"I went into town."

Seth shifted his weight to his other foot. "We thought you were in there helping Buck."

"You sound disappointed."

"Stop it. Both of you." Jenn said through clenched teeth.

"Sorry," I said to no one in particular, then walked to the house. The sheriff pulled up as I reached the front porch. I figured Jenn and Seth could handle it. I wasn't even there when it happened.

I found Alex inside playing video games. Normally, Mama kept an eye on him for us. I'd given her my blessing to leave. While I was grateful that she'd asked for it this time, I wish she'd cared enough to stay.

Jenn had her tail up when she pushed through the front door, and I had a feeling I was about to find out why.

I took a deep breath and braced myself.

"I don't know how that burr got up under your saddle, but you better find a way to get it outta there. We've got a man down. The rest of us need to stick together. For all we know, someone has just declared war against this family."

"I take it you don't think this was an accident."

"At this point, I'm not ruling anything out." She folded her arms across her chest. "What's your problem with Seth?"

"I'm not sure. Somethin' about him has been rubbin' me the wrong way. He's been ordering me around like I'm one of his employees."

"Well..." Jenn suddenly looked like she was about to burst into tears. "I'm glad you didn't listen to him this time."

"You and me both." I held her in my arms for a few moments.

Jenn leaned back and wrinkled her nose. "Where did you say you've been?"

"I didn't."

She opened her mouth, but before she spoke, I said, "We should get to the hospital and check on Buck."

Jenn lingered for a moment, a curious expression on her face. She nodded her agreement.

***

Having survived seventy years without ever spending a night in a hospital made Buck a less-than-ideal patient. Fortunately, none of his injuries were life-threatening. He'd spent two nights there and had given everyone a hard time. The doctor released Buck a couple of days early. Rumor has it, the nurses offered to chip in and buy the doctor a new set of golf clubs.

Buck's doctor recommended limited duty for at least the next week. He wasn't allowed to work more than four hours per day or lift over fifteen pounds. Jenn took it upon herself to enforce the rules and to prepare his meals.

I stayed clear of the patient for the first three days. On the fourth day, Jenn caught on to my plan. She sent me to deliver lunch to Buck's cabin, presumably under the impression that Buck needed someone to feed him lunch and put him down for a nap. Even if by some stretch of the imagination Buck would allow something like that, she picked the wrong man for the job. I set the tray down on Buck's porch, but before I knocked and ran, my conscience got the better of me. If only Hattie had kept her mouth shut, I could've been halfway back to the house.

I imagined what it must have taken for Buck to help Hattie bury Roy's baby. For what? To spare the man who'd stolen his woman the agony of losing a child? To protect the reputation of the woman who'd betrayed him?

I picked up the tray and gave the door two sharp raps.

"Come in."

Buck's expression fell when I opened the door. He'd no doubt been expecting Jenn to walk in.

He pointed to the kitchen table. "You can leave it over there."

I set the tray down and gave the old man the benefit of the doubt. I turned. "How ya feelin' today, Buck?"

"I'm fine. Don't let the door hit you in the ass on the way out."

I took a couple of steps toward the living room chair where he sat. "I'm not sure who you think you're fooling, but you can drop the tough old fart act around me. I know who you are."

His bushy gray mustache shuddered as the muscles in his face tightened. "You don't know jack shit."

"I know you're not as much of an asshat as you let on. I know you're still carryin' a torch for Hattie Scott. And I'm pretty sure Romeo was your horse. You rescued him, you trained him, and you gave him to Alex when Apollo died."

Buck stared at me for what seemed like an hour. As I turned toward the door, he said, "You want a drink?"

I stopped. Time to cowboy up. "I sure do."

Chapter Nineteen

Buck walked to the kitchen, and I followed. He set two glasses and a bottle of whiskey on the table.

"What was the hospital like?" I asked as he poured the first shot.

We emptied our glasses.

"I reckon I gave everyone a real show," he said, "until one of them nurses told me I had that skimpy hospital johnny on backwards. I never spent a night in a hospital in my life. What do I know about anything? If they hadn't gone and hid my clothes…"

I shook my head to clear the image that his story had conjured up.

"I get six hours sleep every night," he continued. "I can't lay in bed all day or I'll get saddle sores."

"I'm sure everyone there was counting down the hours until your discharge."

He nodded and flashed a crooked smile. "They sent me home early."

"I can't say I'm surprised."

Buck had suffered burns on his left arm and took a piece of shrapnel in his gut. His face had been cut in a half-dozen places. Two of them required stitches.

"Are you supposed to be drinking?" I asked.

Buck picked up the bottle. "Do you want another? Or do you need to go home and change your diaper?"

He was one tough monkey. I slid my glass across the table. "My diaper should be good for another half hour."

I thought I noticed the corner of his mouth turn up as he poured the next round.

"So, Hattie's been runnin' her mouth again," he said without looking up.

"We've had a conversation or two."

"You can't believe everything that woman says." He shifted in his chair and winced with pain. "Especially if she's been smokin' that wacky tobacky."

"Good to know." I smiled. "She implied you had a rough go of it. I suppose that's why you're such a pain in the ass."

He brought his glass down firmly on the table. "By the looks a you, you wouldn't know a rough life if it crawled up your pant leg and bit you on the pecker."

He picked up the bottle, and I slid my glass across the table. He poured, and I drank.

"My mama left us when I was twelve," I said. "Six years later, my younger brother disappeared. Then, before my broken old man could drink himself to death, a friend murdered him over a stinkin' piece of dirt." I slammed my glass down. "You can show me your hand, or you can fold right now."

"I never knew my mama," Buck said, his voice low and gravelly. "She died birthin' me. My daddy tried his best to raise my brother and me, but he was a snot-slingin' drunk." He poured another and held up his glass. "Taught me everything he knew."

I watched him empty his glass and slam it on the table.

Buck leaned in. "That's just my childhood. There's plenty more after that."

I already knew some of the gory details, and perhaps a thing or two he didn't. "How about we call it a draw?"

Buck nodded.

"You should probably eat your lunch," I said, then walked into the living room.

Jenn had made him a sandwich. He picked it up and took a bite.

A collection of record albums filled two shelves on the west wall above a phonograph that had probably been all the rage back in the late fifties or early sixties. I leaned in for a better look. Before I touched anything, I turned to Buck for permission.

He waved his free hand in agreement as he took another bite of his sandwich.

I didn't find a collection of old country and western tunes as I'd expected. Joe Cocker, Janis Joplin, Richie Havens, Arlo Guthrie—they all played at Woodstock. This wasn't just his music. These were his memories.

"I heard you were at Woodstock," I said over my shoulder.

"Best weekend a my life."

I didn't have the heart to spoil it for him.

On the corner of the top shelf, I spotted a small tin ring, the kind a child might wear. I held it up for Buck to see. "What's this?"

"It's nothin'."

"If it was nothin', you wouldn't still have it after all these years."

A flicker of a smile crossed his lips. "It's a Wild Bill Hickok Deputy US Marshall Ring with Secret Compartment. Saw it in the back of a comic book in 1953, an' I had ta have it. My brother Billy had one just like it."

I held it between my fingers and examined it—a raised five-point star surrounded by the words *Deputy US Marshall*.

His expression fell. "We used the secret compartment to pass notes. When the old man got drunk, it was the only way to communicate without sufferin' the back a his hand."

"Where's your brother now?"

"He lives near Cripple Creek. Works in one a them casinos."

"Are you close?"

"Close enough."

I set the ring back on the shelf.

I wanted to believe that, like the Wizard of Oz, there was a man behind the curtain. A good man who pulled levers and pushed buttons and hid behind the bluster. I had a feeling that's what I'd stumbled upon today.

I turned to find Buck watching me. "As soon as I leave, you're going back to being the same pain in the ass that you've always been, aren't you?"

When he didn't reply, I walked back into the kitchen and sat. "Okay then, before I go, tell me what happened in the barn."

"I don't know."

"Tell me what you do know."

"I was cleanin' the carburetor on the John Deere when I heard a big bang. Next thing I know, I'm on my back. My arm's on fire and I can see a piece a tractor stickin' outta my gut."

"Were you working with an open flame or a heat source that could have ignited the blast?"

"No."

"Is there anything you did that could have created an explosion?"

"I reckon it coulda had somethin' to do with the bomb I was buildin'."

"What?"

"No, goddammit, I didn't set off that blast. Somebody's tryin' to kill me."

"Or me." I pushed a hand back through my hair. "I was supposed to be in there helping you."

"Says who?"

"Seth."

"Why weren't you?"

"I didn't like him ordering me around like he runs the place."

"He pretty much does."

"I went to Hattie's to blow off steam."

He eyed me suspiciously. "Remember what I said about her."

"I'm more concerned about what happened in the barn. You could have been killed."

Buck opened the bottle and held it above my glass, eyebrow raised. I held up my hand and shook my head.

"Don't worry about me." He poured himself another. "I'm like a cat with nine lives. That was number seven."

CHAPTER TWENTY

Jenn sent me out to the barn the next day to check on Buck. She thought I might be able to shadow him and make sure he was following the doctor's orders. I knew that I'd be as welcome as a skunk at a lawn party, but I agreed to at least check in on him from time to time.

Buck wasn't in the barn, so I went outside to check the paddock. Buck and Seth stood toe-to-toe near the gate. They took turns cussin' at each other. I ducked out of sight behind the barn, then peeked around the corner. Buck pitched a fit about something, and Seth appeared to give it right back to him. I stayed and watched to make sure that it didn't come to blows. They both stomped off in opposite directions. I followed Buck into the barn.

"Hey, Buck. How you feeling today?"

"If you're fixin' to babysit, you best make other plans."

"I just want to be sure you're alright."

"Why wouldn't I be alright?"

"It's your first day back to work and—"

"I appreciate the concern, but I'm fine."

"You didn't look fine out by the paddock a few minutes ago."

He turned and walked toward his workbench. "You saw that?"

"Sure did." I followed and leaned back against the bench next to him so I could see his face. "What's going on?"

"It doesn't concern you."

"Goddammit, Buck, everything that goes on at this ranch concerns me now."

He turned and his eyes narrowed, like he was sizing me up. "If that's the case, you best not believe a word that comes outta that man's yap."

"Seth?"

He nodded. "If he tells you the sky is blue, you better look up and see for yourself. Don't take his word fer nothin'."

"What did he say to you?"

"It's what he didn't say. "Maybe you should find those two ranch hands and ask them why they up an' quit."

"Do you know why?"

"He's up to no good, but I ain't sayin' no more till I got proof. Otherwise, it's just some crazy ol' cowboy and his conspiracy theories." His brows edged close to each other as he spoke. "Ain't that what you said?"

I hesitated. "I might have at one time or another."

"I don't want to be stirrin' up a pot a trouble for you and the missus. Despite your shortcomins, I think you're probably an upstandin' young fella."

"Thank you... I think."

"Now get outta here." He gave a dismissing wave. "I got work to do and so do you."

He was right. I took Chance and Romeo outside for a little workout. After I cooled them down and brushed them, Seth asked me to ride the fence in the upper pasture, looking for any yew bushes or other poisonous plants. I was pretty sure

I wouldn't find any growing there. Someone poisoned those horses. I had it on my to-do list to find out who.

I circled back to the barn when I finished to make sure Buck was obeying the doctor's orders. The place was closed up for the night.

***

After a hearty dinner of meatloaf and mashed potatoes, we cleaned up the kitchen and tucked Alex into bed. Saturday night had become movie night at the ranch—the closest thing to a date since we moved to Colorado. On Sundays, the three of us watched something together, Alex's choice.

I let Jenn pick the movie tonight. My mind wouldn't let go of the showdown I'd witnessed earlier between Buck and Seth. I felt some responsibility to help things run smoothly, however, not enough to bring it up yet. After a couple beers, those thoughts subsided, and I enjoyed the rest of the evening with my girl.

I awoke early Sunday morning to gunshots. Turns out the unusually hot, dry weather had caused some of the local predators to venture down from higher ground in search of food and water. Seth shot a wolf just outside the turnout pen. If Jenn had seen the wolf first, they'd have had a nice little chat, and he'd be on his way back home by now.

As you might imagine, Jenn was fit to be tied. While I hated to see her like that and did my best to settle her down, Seth's stock had just taken another dip. I helped Jenn bury the animal in a brief ceremony rather than risk Seth dumping it out in the woods for the buzzards to take it piece by piece.

On the way back to the house, I asked Jenn if she'd ever visited Roy's grave. She told me she wanted to, but didn't know exactly where it was. I agreed to take her there sometime.

I wanted to learn more about the circumstances of Roy's death, but I had no contacts in Colorado. It bothered me that I'd been stumbling around like I just fell off a turnip truck. I needed to get my bearings. Hattie knew everybody's business in the entire county, so I reckoned that was a good place to start.

I grabbed my truck keys, kissed Jenn, and told her I'd be back before dinner. She recognized that look in my eyes and told me to be careful.

When no one answered after the third knock, I walked around back and found Hattie reclining in a lawn chair.

"Dillon. How nice to see you." She pointed to an empty chair. "Come sit for a while."

"Thank you. I hope I didn't interrupt anything."

"No. Just a memory." She smiled as she fixed her gaze on the pond a little further down the hill in her yard. "My husband, Jim, loved to fish that pond."

A wooden dock extended about ten feet out into the water. I pictured Jim sittin' on a chair, maybe even the one where I presently sat, with a fishin' pole in his hand and a cooler at his side.

"He worked a lot of nights. But every Sunday morning, he'd walk out the bedroom door in his boxer shorts and park himself on that dock down there. I'd wake up a couple hours later and bring him his breakfast and a pair of pants."

Jim had clothes on in my picture. "Is he…"

"Passed away sixteen months ago today."

"I'm sorry."

"All in all, he was a good man. Probably fishin' with James Jr. in heaven as we speak."

The first time we met, she'd mentioned a son who'd drowned. I wondered if it happened right here in her own backyard, but I couldn't bring myself to ask. I studied her as she stared out over the water, lost in a memory.

I pointed to the fifth wheel parked in a pull-off near the garage. "She's a beauty. Do you travel a lot?"

"Used to. Twice a year. Yellowstone, Grand Canyon, Sedona, Tahoe. I'd close the store for a week, hook it up to Jim's F-350, and just take off." Her eyes drifted. "We had some good times in that there RV."

I let her sit with her memories for as long as she wanted.

"I'd show you around, but I haven't been able to set foot inside since Jim died. You're welcome to take a look."

"Maybe some other time."

She rubbed her eyes before she met my gaze. "So, what brings you here this morning?"

"I come from a small town where everybody knew everybody. I knew how things worked and who to see when I needed something, but I feel a little like a fish out of water out here."

"Honey, towns don't get much smaller than Redfield. And we don't just know everybody, we know everybody's business."

"Maybe someday it will feel like that, but right now, I'm on the outside looking in." I paused. "Back in Bradley, Pop's friend Bill McCutchen was a retired Texas Ranger who had connections and access to things like a crime lab and friends in high places. In the end, he turned out to be more trouble than he was worth, but that's a whole other story."

"If you need a crime lab, you might have bigger problems than I can help you with."

"So, who's the top dog around here?"

"That would be the county executive, Jack Higgins."

"Who's next?"

A Mona Lisa smile crossed her lips as she straightened a little in her chair. "You're lookin' at her."

"What?"

"Teller County Clerk Hattie Scott at your service."

"No way."

Her expression fell. "Why is that so hard to believe?"

"I... I... didn't mean any disrespect. I guess I was just surprised that it never came up."

She reached over and patted my knee. "That's okay. I'm just messin' with you. I get that reaction a lot. If I was a man, you probably wouldn't have batted an eye."

I kept my big yap shut so as not to make matters any worse.

"Actually, there's a council, but Jack and I go way back. He doesn't do much without askin' me what I think. So I'd say we pretty much run this one-horse town."

I nodded. "Good to know."

"Well, now that you know, what can I help you with?"

My mind went blank.

She waited for an answer that didn't come. "I'm gonna get me somethin' to drink. You want a beer?"

"It's Sunday morning."

"What... you think the Good Lord doesn't throw back a few once in a while? He must have been rip-roarin' drunk when he came up with the idea for this place."

I hesitated, then gave her a quick nod. "Aw, what the hell."

She laughed all the way to the house.

She returned a few minutes later and handed me a tall, cold one.

I took a long draw and my words came back. "When Roy McDonald died, was an autopsy performed?"

Her brow furrowed. "Why do you ask?"

At this point, everything was just hearsay. "Just curious."

"They didn't do an autopsy. He'd been sick and died while under a doctor's care, so it wasn't required."

I watched a drop of condensation drip off my bottle onto my boot. "So, nobody thought his death was suspicious?"

"I'm sorry, Dillon, but the answer is no. The coroner determines cause of death and files his report."

"Who orders an autopsy?"

"If it's not required under state law, the coroner, the sheriff, or district attorney."

"So, all they have is a report?"

"I'll see if I can get you a copy."

"I guess it's better than nothing."

"Autopsies are expensive," she said. "They set you back three-thousand dollars or more, so if there isn't a good reason..."

"Who pays the bill?"

"It would have been the responsibility of the next of kin."

CHAPTER TWENTY-ONE

Buck didn't waste any time getting back to work full time, which was fine by me. He'd been out three full days and another week of half days. Jenn and I took over most of his daily chores, but we were glad to have our go-to guy back in the saddle.

To celebrate his return, Jenn made her famous pot roast and planned a celebratory dinner Saturday night.

Seth arrived just as we were about to take our places at the table.

"Where's Buck?" Jenn asked.

Seth shrugged. "I haven't seen him."

"He's probably just running late," I said, eager to fill my plate and get started.

"I hope so." Jenn pulled out her chair. "Well, I guess we better eat before it gets cold."

After grace, Seth took a few bites, then pushed the food around on his plate. I watched Jenn eat like she didn't feel the air in the room bristle with electricity. Something was about to explode. She raised her water glass to her lips.

"Buck's not coming," Seth said without looking up. "I fired him."

Jenn covered her mouth to keep from spraying water across the table. She set her glass down. "I thought I heard you say that you fired our foreman without consulting me." Her eyes flared. "But I must be mistaken."

"That's what he said." I jumped at the opportunity to hold his feet to the fire. I didn't trust Seth all that much. It wouldn't break my heart if he just packed up his shit and moved on. Truth be told, I wouldn't lose any sleep over Buck's sudden departure either, but I still had a few questions for him.

Jenn glanced around the table, stopping at Seth. "Your timing sucks."

I'd seen that look on her face before, the blue laser stare that could burn holes in your face. I felt the heat of her glare for a second before she turned it on Seth.

"You think that's a good idea?" I said, feeling the need to show my support for Jenn. "He's been running this ranch a long time. He knows where all the bodies are buried."

"That might be the problem." More food pushing before Seth slowly lifted his head. "I think he buried them."

"What do you mean?" Jenn asked.

"I mean Buck's been stealing from us."

"Mama?" Alex interrupted.

"Not now, Alex," she replied, her eyes fixed on Seth. "How can he do that?"

"When Roy ran the ranch, he let Buck handle most of the purchasing. Gave him access to the operating account. Buck's been making feed and equipment payments to bogus companies and pocketing the cash."

"For how long?"

"It started after Roy got sick. Probably figured he wouldn't notice. He kept it going after I took over."

"After WE took over," Jenn corrected.

Seth pushed his plate away. "I told you the ranch was losing money. Now we know why."

"I don't like the way you handled it."

"I handled it quickly and quietly," Seth replied, dodging her lasers. "I don't want word of this scandal getting out."

"Are you also going to pick up the extra workload?"

"I won't have to. I hired a new foreman."

"Again without consulting me?" She shook her head. "You can't keep doing this."

The shit had hit the fan, and I knew enough to keep my head down.

"I ran into an old friend who was passing through on his way to the coast to find work. I convinced him to stay and take the job. He's well qualified, and we needed someone right away."

I watched Jenn's shoulders relax a bit and wanted to tell her not to get her hopes up. I got the feeling Seth had just evened the teams.

"Fine." Jenn's voice returned to its normal level. "But you have to stop making these unilateral decisions. This ranch is a fifty-fifty proposition. We each get a say in what goes on here."

"Understood."

"And... I'm taking over purchasing. Your guy is going to have to run everything through me."

"That won't be necessary. He—"

"You made your decision. Now it's my turn."

I cleared my throat. "So, what's the new guy's name?"

Seth inhaled slowly, then exhaled sharply. "His name is Frank Snyder. We met years ago when I lived in Kansas City. He agreed to start tomorrow, and I'll personally handle his orientation. He'll be up to speed within a week. You'll see."

"Where is Buck now?" I asked. "I want to talk to him."

"I don't know. He packed up his things and moved out last night."

"I still don't like it." Jenn picked up her plate and walked to the kitchen.

I watched Alex slump in his chair. "What's wrong?"

"I'm sad," he said. "I like Buck. He was always nice to me."

I pointed to his plate. "Are you going to finish that?"

Alex shook his head.

"You're excused."

I turned to Seth after Alex was out of earshot. "Do you think Buck's been causing all the other trouble around here?"

"I don't know." Seth stood and picked up his plate. "I think he's the reason the hired hands quit."

I'd never been good at math, but even I knew something wasn't adding up. I needed to find Buck.

Jenn began clearing the table. Seth handed her his plate.

"Buck's always been a loyal employee," she said. "He barely ever missed a day of work."

"Look how fast he was back on the job after the explosion," I added. "He's motivated."

Seth snorted. "He's motivated, all right."

"What's that supposed to mean?" Jenn asked.

"It means he's hiding something." Seth folded his arms across his chest. "If you work at a bank, you have a mandatory two-week vacation, and you're required to take both weeks at the same time. You can't split them up. Do you know why?"

I glanced at Jenn before I shrugged.

"When you're away for a week, most of your work can probably wait until you get back. But two weeks? In most cases, you just can't let your work go that long. Someone needs to step in and do it for you. If you've been stealing money or doing something underhanded, there's a good chance they'll find it."

Jenn nodded. "Okay, but—"

"Don't you see? That's why Buck didn't want to stay in the hospital. And why he was so stubborn about getting back to work. He didn't want anyone to uncover his scheme."

I struggled to come up with a rebuttal.

"He's lucky I only fired him."

I felt Jenn's stare as Seth left the room. I waited as long as I could before our eyes met. No one spoke. I followed Jenn into the kitchen.

"Did you know Seth has been living here for three years?"

"I knew he got here before me, but I thought it was after Uncle Roy got sick."

"Don't you think that he might have said something about that?"

"Everything's not a conspiracy, Dillon. Why don't you just ask him?"

"I'm gonna go look for Buck tomorrow."

Jenn stopped and turned. "I don't know about y'all, but I've been busting my ass around here taking care of Alex and trying to keep this ranch afloat. Now I find out that our foreman has been stealing all the profits. Excuse me for not wanting to wish him a fond farewell."

"So, you've already tried and convicted him?"

"I don't think I could even look at him right now."

"Then, I guess it's a good thing he doesn't work for you anymore." I stood. "I think the wrong man got fired."

"What's that supposed to mean?"

"Alright, I'll say it. I don't trust Seth."

"Well, I do. He's family."

"Not my family." I turned and left the room.

***

I couldn't sleep straight that night. Probably should have had a cup of rain dance tea before I went to bed. I tossed and turned half the night thinking about how Buck got run off the ranch. He put up with a gigantic pile of shit from Roy, and as far as I could tell, another one from Seth, and he still showed up for work every morning. He didn't deserve what he got in the end.

Jenn seemed to think otherwise, so I needed to find a way to keep her on my side. We needed to stick together now more than ever. We had Seth outnumbered, but the new guy made it two against two. I had a feeling things were about to go sideways.

CHAPTER TWENTY-TWO

The next morning after chores, I retreated to my Fortress of Solitude to take a step back and try to process everything that had happened. I moved to Colorado to get away from the drama, but apparently, the trouble that I thought I left behind in Bradley had followed me here. The names and the places were different, but it was shaping up to be another shitstorm.

Maybe it was me. Maybe I was sticking my big nose somewhere it didn't belong. I'd told myself I'd never set foot in Bradley, Texas, again. I got sucked into that mayhem because I was family. I'd never met Roy McDonald and didn't know the man existed until a couple of months ago.

I had to tap the brakes. Things were happening fast, and I didn't want to overlook anything. I could sure use Coop right about now. He should have been a detective. He tells me I don't watch enough TV. Maybe he's right. But he wasn't here, so I needed to step up. People were getting hurt. I had a new family to protect.

I took a deep breath. It appeared to have all started when I met Cassidy in the makeshift cemetery up on the ridge. She pointed the finger at Roy for her sister Asha's death. That didn't make any sense. Why would Roy want to kill his fiancée on the way to his wedding? Maybe he got cold feet, but there are safer ways to back out of the nuptials than killing the bride in a car accident. He could have been killed himself. Why take such a chance?

Asha's sons didn't think it was an accident. Admittedly, those two didn't have half a brain between them, but they were convinced that Roy was guilty. Why? Was there some evidence I didn't know about?

Why did Buck have his hackles up when it came to those boys? They burned down Roy's barn and went to jail for it. I didn't see why Buck would go to battle for the man who'd knocked up his girlfriend. Nobody is that loyal. Poor Buck was in love with Hattie, and she got pregnant by his boss. Sad enough to bring a tear to a glass eye.

If that wasn't confusing enough, we had Roy McDonald pushin' up daisies up on the ridge. Was he a murderer or a murderee? Both, according to Cassidy. If he was murdered, Buck had to be on the shortlist for motive along with the Whitehawk brothers. Add Seth, and the list wasn't so short. He'd fired Buck to cover his tracks. Buck didn't strike me as the type that could spell embezzlement, let alone know how to pull it off. Now he was gone, leaving me with more questions than answers.

Whenever I got stressed, my thoughts drifted back to a Cherokee medicine woman named Leotie who helped me get my shit together. Well, not all of it, but enough to make a difference. After I'd returned to Bradley the wheels fell off, and I feared I'd lost control of my life. The PTSD meds I'd been taking helped, but I was treading water at best. Mama, who was part of the problem, convinced me to go see Leotie, the woman who had helped her regain balance in her life.

I reluctantly agreed to see Mama's witch doctor. She was all sage and eagle feathers with a couple animal skulls thrown in for good measure, but she could look into your soul with those deep-set onyx eyes. I resisted at first, but she had a way about her. She knew things she couldn't possibly have known. She suggested I replace my meds with some herbs and berries she gathered and blessed.

I closed my eyes and remembered her weathered face as she handed me a cloth sack.

"Custom blend," she said. "Only for you."

I smiled and felt special.

"When your body is out of balance," she continued, "so is your life. I treat cause, not symptoms. The herbs will help restore your natural balance. You think you need chemicals, but nature provides everything you need."

I opened the sack and looked inside. It reminded me of pot, but with a strange minty smell, aromatic like a menthol cigarette. "Do I smoke it?"

Leotie smiled for the first time since I'd met her. "You could... but I wouldn't recommend it. Make a cup of tea and drink it before bed."

"Will it help me sleep?"

She nodded. "Your dreams may become more vivid."

I closed the bag. "My dreams are vivid enough, thank you."

"Dreams are visions of your inner life."

"Then I'm in big trouble."

"No." Leotie shook her head. "Out of balance."

"You say tomato..."

"The Creator takes care of us like a mother takes care of her children. She sends abundance and good fortune at every opportunity. You would be wise to view life through the eyes of a child."

"How do I do that?"

"When water falls from the sky to cleanse the Earth, don't curse the rain. Dance in it."

A smile crossed my lips as I opened my eyes. I drank her rain dance tea, as I called it, a few nights before bed and it worked. I needed to buy a lifetime supply. A few days later, I had a strange dream in which Leotie took me to a special place that I later found out to be Jenn's special place here in Colorado. It became my Fortress of Solitude. In the dream, Leotie convinced me to throw my pills into the canyon below. When I did, she bid me farewell and jumped into the abyss. I watched her morph into an eagle that spread its mighty wings and flew up into the heavens.

The next day, Mama told me that Leotie's spirit had left this world during the night. I told Mama about the tea. She said not to worry. Leotie knew exactly how much to give me. Her intention was not to replace one crutch with another but to provide a way for my body to transition back to its natural state. I should have believed her, but I rationed the tea.

I might need a cup tonight.

***

Buck came with the ranch when Roy bought it, so I couldn't believe he was gone. I had to see for myself.

His place had been stripped bare except for a few pieces of tattered furniture. Light-colored shapes on dingy walls where pictures had once hung and worn hardwood floors were the only memories of a life lived in this place. I wondered what stories they had to tell. I couldn't recall if Hattie's image had occupied one of those spots. Perhaps she'd required a more private place for fear of reprisal from his old boss.

The shelves where he'd kept his records were bare, the Woodstock poster conspicuously absent. His music may have been his only solace, memories of better times pressed in vinyl. Memories of her.

I had a feeling that his crusty, often abrasive shell protected a once wide-eyed child that the years had left disappointed and unfulfilled. Exposing that raw interior would be a painful admission of his failures. Perhaps I'd been too quick to judge the man.

The kitchen looked like a thrift store, with cabinets full of mismatched plates and glasses. An old coffee can sat next to a dirty toaster oven on the counter. The sink looked like it hadn't been scrubbed clean since the Reagan administration. It didn't fit. This was the home of someone waiting to die. Not what you might expect of someone who'd embezzled nearly $100,000 over the last four years. Show me the money, Buck.

I picked up the coffee can and shook the contents. Paper clips, broken pencils, a few old coins. I dumped them on the counter. The coins were tokens from a casino in Cripple Creek. I pushed the pile around on the counter, wondering why Buck hadn't just thrown it all away. Then I saw it. A slightly tarnished Wild Bill Hickok Deputy US Marshall Ring with Secret Compartment.

You'd have thought that little tin ring was made of gold. I held it in my hand and imagined how a young Charlie Owens felt the first time he laid his eight-year-old eyes on it. I opened the secret compartment and removed a tiny piece of paper, wondering how Buck's sausage fingers could have possibly folded something so small.

The words, *I'm innocent* were scratched on the paper above a phone number. I instinctively glanced around the empty room before slipping the ring and the paper into my pocket. Who else knew about the ring? The message, I decided, was meant for me. I brushed everything else back into the can and left the building.

CHAPTER TWENTY-THREE

A hot, dry wind whispered its way through the pines, making it feel more like August than October. We hadn't had any rain for two weeks, which was unusual for this time of year. The grass in the upper pasture had turned brown and brittle and the pond looked to be down a couple of feet.

I sat barefoot on the porch swing. My thoughts see-sawed between calling Buck and minding my own damn business. After some deliberation, I dialed the number he'd written below his not-guilty plea. I wasn't sure I had anything to offer besides moral support. His work had been his life after Hattie tossed him to the curb.

After the second ring, I heard, "Hattie's Hardware. How can I improve your day?"

I pulled the phone from my ear and stared at it for a moment. "Hattie?"

"Speaking."

"Uh... I'm confused."

"We all are, honey. Who is this?"

"Dillon."

"Why didn't you say so. What's got you confused?"

I felt her smile through the phone.

Twenty minutes later, the bell jingled as I walked through Hattie's front door. She ushered me into the back room and poured two cups of coffee. A man sat at one of the small tables on the other side of the room. He appeared to be finishing a meal.

"Smells good in here," I said.

"I got a nice roast over there in the slow cooker. Want some?"

"I'm good. Thanks, anyway."

"It can get pretty busy in here closer to dinnertime."

I leaned against the edge of the table. "So, you heard Buck got fired?"

She nodded as she sipped her coffee slowly. "What's going on over there?"

"Someone's been targeting the ranch. Buck swears it's the Whitehawk brothers, but I'm not so sure."

"He's got a point. They burned down Roy's barn. Went to prison for it. You think that was enough to stop 'em."

I shrugged. "I'm pretty sure the explosion that sent Buck to the hospital was supposed to send me there with him. It just got personal, and I'm not going to sit around and do nothin' about it.'"

"What are you fixin' to do?"

"I'm gonna find Buck. I don't think he stole that money, and I have a feeling he knows more than he's lettin' on."

"He was here."

"Buck? When?"

"Yesterday. We talked for a bit. He was mad as a hornet. Swore up and down and in every compass direction that he was innocent."

"I need to find him before he does something stupid. Did he say where he was headed?"

"No, but he told me to expect a call from you. I think he just wanted you to know he's okay."

"The other day, he mentioned something about a brother."

"Billy. Lives in Cripple Creek, but I don't think they've spoken in years."

The other man in the room approached our table. He tipped his hat to Hattie. "Thank you, Ma'am. Much obliged for the grub."

Hattie nodded with a smile. "You come back anytime, dear."

He turned to me. "Don't mean to intrude on your conversation, but you folks talkin' about Bucky Owens from Red Valley?"

I studied him. Mid-sixties, scraggly beard, Indiana Jones hat that, like him, had seen better days. "I reckon we are. What's it to ya?"

"I seen him here yesterday. I was comin' in, he was comin' out. Jumped in his truck and headed south."

"I appreciate the information."

He nodded a couple more times, then left.

I looked at Hattie. "You know him?"

"Sorta. He stops in for a meal now and then. He's a local. Works in the greenhouses during the off-season. Don't know what he does the rest of the year."

"Greenhouses? You mean RMA?"

"They don't pay much, but there's not a lot of work in these parts, especially during the winter months. A man's gotta make a living somehow. I do my part by feeding them once in a while."

I polished off the rest of my coffee and set the cup down. "Indiana Jones said Buck was headed south. Maybe he's going to see his brother after all."

"He bought some camping gear when he was in here. I imagine if he thinks the Whitehawks are after him, he'll lie low. Everybody knows those boys can track a rattlesnake through the Grand Canyon."

Everybody but me. That gave me an idea. "Thanks, Hattie. I'll let you know if I find him."

"My son, Ziggy, is the deputy sheriff here in Redfield. I'll ask him to keep an eye out."

***

"What do you think of the new foreman?" Jenn asked as we watched Alex ride Romeo around the pen.

"He doesn't say much, but neither did Buck till I got to know him. He seems to know his way around a horse ranch."

I just don't like Seth making those kinds of decisions without me." She sighed. "Makes me wonder what else he's been deciding."

"Sounds like you're changing your tune with the whole trusting family thing."

She hesitated. "I might have been a little pigheaded the last time we talked about it."

"A little?"

She looked at me with folded arms and raised eyebrows. "I'm agreeing with you, honey. Don't push your luck."

Jenn and I were sitting on the couch after dinner, sharing a couple of memories, when I decided to give my best friend Coop a call. We hadn't spoken since I left Bradley a month ago, and I'd been feeling bad about that.

I held my phone out between us. "Can you show me how that face thing works?"

Jenn smiled. "FaceTime. Sure." She straightened up and took my phone. "Who do you want to talk to, Coop?"

I nodded. Jenn had bought me an iPhone shortly after I'd arrived to keep in touch with friends back home. Well, not all of them, mostly just Coop and Jolene. Apparently, this Face-

Time app allowed you to see the person on the other end of the conversation while you talked. She thought it might ease the transition, as well as enable me to keep tabs on the fledgling Bishop Oil, which I'd hired Coop to manage in my absence. I needed to let him know that Mama would be back in Texas soon to take some of the pressure off.

Jenn walked me through placing the call and bringing up the video. In a few seconds, Coop stared up at me from the screen.

I must have sounded like a little kid. "Hey look at that. It's like you're on TV. Cooper Hill, Private Eye. Right?"

"I wish." His smile disappeared. "So, you've been gone a month, and you're just calling me now?"

"The phone works both ways."

He tilted his head and raised his brow. "Not if I don't have your number."

"Good point. I guess I've been busy settling in. You've got it now."

I relaxed, unaware that I was providing Coop with a great view of the ceiling. Jenn adjusted my hands so that my face returned to the frame.

She pointed to the thumbnail image at the bottom of the screen. "That's what he sees."

I nodded.

Jolene, all smiles, joined Coop on-screen to say hello. It amazed me how quickly we'd become close again after I returned to Bradley, like we'd simply picked up where we'd left off after I'd disappeared for ten years. Seeing Coop and Jolene nearly brought me to tears, and I needed Jenn's touch to ground me. I tilted the phone to let Jenn get in the picture as I slipped my free hand into hers and our fingers intertwined.

The last two months in Bradley with Coop hadn't been all sunshine and rainbows. At one point, I'd let my relationship with Nicole, whatever that was, come between us. But in the end, our friendship prevailed. So much so that he'd taken a bullet for me. That's something you never forget.

I'd introduced Coop and Jolene to Jenn during my brief stay in Bradley, and they took a real shine to her. They were sad to see us leave, but happy that I was finally moving on with my life.

"So, what are you doing for Thanksgiving?" I asked them. It just came out, and I shot a glance at Jenn that must have looked like a ten-year-old girl asking her mother for a sleepover with her BFF.

Jenn smiled and nodded.

"Well?"

"That depends," Coop replied warily. "Was that an invitation?"

"We'd love to come out to see you guys," Jolene interjected.

"Then it's settled. We can talk some business while you're here, so you can charge it all to the company."

"Thanks, Bish."

"You can catch a flight if you'd rather not drive."

Coop turned to Jolene. "See, Jo, I told you there's a heart in there somewhere."

"I have more good news. Mama's on her way back to Bradley. Apparently, she got cozy with Mort before she left. Who knew, right? Anyway, she's going back to live there and run the company."

Jolene commandeered Coop's phone. "That's great news on this end. How do you feel about it?"

"I'm going to miss her, but her leaving was different this time." Another sideways glance at Jenn. "I'm inviting her and Mort for Thanksgiving, too."

Again, Jenn nodded her approval.

"Great. I can't wait."

Coop returned to the screen. "Same here."

We said our goodbyes and ended the call.

I looked at Jenn. "Sorry to put you on the spot like that, but I hadn't planned to invite them... until I did."

"It's fine, honey. I figure it's the least I could do after draggin' y'all so far away from home."

I'm sure she caught the wave of relief that must have washed over my face. "Home is wherever you are, Babe. That's a fact."

"Good answer." She stood. "I've got some things to do. You should call your mama and tell her the good news."

It surprised Mama to hear from me so soon, and she was happy to accept my invitation. I said hey to Mort and told him to take good care of Mama. He promised he would.

I had one more call to make. I checked on Jenn to make sure she was busy in the kitchen, then slipped out the front door.

CHAPTER TWENTY-FOUR

I found a secluded spot under a cypress tree and dialed Coop's number.

"Cooper Hill, Private Eye. When you're in trouble, we charge double."

"Hey, Coop."

"Who *is* this?"

"Very funny."

"I don't hear from you in over a month, then twice in one day. What did you get yourself into this time?"

"About the flight out here..."

"I knew there'd be a catch."

"I need you to stay a little longer. Maybe a week or two."

"Why? What's the matter?"

I looked around to make sure no one was within earshot. "Something doesn't add up with how Jenn's Uncle Roy died."

"I thought you said it was a heart attack."

"That's what Jenn told me, but since I got here, I've been hearing other things. The ranch foreman knows more than he's sayin', but he went missing a couple of days ago."

"You think Roy was murdered?"

"I don't know, but if he was, I'm gonna need some help figuring out who did it."

"Another mystery?" He paused. "You're just messin' with me, aren't you?"

"I'm serious. Things are going sideways faster than I can figure out why."

"You're like a trouble magnet."

"You think I'd offer to fly you and Jo out here for two weeks if it wasn't serious?"

"You've got a point, Ebenezer." He laughed at his own joke, as he often did. "You can count on me. I hate to think what would have happened last time if Cooper Hill, Private Eye, hadn't take a bullet for you."

"You're never going to let me forget that, are you?"

"No, I am not." He let that hang there for a moment. "It sounds like you need me sooner rather than later. What if we came out two weeks before Thanksgiving instead of staying after?"

"Could you?"

"Let me bring the girls and you've got a deal."

"Done. We've got plenty of room."

***

When Hattie told me that the Whitehawk brothers could track anybody or anything, it gave me an idea. I would enlist their services to help me find Buck. However, I had a big problem. They hated my guts.

I couldn't do it alone. I needed a wingman, or in this case, a wing woman. I drove to the Cheyenne village that Roy had helped establish on the eastern end of the property. I wasn't sure what to expect, even though my mind painted a picture of smoke signals rising from a bunch of teepees. Instead, quaint little shops lined the paved main street, which was intersected by two cross streets that appeared to lead to small residential developments dotted with small homes and trailers.

I pulled into a parking spot in front of a saloon that looked like it came from the set of a John Wayne movie. I decided it might be better to inquire at one of the other shops. The dry goods store across the street seemed like a safer bet. The woman behind the counter eyed me suspiciously when I entered. I don't imagine they get many white folk walking through their door.

I thought of using Roy's name as a reference, but my gut told me he might not be that highly regarded despite his generosity. When she told me Cassidy worked at the coffee shop a couple doors down the block, I thanked her and moved on.

I stood at the door of the Whitehawk Café, unsure how I missed it when I drove in. The stenciled glass door read, Cassidy Whitehawk, proprietor. I noticed her watching me through the glass from behind the counter. Her big ebony eyes held a mixture of surprise and apprehension. The little bell that jingled when I walked in reminded me of Hattie's. A handful of patrons occupied three of the dozen or so tables. I felt their stares as I read the large menu on the wall behind the counter, which indicated that they served a variety of caffeinated beverages along with light breakfast and lunch fare.

"What are you doing here?"

"I'd like a medium coffee. Black."

"Is that to go?"

"No. I'll drink it here if that's okay."

"We don't get many white men coming in here for coffee."

"Really? What do they usually order?"

She tried to hide the smile that flashed across her face. "I meant—"

"I know what you meant." An awkward moment passed. "If you sit with me, I'll buy you one, too."

"How could I resist an offer like that?" She poured two cups and led me to a table in the corner. She scanned the room before she sat.

"Nice place you've got here." I took a sip.

"You wouldn't risk coming down here if you didn't want something. So, what is it?"

"I need to talk to Jacob and Jeremiah. Do you know where I can find them?"

"If they're not across the street, you can probably find them at the Wet Whistle."

"Noted." I raised my cup and took another sip. My eyes never left hers. "I kinda got off on the wrong foot with your nephews. I need their help with something, so I was hoping you'd be around when I talked to them."

A second smile flashed across her face. "You're a funny man, Mr. Bishop. Funny and brave."

"Thanks... I think. You can call me Dillon." A silence descended upon us for a moment. "Will you help me?"

"It's a big ask."

"It wasn't easy coming down here."

She kneaded the muscles in her upper arms. "My arms still hurt where you knelt on them."

"You shouldn't go around jumping people from behind."

Her expression softened. "Meet me back here tomorrow at three. The boys will be here. I can't promise you anything beyond that."

"Thank you. I'll make it worth your while."

"I hope you're not hitting on me."

I had to chuckle. I stood. "Tomorrow," I said with a polite tip of my hat.

***

On the way home, Hattie called with news that the coroner had a copy of Roy's report, but he wanted to deliver it in person. He offered to swing by Hattie's Hardware in a half hour. I told her I'd be there.

Sam Higgins had been the Teller County coroner for going on forty years. His son, Jack, currently held the county executive position. Of course, Hattie Scott was a close friend of the family.

Sam wore a worried look when I arrived at Hattie's. We walked to the back of the store in silence, and she ushered us into a room that appeared more like a full kitchen than a break room. After introductions, Sam got right to the point.

We sat, and Sam placed a manila envelope on the table. "I'm taking a huge risk giving you this, but Hattie here is an old friend, and in my business, it's all about getting to the truth. I've been doing this for nearly forty years, and this case is only the second one where I don't believe that's what happened."

"What was the first?"

"It doesn't matter." He tapped the folder with his finger. "There are two reports in here, my original, which I kept a copy of, and the official report that was filed. You'll notice some significant differences. Sheriff didn't like the preliminary report."

I glanced at Hattie, then urged Sam to continue.

"He made me edit the report before I filed it. I didn't want to do it, but I'm too close to retirement to jeopardize my pension."

"I appreciate your honesty."

He nodded, his eyes darting around the room like the sheriff might come busting in.

"So, can you tell me about the differences?"

He slid the envelope across the table. I opened it and scanned the two reports. "I'm not sure I understand all the medical jargon. Can you give me a summary in layman's terms?"

"Well, they told me it was a heart attack when they brought him in."

"And you don't think that's true?"

"It certainly looked like it, but I don't think it's that simple." He shook his head. "But the sheriff didn't want to hear anything to the contrary."

"What makes you think there was more?"

"There were several things that I was told to leave out of the report." He pulled a handkerchief from his pocket and wiped his forehead. "For instance, there was a contusion on the side of his head just above the ear, and more on his arms. The marks on his arms were consistent with someone kneeling on them."

Hattie closed her eyes and hung her head.

I flashed back to my struggle with Cassidy in the woods. "Like someone held him down?"

"That's a reasonable assumption." He pointed to the papers in my hand. "The official report lists the cause of death as cardiac arrest, same as mine, but any mention of other injuries has been removed."

"So, he died of a heart attack?"

"Yes, but I wouldn't exactly call it natural causes."

"You think Roy McDonald was murdered?"

"I will deny it publicly, but in this room, yes, I believe Roy's death was the result of foul play."

Hattie excused herself and walked to the refrigerator in the corner of the room. She retrieved a bottle of water and took a long drink. I'm sure she wished it was something much stronger.

"I really should get back to work," Sam said as he stood.

I thanked him for his candor and offered to do my best not to reveal the source of this information. Unfortunately, I couldn't promise him the same.

Hattie pulled two more bottles of water from the refrigerator and put them in a paper bag. She handed them to Sam.

"If anyone sees you leaving, just tell them you had to buy some supplies."

I'm getting too old for this," he said with a shake of his head. He took the bag from Hattie and left.

Hattie turned to me and pointed to the envelope in my hand. "What are you going to do with that information?"

"I don't know yet."

"Please be careful."

Unfortunately, no one ever got to the bottom of anything by being careful.

Chapter Twenty-Five

I slipped my boots on by the door, dropped my phone into my shirt pocket, and stepped outside.

Jenn's voice startled me from the porch swing. "Going somewhere?"

I stopped in my tracks, and my head snapped in her direction. I must have looked like a deer in her headlights. "Gotta run an errand."

She smiled and patted the seat next to her.

I checked the time on my phone before I sat. I didn't want to be late.

"What kind of errand?" she asked.

"The kind you're better off not knowing about." I forced a smile.

"Unless you're meeting another woman, you better spill it. And if it is another woman, you best find yourself another place to live."

"What if it's a little of both?"

She raised an eyebrow as if to say, *You've got to be kidding.*

"Cassidy Whitehawk agreed to broker a deal between myself and her nephews."

"What kind of deal?"

"To help me find Buck."

"God help me. Not Buck again. I asked you to drop it, Dillon. Why is that so hard?"

"Because he got railroaded, and I think Seth is driving the train."

I waited for a tongue-lashing that never came.

"I'm going with you."

"What?"

"You heard me. Where's this meeting supposed to take place?"

"Cheyenne Village, but I don't think you tagging along is a good idea."

"Well, I think it's an excellent idea." She stood. "Don't make me pull rank on you, Sergeant."

"We're going into enemy territory. It might get rough."

She folded her arms across her chest. "And what part of rough do you think I can't handle?"

I'd seen her in action. I wouldn't bet against her, no matter the opponent. "You can ride shotgun."

"Alex is inside playing video games. I'll go tell him we're leaving and to find Uncle Seth in the barn if he needs any-thing."

That was a little like letting the fox guard the henhouse.

I explained my plan in the truck on the way to the village. If she had any reservations, she kept them to herself. I only hoped she'd be as restrained when we met with the Whitehawks.

We parked in front of the café and walked inside. Cassidy waited on a customer at the counter. After her initial surprise, presumably at seeing Jenn by my side, she nodded toward the corner where the boys sat. They stood and greeted us as we approached. Well, neither of them looked at *me* as they spoke. For a couple of hoodlums, they seemed well-behaved. I guess bringing Jenn wasn't such a bad idea after all.

Fortunately, Cassidy joined us as soon as we sat down across from Jacob and Jeremiah. She offered us something to drink. I passed, but Jenn asked for a glass of water. I wanted to kick her under the table. We made small talk until Cassidy returned.

"I offered to arrange this little get-together at my place of business, so I trust everyone will be on their best behavior."

The comment had clearly been aimed at the other side of the table, and I guessed it wasn't the first time they'd heard it.

I jumped right in. "First, I'd like to apologize for us getting off on the wrong foot the first time we met."

"First two times," Jacob said.

"I stand corrected. Anyway, I ask that you hear me out before making any rash decisions."

No one spoke, so I continued. *Start with a compliment.* "I understand you boys are good at tracking things. Someone told me you could track a rattlesnake through the Grand Canyon, and I believe her. So I'm asking you to locate my friend Buck, that crazy old cowboy I tossed out of the bar the first night we met."

When they heard Buck's name, they both wrinkled their noses like they'd just smelled a steaming pile of roadkill in the middle of July. I glanced at Jenn in case we needed to make a hasty exit.

"I know he's not one of your favorite people, he's not even one of mine, but he has some information that might help us get to the bottom of some shady business that's been going down at the ranch, including that unfortunate car accident."

"It wasn't an accident." Jacob leaned closer. "Roy McDonald killed her."

"I don't think he did."

"Prove it."

"That's what I intend to do if you'll help me." I had no idea how I might do that, but I was desperate.

Jacob eyed me suspiciously while his brother's eyes were busy with Jenn. I buried the urge to gouge out one or both of them.

"It seems pretty fair to me," Cassidy offered.

The boys glanced at her, then fixed their gaze on me. Jacob spoke first. "If Roy didn't do it, I want to know who did."

"Okay." My eyes alternated between the two brothers. "Do we have a deal?"

I'm sure Jenn wanted to kick *me* under the table.

"Deal." They said in unison.

Jenn remained silent, but I was sure I'd hear plenty about this when we got outside.

Jenn waited until we were back in the truck. "You mind telling me what just happened in there?"

"Okay, so I over-promised a bit, but I need to find Buck."

"And what happens when they find him and it's your turn to pony up? Huh? Those boys don't strike me as the kind that look the other way if you renege on a promise."

"Yes, but I have an ace up my sleeve."

She eyed me suspiciously. "You're not seriously thinking about dragging Cooper and his family into another one of your messes, are you?"

"We make a great team, like Butch and Sundance or Starsky and Hutch."

"More like Dumb and Dumber." A faint smile played on her lips before her expression fell. "The last time you two did something crazy like this, Cooper got shot."

"He knew what he was getting into… I think. Besides, he was wearing a vest at the time."

"You didn't know that."

"Obviously, Coop is the brains of this outfit. All the more reason I need him."

Jenn stared out the window as I started the truck and pointed it toward home. I knew she'd have more to say.

"He's only here for the holiday. What do you think you're going to accomplish in one weekend?"

"Here's the thing... I kinda invited Coop to stay for a couple weeks."

"Seriously?"

"They're bringing the girls."

"Dillon!" She blew out a breath. "It would be nice if people started asking me before going off and making plans that affect me or my ranch."

"I'm sorry, Babe. Everything's been happening so fast, I wasn't thinking straight."

Jenn's expression softened. "I love you, Dillon, but sometimes you're as dumb as a watermelon."

I was okay with that. There are worse things she could have called me.

At one point on the ride home, Seth's name came up in conversation.

"He's another one." Jenn had her tail up again. "What makes him think he can make all these important decisions without consulting me? He's actin' like he owns the place, and it's pissin' me off." She turned to me. "What am I gonna do?"

"Do you really think you should be takin' advice from a watermelon?"

"I'm serious, Dillon. We can't just let him go on like this. He's not the same person I knew way back when. He's changed, and frankly, I'm beginning not to trust him anymore."

"I'm way ahead of you. You didn't want to hear it when I told you he threatened us."

"He threatened *us*? I figured he just didn't care for *you* movin' in, like he might have felt outnumbered." She paused, her eyes locked on mine. "What exactly did he say?"

"He said Mama and I should go back where we came from, or somebody might get hurt." When that didn't have the desired effect, I said, "He also told me the ranch was no place for *that* boy."

"He said *that* boy?"

"Sure did. Said boys like him have a way of gettin' into trouble. That's when accidents happen." I made up that last part so she might start watching her back around Seth.

"When we get home, I'm gonna sucker punch that two-faced son of a bitch."

"Now who's the watermelon?"

"What's that supposed to mean?"

"It means that's a bad idea." As much as I'd like a front-row seat for that show, I couldn't let her tip our hand to Seth. "We don't want him to know that we're on to him."

"What are we supposed to do, wait around till somebody gets hurt?"

"The coroner thinks Roy was murdered."

"I think I would have heard about something like that."

"Sheriff shut it down."

"Who would want to kill Uncle Roy?"

"Seriously?" I took a deep breath. "Let's see... There are the crazy Whitehawk brothers who want revenge for their mother's death. There's Buck who maybe never forgave him for knockin' boots with his girlfriend and getting her pregnant. Finally, there's Seth who appears to have his sights set on turning this place into a big marijuana farm." I paused to let her catch up. "Those are only the ones I know about."

"Okay, you made your point."

I had her on the ropes as I parked the truck in front of the house, so I made no attempt to exit the vehicle. "How do we know this new foreman he hired isn't one of his cronies, here to help him squeeze us out?"

"What are we gonna do?"

"You know who can help us with this, don't you?"

"Why do I have a feeling you're gonna say Coop?"

I folded my arms across my chest triumphantly. "I'm just sayin'..."

Jenn shook her head before opening the door. She turned and looked at me with a good measure of resignation. "Well, if you really think so, he can stay as long as he likes."

Chapter Twenty-Six

It took a week before I heard from Jacob Whitehawk. He assured me they had picked up Buck's trail and could tell me where he was in a day or two. They promised to keep their distance and let me make first contact. I took a risk believing them, hoping Buck wouldn't be a bloody mess by the time I arrived.

In the meantime, I enlisted the help of Deputy Sheriff Ziggy Scott to help me track down Ben and Sadie, the two ranch hands Buck had suggested I talk to. However, when his boss, Sheriff Decker, got wind of it, he shut it down. The fact that Sheriff Pecker, as Ziggy liked to call him, knew Seth probably had something to do with it.

"Does everybody call him that?"

He smiled. "Just the people who know him."

I took a shine to Ziggy, who offered to help me on his own time. He had his mama's eyes.

Sadie was easy to find. We paid a visit to her trailer at the edge of town. Ziggy was takin' a big enough risk wearing his official uniform on unofficial business, so I drove. We rolled up in the Silverado around dinner time in case she'd started a new job since she left the ranch. Turns out she hadn't.

She opened the door, looking about as scared as a cat at the dog pound. I'd seen her around the ranch a couple of times, maybe even spoke to her once. But I believe it was Ziggy's uniform that got us in the door. We introduced ourselves, and Ziggy explained that we were looking for information surrounding her departure from the Red Valley Ranch.

"Seth McDonald doesn't know we're here," I said. "He claims you and Ben just up and quit, but I think there's more to it than that. Am I right?"

She met my gaze, and I saw recognition in her eyes. "I know you. You're the boyfriend."

"I guess I am."

"You're not in any trouble," Ziggy offered. "We're just trying to get to the truth."

"Why would I be in trouble? Can't a person quit a job without it being a federal case?"

I shot a glance in Ziggy's direction.

Ziggy straightened up. "Can you tell us why you quit?"

Her eyes darted around the small room like she hadn't expected anyone to show up asking questions. "Uh... I got another job. A better job."

"That's good. Mind if I ask where?"

More eye darting. "I do mind. I'm not sure what business it is of yours."

I scanned the room while Ziggy continued to question her. I didn't see anything that sent up a red flag or didn't belong in a young woman's trailer.

"What about Ben? Did he have another job to go to?"

"You'll have to ask him."

One of her hands trembled. She placed the other one on top of it. "I'm afraid I'm gonna have to ask you to leave."

This girl was either really scared or really stupid, or maybe both. She couldn't have known that Ziggy wasn't there on official police business.

I looked at Ziggy and then Sadie. We thanked her and left quietly. Once inside the truck, Ziggy offered to keep an eye on the place for the next couple of days. She watched us through parted curtains in the trailer's front window. I started the truck and backed out of her drive.

"She's scared and in some kind of trouble," Ziggy said. "I wish she'd let us help her."

"Maybe she saw something she wasn't supposed to see, and she's being threatened to keep quiet."

"If you're right, whoever that is won't take kindly to you sticking your nose into their business. You'd better watch your back."

"Copy that."

***

Jacob Whitehawk called the next day to tell me they'd found Buck. He'd holed up in an abandoned building on the other side of Victor, about twenty miles south of here. I told him to sit tight, and that I'd be there in a half hour. With my truck headed south, I had about twenty minutes to figure out what to say. Buck was one bubble off plumb when he had a job and a place to live. I wasn't sure what to expect now.

I didn't want to go in there asking for something without anything to offer in return. I could offer him his job back, but that's something I needed to run by Jenn first. Her being left out of ranch decisions was too sore of a subject right now.

I assumed Buck had information in that thick skull of his that could blow this case wide open. Why else would Seth have fired him? I envisioned a turning point, much like what finding Pop's journal had done to my little brother's case. Note to self: look for Roy's missing journals again.

I stopped at a little pizza shop in Victor and picked up a couple slices and a bottle of Coke. About a mile out of town, I spotted Jacob's pickup in an emergency pullout on County Road 67. I pulled alongside and rolled down my window.

"Where is he?"

"Quarter mile on the right. Abandoned mine building. His truck's around back."

"Thanks."

"We held up our end of the deal." They both nodded like a couple of bobblehead dolls.

"Yes, you did. And I'll hold up mine, but I need some time."

"Don't wait too long."

"You can go now. I got this." I rolled up my window and sped off.

The building came up quickly, set back from the road around a big bend. If I wasn't looking for it, I probably would have missed it. I wondered how in the world those two bobbleheads found him.

I pulled in behind the building and parked next to Buck's truck. The greasy shell of a building had seen better days. One corner of a condemned sign flapped in the breeze as I pounded on the rusty metal door. I knew he was in there. I pounded again.

A low voice rattled inside. "Nobody's home."

"Really, Buck? It's Dillon. Let me in." I waited.

After a few moments of silence, the door opened a crack.

"What do you want?"

I held up the food. "Pizza delivery."

The door closed, then opened a few seconds later. Buck looked like a miner standing in a cave. A pissed-off miner. I stood my ground, hoping his empty stomach would overrule his fool head.

He took a step back. "Well, don't just stand there."

I walked inside the dimly lit cave of a building that smelled of mold. Filtered light entered from three upper windows. The lower windows had been boarded up.

"Nice place you got here."

"How'd you find me?"

I handed him the food. "I thought you might be hungry."

He grabbed it from my hand and walked over to a lawn chair set up next to a sleeping bag and camp stove. "Thanks," he said as he sat.

I walked around, checking the place out as he devoured the first slice.

"Better stay on this side. That's the toilet over there."

As soon as he spoke, my nose confirmed his warning. By the time I walked back to where he sat, the food was gone.

"Now I'm gonna have to move." His eyes widened and his ruddy complexion lost its color. "I seen Jacob Whitehawk sniffin' around the building earlier. They nearly killed me with that explosion. Now that they found me, they'll finish me off fer sure."

"The Whitehawks didn't blow up the barn."

He looked at me with squinted eyes. "And how would you know somethin' like that?"

"Because I hired them."

"*You* tried to kill me?"

"No, you idiot. I hired them to find you."

"Are they here now?"

"I sent them home."

"If they didn't try to kill me, who did?"

"I was hoping *you* could tell *me*."

Buck took another hit off the Coke bottle. He held it up between us. "You got anything stronger than this?"

"Not with me."

"You should leave, then. I can take care a myself."

"Clearly." I shook my head slowly. "I was right about you. You're a mean old fart who doesn't have enough sense to spit downwind."

"Go on now, get outta here."

"Here's what we're gonna do. I'm gonna put you up in a five-star hotel and you're gonna tell me why you got fired. Then you're gonna come clean about all the rest of the shady stuff you been doin' at the ranch."

He laughed and took a big gulp of the two-liter bottle of Coke. "A five-star hotel, huh? Where you gonna find one a them in these parts?"

A doghouse would be an improvement over this place. "I have reason to believe that Roy was murdered."

"Really, Sherlock? That's what I been tryin' to tell ya."

"I kinda think you did it, but maybe you just stole all his money."

He jumped up from his seat and thrust a grubby finger in my face. "I didn't do none a those things."

"Well, somebody did, and I think there's shit you're not telling me."

His bushy, gray mustache twitched as he inhaled a long breath and studied me. "You were sayin' something about a five-star hotel?"

I glanced around the black hole where we stood. "You probably don't deserve it, but I can't leave you here. Pack up your shit."

He tried to stare me down. When I didn't flinch, he started packing.

"Your place was empty," I asked. "Where's all your belong-ings?"

"I rented a storage locker."

Apparently, he hadn't intended to go very far when he left town.

I told him I'd come back later for his truck, and we drove off in mine. Buck hunkered down in the passenger seat on the way. I parked the truck in Hattie's driveway about a mile outside of town.

Buck sat up. "What are we doin' here?"

"Remember that five-star hotel I told you about?"

"Yeah, but this—"

"Technically, it's a *motel*. It's out back."

He mumbled something I didn't catch. I'm sure I was better off.

I told Buck to stay in the truck while I went inside to talk to Hattie. Five minutes later, I was back with the keys to the RV. Hattie waved to Buck from the doorway.

The RV wasn't top of the line, but it was close. I watched Buck check everything out when we stepped inside. Hattie had mentioned how to hook up the electricity in the garage, so I took care of that first. I got Buck settled and told him to keep the shades drawn, then went into town to get some provisions. He didn't care what food he ate as long as it came with a side of bourbon.

After I dropped everything off, I had to get home for dinner. He seemed to like his new digs, so I didn't think he was a flight risk. He looked like he needed a good night's sleep. I planned to talk again in the morning after chores.

"Only three people know you're here," I said before I left. "You, me, and Hattie. You'll be safe here." I pointed a finger in his direction. "Just stay put."

Chapter Twenty-Seven

I blew through chores the next morning and parked my truck at Hattie's house. I ran around back to find the RV empty. He couldn't have gotten far without a vehicle. I hoped to God that I wouldn't find an empty bourbon bottle in the RV and have to dredge the pond to find his drunken carcass. He had some explainin' to do first.

"Buck." I scanned the yard. "Buck."

The back door to the house opened, and Hattie stuck her head out. "He's in here."

I blew out a breath and my heart rate dropped to within normal range.

"Before you say anything, I invited him in for breakfast." She waited for an acknowledgment before she let me in.

Buck sat at the table and looked up with a mouthful of bacon, eggs, and hash browns. He gave me a quick nod.

"Can I get you some breakfast?" Hattie asked.

"Maybe just a cup of coffee if you have one."

I took a seat at the table across from Buck, and Hattie set a steaming cup in front of me.

I took a sip and looked at Buck. "How'd you sleep last night?"

"Best sleep I've had in a week."

Hattie pulled out a chair. "I told him he can stay as long as he wants."

I looked from Hattie to Buck. "Don't get too comfortable. They might be holdin' a cell in Fremont with your name on it."

"Dillon. Why would you say such a thing?"

I pointed across the table. "Maybe you should ask him."

Buck swallowed hard. "I told ya, I didn't do nothin'."

"Tell me some more. Like how you got yourself fired."

"I'm sure Seth already told you his version."

"I want to hear yours."

I waited while he finished the last couple of bites from his plate. He appeared to be stalling while he made up a story. It didn't look like he'd be much help. I took a sip of coffee and glanced at Hattie, but her expression was unreadable.

"Well?"

"Whatever he told you, I didn't do it. I've got his number now, so he wants me gone."

"Buck, what does that mean?" Hattie looked almost as interested as me.

"It means he's the one who poisoned the horses."

"So, you don't think it was the Whitehawks that poisoned the horses?"

"Not anymore."

"How do you know that?"

"I overheard him talkin' on the phone. I think he's fixin' to do it again."

"That's a pretty strong accusation. What did you hear?"

"He said he would take care a you and Jenny Lee one way or another."

"Who was he talking to?"

"That I don't know." He looked at Hattie. "Can I get another cup a coffee?"

Hattie nodded and left the table.

"Can you put a little somethin' in this one?"

"I've got some fresh cream."

Buck shook his head. "I was thinkin' more like a shot a whiskey."

"What do you think he meant by *take care* of us?"

"Well, I don't think he meant readin' you a bedtime story and tuckin' you in every night."

Hattie set a fresh cup of coffee in front of him. "Be nice, Buck. He's just tryin' to help."

"Seth's tryin' to drive you two off." He sipped the coffee and looked disappointed.

"Why?"

"You two ain't supposed to be there."

I frowned. "He pretty much told me that the day I arrived."

"Let me give you a little history lesson." He leaned back in his chair. "Seth showed up about three years ago. He made a deal with Roy to work for room and board and maybe a little pocket money. He seemed like a nice enough fella, a real hard worker. Word around town was that Roy put him in the will."

I waited while Buck took another drink. He turned to Hattie with big sad eyes and held out his cup.

She got up without a word and returned with a whiskey bottle. She poured a shot into his coffee. He smiled like a little kid with an ice cream cone.

"I think that was his plan all along," he continued. "The ranch fell on hard times right about when Roy's drinkin' caught up with him. Then, just as I start thinkin' that maybe Seth had somethin' to do with the financial troubles, he brought in some fancy doctor, and far as I can tell, started takin' good care a Roy. I wouldn't have believed it if I hadn't seen it for myself."

"So, you never found any evidence of wrongdoing?"

"That's right, but I never seen Seth so mad as when he come back from the lawyers the day they read the will. He was in a horn-tossin' mood, so I stayed clear for a couple days."

"Seth got half the ranch, and Jenn got the other half. Wasn't that the plan?"

"I wouldn't know, but it looked like he thought he was gettin' the whole thing."

Hattie frowned and shook her head. "Seth was always so nice when he came into the store."

I leaned over the table in Buck's direction. "Do you think Seth could have killed Roy?"

He spoke without hesitation. "I think them Whitehawks was the ones that killed Roy McDonald."

***

I left Buck with Hattie, who agreed to keep an eye on him. They would probably both be high by this afternoon. Buck was still a suspect in my mind, but Seth's stock just took another dip. I wouldn't rush to judgment without verifying the things Buck had said, but truth be told, I wanted Buck to be innocent. Sure, he had an abrasive personality, but Buck wasn't trying to be something he's not. I had a feeling Seth had horns holdin' up his halo.

I filed a Colorado Open Records Act (CORA) request to get a copy of the police report from the day they found Roy. If the sheriff signed off on it, I didn't expect it to be any more accurate than the official coroner's report, but I needed to keep trying.

Alex had just left for school by the time I got home. Jenn agreed to take a ride with me to see Roy's grave.

"We can drive as far as the overlook," I said as I steered the Jeep along in the direction of the ridge.

"The overlook?"

"Yeah. That's what I call the special place you showed me. It overlooks the entire valley. I go up there sometimes when I need some space to figure things out."

"You'd tell me if the flashbacks are starting again, right?"

"Yeah. It's not that."

I pulled the Jeep off the trail. "We're on foot from here."

We hiked about a quarter of a mile before we reached the clearing.

"I've never been up here," Jenn said when we got there. "It's beautiful."

She walked a little further and stopped just outside the circle of rocks. "Y'all did this?"

"No, it was here," I answered from near the graves. "Check this out."

She walked up beside me. "There's two."

"The one with all the trinkets is Asha. Cassidy put them there."

She pointed to the other grave. "That's Uncle Roy's?"

I nodded.

"He should have a headstone. You can't even tell who's buried there."

"I'm not sure who did it. Seth, maybe."

"I'm going to make sure he gets a proper marker."

I walked over to the unmarked grave. "There's another one here. Hattie had a stillborn son."

"There's no marker. Why is he up here?"

"It was Roy's."

"What?" Her brow furrowed, and she chewed her bottom lip. "I didn't know he had a son."

"Neither did he."

"What do you mean?"

"Hattie never told him."

"Then how did he get buried up here?"

"You're not going to believe this, but Buck helped her."

"Come on, Dillon. Y'all are just messin' with me now."

"I shit you not." I turned to her. "Buck and Hattie were an item until Roy moved to town and bought the ranch. She kicked poor ol' Buck to the curb and took up with Roy. She got pregnant and didn't tell anyone. She called Buck, who was still carryin' a torch for her, when she lost the baby six months later. He helped her bury her son up here to save her the embarrassment."

"That was sweet of him."

"Yeah, he's a real sweet guy." I blew out a breath. "That's not the point. It was his boss for God's sake. Don't you think he wanted to tear him limb from limb? I would have."

"If you're trying to make a case for Buck killing Uncle Roy, I don't buy it. Besides, it was years later."

"Buck swears the Whitehawk brothers did it."

"Maybe they did." She stared down at Roy's grave as she pleaded her case. "Those boys thought Roy killed their mama, so it was an eye for an eye. Like the Bible says."

"Maybe, but can you imagine how Buck must have felt after what Roy did to him? How it must have festered over the years until one day Buck snapped and killed him?"

She raised an eyebrow. "What if Buck just started stealing money from Uncle Roy, like payback or something?"

"Hmm... I didn't think of that."

We walked back to the overlook in silence and stopped to take in the view.

"Speaking of Hattie and Buck, when I got to Hattie's this morning, they were having breakfast inside the house."

Jenn raised an eyebrow. "You think they...?"

"Don't say it." I closed my eyes and shook my head. "That's something I can't unsee."

"Wouldn't it be wonderful if after all this time they ended up together?"

"I reckon it depends on who you ask."

On our way home, I got a call from the coroner.

"This is Sam Higgins. I thought you should know that Roy's case was just reopened."

"That's good news, right?"

"I hope so, but it doesn't make sense."

"Who reopened it?"

"Sheriff."

"Didn't you say he buried evidence on the original report?"

"That's what bothers me. I seriously doubt he had a sudden case of conscience."

He's right. This didn't make sense. "What would he have to gain by telling the truth now? I thought he wanted to cover up Roy's murder. Won't his make him look bad?"

"You don't understand. He'll blame it on an inept coroner, or worse, implicate me in a cover-up. Either way, I'm out of a job and possibly looking at jail time." His voice cracked. "I never should have told you anything."

"How is this my fault?"

"Whatever you're planning to do with that information, leave me out of it."

I set my phone on the seat and looked at Jenn. "Did you know they reopened Roy's case?"

She frowned and shook her head.

"That could be a good thing."

My phone vibrated with a text message, and Jenn picked it up off the seat.

"Don't count on it." She held up the phone.

I read the message. *Your CORA request has been denied because the records requested pertain to an open case.*

Chapter Twenty-Eight

The rest of the week went by without incident. It gave me a chance to slow down and spend some time with my family, but I couldn't help feeling like this was the calm before the storm. I'd tried my best to make a case against Buck to Jenn, just to see if I could. She poked holes in it, which didn't bother me, other than it made Seth's claims that Buck had been stealing from the ranch a little more plausible.

I counted the days until Coop arrived. Meanwhile, Jenn and Alex were preparing for Halloween. Jenn enlisted my help with the front porch decorations. While it seemed like a waste of time to me, I was happy to oblige for Alex's sake—eleven years old and looking forward to his first Halloween.

Growing up in Bradley, we'd go from door to door in the neighborhood collecting treats. Out here, there weren't any neighborhoods. Our nearest neighbors were well beyond walking distance.

Alex had his Captain America costume all ready for the school party on the 31st. That night the kids could trick-or-treat in town at local businesses to make up for them not bein' able to do it at home. Jenn and I had agreed to take Alex.

On Sunday afternoon, Alex and I went for another ride on the ATVs. We packed a lunch and headed north to Fletcher's Pond to do a little fishin'. We still hadn't had any rain, and the grass crackled like broken glass beneath our tires. Alex asked me if we planned to kill anything today. I told him we might bring a fish or two home for dinner, but if he'd rather we throw them back, that I wouldn't object.

The pond was down a good four feet, and we stood on the bank and stared in disbelief.

"If it doesn't rain pretty soon, we're gonna be in trouble. The horses won't have any grass to eat, and the fish won't have enough water to swim in."

Alex shook his head. He looked like he was about to burst into tears.

I had to say something. "Maybe we can help."

"How?"

"When the Indians needed it to rain, they did a special dance called a rain dance."

He thought about it for a few moments. "We got Indians on the ranch down in Cheyenne Village."

"What if they've been dancing already? It might be raining over there right now."

Again, he took a moment to think. "Do you know any rain dances?"

"Why, yes, I think I do. A medicine woman named Leotie showed me once." I looked at him with wide eyes and a feigned sense of urgency. "I'm willin' to give it a try if you are."

He nodded his head like there was only one answer to that question.

I threw my hat on the ground, and we danced around it. Soon we were hootin' and hollerin' loud enough for the rain gods to hear. I had checked the forecast before we left—a chance of rain later in the day. Even if we only got a little, I could blame it on our dance.

Alex held out his hands, palms up, as soon as we finished. He looked up at the puffy white clouds that momentarily blocked the sun.

"You've got to be patient," I said. "Nothing usually happens right away."

We had to climb down the bank to get close enough to the water.

"Where does all the water go?" Alex asked.

I told him what I remembered from school about evaporation and such. It appeared to satisfy his curiosity for the time being.

We sat and talked for a spell before he got a pull on his line. I helped him reel in his first fish.

"She's a beauty. Pretty near ten inches long, wouldn't you say?"

Alex nodded.

"What do you want to do with her?"

He stared at it without saying a word. A panicked expression washed over his face like he didn't know what his choices were.

"If we catch a couple more like that," I said. "We'll have a nice fish fry tonight."

More thinking before he shrugged. "Maybe we could have hamburgers instead."

"That works for me." I unhooked the fish from the line and tossed it back.

Alex smiled as he watched it swim away.

We didn't have much luck for the next hour, so after lunch, we packed up and moved about a hundred yards around to the west side. As we climbed down the bank to set up, Alex called out.

"What's this?"

I stood by his side and studied the end of an eight-inch pipe that stuck out horizontally from the bank into the shallow water. I estimated it to be a good five feet below the normal water level. If it weren't for the drought, we'd never have known it was there.

"Looks like some kind of pipe." That was the easy part. "Not sure why it's here."

Alex walked past it and found us a spot nearby. I guess that's all he needed to know. I needed a little more information.

We caught seven more fish over the next two hours. I'd promised Alex we would catch and release for the rest of the day, and I kept my word. I stared at that damn pipe when I wasn't busy unhooking fish and tossing them back. My first thought had been that someone was dumping shit into the pond, but it appeared that water flowed out of the pond rather than into it.

Buck had never mentioned a pipe. He'd told me when we met that there wasn't a leaf that blew 'round here that he didn't know about. I wondered if the same applied to pipes.

Before we left, I used the compass app on my phone to determine that the pipe headed off in a northwesterly direction. I wasn't sure what was out that way, but I was going to find out.

It rained a little that night after dinner. Alex watched from the window. At one point, he turned to me, and I gave him the thumbs-up sign. He smiled so hard, I thought the top of his head might fall off.

***

Halloween appeared to be something of a big deal 'round these parts. The most people I'd seen since I arrived in Colorado descended on the business district in the center of town. People milled about on Main Street, which had been closed to traffic for three blocks by the sheriff's department. A bandstand anchored one end where a local country-rock band played their hearts out. Several food and beverage vendors had set up booths at the other end. They had cider and donuts, coffee, and all manner of pumpkin-flavored treats.

Jenn and I sat on a hay bale, one of many scattered around Main Street, while Alex and a couple friends from school filled their bags with candy from many of the store owners.

Hattie approached, smiling like someone had just filled her trick-or-treat bag full of candy. "Well, if it isn't little Jenny come home after all these years. Aren't you a sight for sore eyes?"

"Hi, Miss Hattie. So nice to see you again."

"You too, dear. It's been too long."

She nodded in my direction. "I see you found yourself a keeper."

"Is that what y'all think?" She shot me a sideways wink. "I still haven't decided."

While the girls were busy talking, Sam Higgins walked by and gave the slightest nod.

I returned a courtesy smile as if he was just another stranger in a strange town.

"Oh, Honey." Hattie hugged Jenn again. "I just had to say hi. But I better get back to passin' out candy before one of these little rug rats eggs the front of my store."

"Thanks for stopping by."

"You come and see me sometime so we can get caught up."

"For sure."

Jenn turned to me as Hattie walked away. "I just love her."

"Me, too." I put an arm around Jenn. "Let's see what they've got to eat."

"What about Alex?"

I pointed to Alex walking with three other boys, laughing and stuffing their faces with candy. "He'll be all right."

Sheriff Pecker stopped us just before we reached the cider and donuts booth. I'd been trained in the army to immediately size up potential opponents. The sheriff appeared to be about six foot three, mid-forties, with a full head of dark hair and arrogant eyes. He clearly took good care of himself. I'm sure he fancied himself as a ladies' man. No wedding ring, not that it would have mattered. I didn't like the way he looked at Jenn.

"You two must be new in town."

"That's right." I extended my hand. "Dillon Bishop and Jenny Lee Myles. Jenn owns the Red Valley Ranch up the road about three miles."

"I know the place."

I bet you do. I watched him glance at Jenn's ring finger and I wanted to kick him in the nuts.

He held on to my hand for too long. "People around here don't take kindly to nosy neighbors. I thought you should know."

Subtlety wasn't his strong suit.

"I reckon they wouldn't." I met his steely gaze. "I'm the same way, myself."

He let go of my hand and turned to Jenn. "Welcome to Redfield. I'll let you two enjoy the festivities."

I nodded. "Sheriff." I didn't trust myself with his last name.

Jenn watched with stormy eyes as he walked away. She turned to me. "What was that about?"

"It was nothing."

"It was definitely something. Y'all better tell me what's goin' on."

"And spoil the party?" I gave her a quick nod. "I'll tell you later."

Pecker had just ruined whatever holiday spirit I had left. He somehow knew that I'd been sticking my nose into Roy's business. I didn't know how much he knew, but his message to back off was not lost on me. Sam Higgin's story just got real.

Chapter Twenty-Nine

Alex talked non-stop all the way home. I hoped he would come down off his sugar high by the time we got him ready for bed. We tucked him in around 9:30, which was late for a school night. I left his room before Jenn and retired to our bedroom. Jenn followed a few minutes later and closed the door.

"Now would be a good time to tell me what was going on between you and Sheriff Decker tonight."

I sat her on the bed and told her about the meeting with Sam Higgins. She shook her head like she could make it go away. I'd been asking questions and positing theories, but she never let herself go there. She asked to see the reports and scanned them briefly before she covered her face and cried.

"We need to find out who did this," she said.

"That's what I've been trying to tell you."

"You won't get any help from the sheriff. How did he know you were looking into all this?"

"Another good question. The only one I can think of is Seth. Hattie wouldn't have said anything, and Sam has too much to lose. Besides, he was as nervous as a whore in church when I met him at Hattie's."

"Are you going to say anything to Seth?"

"Not yet. Hattie's son Ziggy is a deputy, I think I can trust him if I need help with anything. But we need to watch our backs."

"I don't like it. I don't feel safe in my own home."

"Right now, it needs to be business as usual around here. Buck might just be our ace in the hole. Seth doesn't know he's back in town, and Buck knows more than any of us about what went on here at the ranch."

"So, you don't think he had anything to do with Uncle Roy's death?"

"I guess I haven't said it out loud, or even admitted it to myself, but I don't believe Buck killed your uncle."

***

"What do you know about Sheriff Pecker?" I asked Buck when I checked on him a couple days later.

"I never cared for him. Near as I can remember, he showed up from Denver about the time RMA started buyin' up all the land 'round here. He had lots a money to spend on his campaign, and I bet most of it came from RMA. He won in a landslide. Been a real peckerhead ever since."

"Why do you think he'd want to cover up Roy's murder?"

"I guess it depends on who done it."

"Did you ever see the sheriff and Seth together?"

"I seen the sheriff at the ranch a couple times, but no more than you might expect in the line a duty."

"Was he around when the barn burned down?"

"Sure was. The only good he ever done was make sure them Whitehawks paid for settin' that fire."

"Was Seth living there at the time?"

"Maybe he was. I don't recall."

I looked around the RV, pleasantly surprised to find the place in good order. I guess I expected it to be a mess by now.

"The other day, Alex and I went fishin' in the pond. The water was down about four feet because of the drought, which I expected. What I didn't expect was to find an eight-inch pipe sucking water out of the pond." I watched his reaction. "Did you know that was there?"

"I most certainly did not."

I believed him. "How does something like that get there?"

"It would have to be dug or drilled."

"And you don't remember that ever happening?"

He shook his head. "Could have been drilled sideways. That pond is only a hundred yards from the property line to the west."

"That's roughly the direction the pipe was headed. What's on the other side of the line?"

"Used to be the Miller ranch. RMA owns it now."

***

I found a number for RMA and called their corporate office in Denver. After being bounced around for twenty minutes, I was referred to the local project manager, Darrin Fuller, and a number in Woodland Park. Fuller acknowledged the pipe existed and there were several such deals made with local ranchers in the area. He referred me to the legal department in Denver.

I eventually found someone who confirmed that a deal had been signed five months ago with Seth McDonald representing the Red Valley Ranch in Teller County. He hesitated when I asked for a copy, but explained that all land, water, or mineral rights contracts were required to be recorded with the county clerk. I told him I'd request it from the clerk and thanked him for his help.

Hattie confirmed what I'd been told and said she'd have a copy waiting for me when I arrived. I called Jenn on the way and told her what had happened. She remained silent, and I could almost hear her blood pressure rise. I begged her not to do anything until I got there. When Hattie handed me the copy, I told her I didn't have time to talk and left rubber on my way out of the parking lot.

Jenn paced on the front porch when I pulled into the driveway. I threw the truck in park and ran to her.

"Where is he?"

She pointed toward the paddock, looking like her anger had hijacked her voice.

"You haven't confronted him yet, have you?"

She shook her head, then pulled the envelope from my hand and scanned the contents. I had only seen her this mad once, and I'd made it a point to stay out of her way.

She handed the papers back to me and we stormed off toward the paddock.

"Let me do the talking," I said, trying to keep up.

"Good luck with that."

Jenn was a bitch on wheels. I mean that in a nice way, but I had a feeling this would not end well for anybody.

Seth turned the corner of the barn and stopped when he saw us coming.

"Hey!" She pulled up about three feet from where he stood. I got a little closer in case I had to step between them. "What's the big idea makin' deals behind my back?"

"I'm not sure what you're talking about."

I wanted to punch the smug expression off his face.

"Y'all are selling the ranch's water to RMA and pocketing the cash."

"Where did you hear something like that?"

"I didn't hear it. I read it." She shoved the papers into his chest.

He took a half step backward, and I stepped between them in case he was thinking of pushing back.

He glanced at the papers.

"That's the ranch's money," I said. "You may be entitled to half of it, but the other half is Jenn's."

"Jenn wasn't around. I didn't know if she was even alive until she showed up here a few months later."

"The ranch was here." Jenn leaned in and I extended my arm to stop her. "It's the ranch's money."

"What have you done for the ranch since you been here?" he asked from behind a smug expression.

He was a real piece of work. I got up in his grille, silently daring him to throw the first punch. "I reckon you owe the ranch about five thousand dollars."

He met my gaze. "This is none of your business."

I bumped him with my chest. "You're makin' it my business."

He clenched his hands into fists, and I saw the venom in his eyes.

"I wouldn't if I were you, Seth." Jenn knew he didn't stand a chance in the circle of death, a four-foot radius around my body. In the army, I had earned the nickname *Teenage Mutant Ninja Texan.*

"If you know what's good for you, you'll take a step back."

The only move he made was the twitch in his neck muscle.

"I'm not askin'."

The dumb son-of-a-bitch threw a punch. I blocked it, grabbed his forearm, and twisted it behind his back.

"You shoulda listened to your cousin." I applied more pressure to his arm, and he winced.

"Damn it, Seth." Jenn was fit to be tied. "What other shady deals have you been making?"

He spit on the ground in her direction and I pushed a little harder on his arm. He attempted to grab my head with his free hand, but I pulled back out of reach. I wrapped my other arm around his neck and squeezed.

I leaned in close to his ear. "She trusted you, which is more than I can say about me."

Frank came running out of the barn. Jenn headed him off and got up in his face.

"This doesn't concern you," she said.

He attempted to step around her, but she blocked his path. Lucky for him, he glanced at me before he made another move. My eyes told him he'd go down hard if he laid a hand on her.

Jenn stood her ground. "You best get back to the barn, or I'll fire your ass."

Frank hesitated, took another look at me, then retreated to the barn.

I threw Seth to the ground, hoping this little skirmish was over.

Jenn looked down at Seth as he gasped for air. "I want to see a deposit receipt for five thousand dollars deposited into the operating account by the end of the week. And from now on, those payments go directly into that account."

Jenn turned on her heel and headed toward the house. I followed and caught up with her in the kitchen. She was hotter than a dumpster fire, and I needed to cool her down.

I took two bottles of beer from the fridge and handed one to Jenn. "You should have fired Frank."

"I don't like him either, but right now I've got enough problems with Seth. I don't need to throw more gasoline on that fire."

I walked over to the window and took a gulp from the bottle as I watched Seth and Frank talking near the barn. I didn't trust either of them as far as I could throw 'em.

Jenn joined me at the window.

I took a long drink. "I reckon we just poked a bear."

Chapter Thirty

Seth had told us that Frank was an old friend from Kansas City that happened to be passing through on his way to California. Nobody *passes through* Redfield. It's a tiny town in the middle of nowhere surrounded by mountains. There's one road in and one road out, and neither of them goes anywhere near California. Also, it was a little too convenient that he showed up the day Buck got fired.

Jenn kept her distance from Seth for the next few days, which made things run less than smoothly at the ranch. Of course, I supported her even as I reminded her of the old saying, *keep your friends close and your enemies closer.* Seth needed more oversight than ever, but lines had been drawn and I feared Team Seth had retreated to lick their wounds and plan their next attack.

Friday afternoon brought a knock on the front door. I opened it to find an envelope on the floor and Seth walking away toward the barn. The envelope had Jenn's name written on the front.

Jenn opened it to find the deposit receipt she had demanded from Seth after our little scuffle earlier in the week. She breathed a sigh of relief. I did no such thing.

"This isn't over," I said. "It's a peace offering, a small price to pay when you're looking at a much bigger prize."

"And I suppose y'all know what that prize is."

"I have an idea."

Another knock at the door interrupted our conversation. Our eyes met and we froze for a moment. Seth? Frank? Whoever it was, they'd caught us off guard. That wouldn't happen again.

I braced myself and opened the door. Jenn watched from the kitchen.

"Cooper Hill, Private Eye, at your service."

My muscles relaxed and the adrenaline rush subsided.

Coop dropped his bag and held his arms out at his sides. "Don't just stand there, bring it in."

I met him on the porch for a real back-slappin' man-hug. Just like the old days.

"Day-um, Coop. Aren't you a sight for sore eyes?" I frowned. "I wasn't expecting you till next week."

"Do not underestimate the element of surprise."

I looked at him sideways. "Sun Tzu?"

He smiled. "No, Cooper Hill."

Back in Bradley when we were in a fight for our lives trying to bring Pop's killer to justice, Coop liked to quote a fifteen-hundred-year-old book called *The Art of War* by a Chinese general named Sun Tzu. I still remember the quote that helped tip the battle in our favor. *He who is prudent and lies in wait for an enemy who is not, will be victorious.*

"You should have told me. I would have picked you up at the airport."

"That's exactly why I didn't tell you. I wanted to rent a car and drive down myself. Get the lay of the land."

"Well, I'm sure glad you're here." I turned around and called into the house. "Hey, Jenn. Look who's here."

She joined us on the porch. Another big hug, minus the back slapping. "Where's Jolene and the girls?"

"Jo didn't want the girls to miss too much school, so they'll be flying in Thanksgiving week."

"Why don't y'all come in and get settled? I reckon we've got a lot of catching up to do."

"We sure do," I said as I slapped Coop on the back.

"You got anything to drink? I'm parched."

"Can't find Lone Star up here, so you'll have to settle for Coors."

"As long as it's cold."

We sat on the front porch for an hour and threw back a couple more as we got caught up. Jenn asked a lot of questions about Jolene and their two girls, Katey Jo and Carrie Beth. I threw in a few questions about Bishop Oil. Two more wells had started producing since I'd left, and the company was growing like jingweed in July. Mama came on board about a month ago and Coop felt comfortable leaving her in control. After everything she'd been through in her life, I knew she could handle whatever they might throw at her.

Coop finally broached the subject of why he'd been summoned to Colorado. I told him we needed to eat first. While Coop and I watched four steaks sizzle on the outdoor grill, I reconsidered. I told him what I knew about the ranch's history up until the time Jenn and I arrived.

"So, two people have died in the last five years?"

"Two that I know of. They're both buried here on the ranch."

I described my run-ins with Cassidy and her nephews and their belief that Roy killed Cassidy's sister. As I told him Buck's theory about the Whitehawk brothers killing Roy to avenge Asha's death, I remembered something that hadn't registered the first time I heard it.

Jacob Whitehawk had said something when we talked at the Wet Whistle. He said he'd just spent a year in prison for something he didn't do—the barn fire. Roy died while he and his brother were locked up.

Jenn poked her head out the back door. "Y'all grilling steaks or tanning leather?"

"He was fixin' to make you a new saddle," Coop replied.

"We're coming in right now. You best be ready."

Coop and I continued our conversation while we ate.

Jenn cleared her throat. She met my gaze and nodded her head toward Alex. "Can you boys talk about business after dinner?"

It sounded like a question, but I knew better.

Jenn joined us on the porch with three cold ones after she cleaned up the kitchen.

"I was just telling Coop about Buck's relationship with Hattie and the third grave up on the ridge."

"Bummer," he said. "Men have certainly killed for less."

I nodded. "I thought so too, until Seth fired him."

"Buck didn't kill him," Jenn offered.

Coop frowned. "And you know this how?"

"I've known Charlie Owens the better part of my life. He may seem rough on the outside, and who would blame him, but somewhere inside is a kind heart. He just needs to trust you enough to let you in."

I rolled my eyes. "Thank you, Dr. Phil."

She gave me a playful slap on the shoulder.

"Seriously, as cheesy as that sounds," I said. "I have to agree with her. I don't think he could kill anyone, not even Roy."

"Okay, either you've got some more suspects, or you flew me out here for nothing."

"I'm saving the best for last." I glanced at Jenn as her expression fell. She didn't want to consider Seth a suspect, but keeping his name off the list was no longer an option.

"Let me guess. Seth McDonald had a farm, E-I-E-I-O."

Despite the tension, a flicker of a smile crossed Jenn's face.

"Technically, it's a ranch, but you guessed it," I said. "His star has been rising fast, and the hits just keep on coming."

"So why did he fire Buck?"

"Buck allegedly overheard a phone conversation where Seth told someone he would get rid of Jenn and me one way or another. He thinks Seth was the one who poisoned the horses, and he's fixin' to do it again."

"Even if you guys went back to Texas, which I personally think is an excellent idea, Jenn still owns half the ranch."

Jenn watched Coop as she took a long draw on her beer.

"That's what scares me the most. If he's got his sights set on the ranch..." I paused to consider how to finish that sentence. "He needs Jenn out of the way. Permanently."

Jenn spit beer on the floor. She met my gaze with a mix of fear and fire in her eyes.

"Maybe we should pick this back up in the morning," I said.

Coop gave a quick nod as Jenn stood.

"You better get a good night's sleep," I told Coop. "You wouldn't want to miss Jenn's biscuits and gravy for breakfast."

"This trip just keeps getting better and better."

"I'm sure they're not as good as Jolene's," Jenn said with a modest shake of her head. "Dillon says Jo's are the best he's ever had."

Coop snorted. "You best be talkin' about biscuits... the kind you put in the oven."

We got Coop set up in one of the guest rooms, checked in on Alex, then retired to our room. Jenn didn't say much until we were in bed.

"Do you really think Seth would kill me to get the ranch?"

"I hope not, but we need to be prepared for the worst."

"I don't want to live my life always looking over my shoulder."

I put my arm around her and pulled her close. "You won't have to. I promise you that. I'm going to figure out what he's up to and put a stop to it. I'm trained in threat assessment and mitigation. I still remember a thing or two."

***

Coop pushed his plate away after breakfast and licked his lips.

I finished my coffee and turned to Coop. "What did I tell you?"

Jenn nudged my arm. "Dillon, stop it."

"As far as the biscuits, I'm gonna have to plead the fifth," Coop replied.

"Good answer," Jenn said as she cleared the table. "Chores are done, your bellies are full, so why don't you boys go do what you gotta do while I clean up in here? Alex is going to help me take the horses up to the north pasture."

"Doesn't he have school?"

"It's Saturday."

I shrugged. Lately, one day blended into the next, and I couldn't remember which one was which. There's no such thing as a weekend on a ranch. There's work to be done seven days a week, 365 days a year.

I'd dragged Coop along to help with chores before breakfast, so he'd seen some of the ranch. After breakfast, I set out to show him the rest.

We were halfway through the stable when Seth walked in the opposite door. We were on a collision course. I didn't feel like talking to him, but I thought it best to introduce Coop early on and let Seth know the teams were no longer even. I tried my best to be civil.

"Seth, this is Cooper, an old friend from Texas. He's going to be staying with us for a few weeks."

Seth's features hardened as his eyes gave Coop the once-over. He turned to me like Coop wasn't there. "Make sure he stays out of the way."

I didn't like how he said it. "He's going to be helping with chores, so I reckon he'll be in the way plenty."

Seth brushed past us without a word, no doubt on his way to set fire to something or poison the rest of the horses.

CHAPTER THIRTY-ONE

Coop looked at me as we walked to my truck. "I'm going to give you my first bit of advice," he said. "Bury the hatchet with Seth."

"I'd like to bury one right in the middle of his forehead."

"That's nice, but remember, *he will win who knows when to fight and when not to fight.* Don't pick a fight over something stupid he might say or do. Pretend if you have to, but make him think it's water under the bridge. He stole some money, he put it back. No harm, no foul."

"Great. Maybe I'll invite him over tonight and we can all make s'mores and sing 'Kumbaya' around the campfire."

"My point is, he's got his guard up. If what you've been telling me is true, we don't want to force his hand until we're ready. We've got a couple of leads, a few assumptions, but we're still pretty much flying blind."

"Roger that."

***

We stopped at the hardware store so I could introduce Coop to Hattie. Ziggy pulled in right after us and parked next to my truck.

"I'm glad I ran into you," Ziggy said when we all got out.

After I introduced him to Coop, he turned to me. "Something you said the other day about Roy's accident prompted me to do a little digging. I contacted the sheriff in Jefferson County who owes me a favor. He remembered the accident and called today to tell me he found Roy's truck in a junkyard in Lakewood. I was on my way to the ranch to give you the good news."

"Did you say anything to Sheriff Pecker?"

He shook his head.

"Good. Next time call me. I wouldn't want Seth to see us talking. He knows the sheriff and could get both of us in trouble."

Ziggy agreed and gave us the directions to the junkyard. He said he'd call the owner and tell him we were coming.

We went inside and had a nice chat. Hattie and Coop hit it off right away.

We left Hattie's a half hour later and headed north to Lakewood. I'd thought Roy's truck was long gone by now, so I was eager to go have a look. Coop ran an auto repair shop in Bradley for nine years before coming to work for me at Bishop Oil. I'm not sure I would have made the two-hour drive to Lakewood if he wasn't with me.

The junkyard owner, a short Black man with white hair, explained where to find the truck in the twelve-acre auto graveyard. Coop said the man reminded him of Fred Sanford. I'd never watched much TV growing up, so I took his word for it.

The accident was two years ago, so we had to walk a way to find the truck. I nearly stepped on a snake that slithered through the jingweed that grew up in and around the metal carcasses.

Roy's F-150 looked like it had rolled down a mountain. I'm not sure how he survived. The vehicle rested on its side in the weeds. The frame and undercarriage remained pretty much intact, the body not so much. Coop began his examination as I watched.

After about ten minutes, he called me over.

"This wasn't an accident."

"How do you know?"

"Someone tampered with the brake lines."

"The lines were cut?"

"No. If they'd been cut, it would be neater. This looks like it melted or was blown apart."

"But the car was moving when the brakes failed."

"I watched a show once where the brake lines on a train were severed using detonation chord."

In the army, our demo squad used a lot of det cord in the field. It's a high-speed fuse that explodes rather than burns.

"They wrapped it around a brake line. It blew out a section of the line when detonated. The result looked similar to this."

I looked over Coop's shoulder. "How would they detonate it?"

"With a timer or some sort of remote detonator."

I pointed to a small device strapped to the rear axle. "Like that?"

Coop turned to me. "Exactly like that."

"So, the Whitehawks were right. Somebody killed Asha."

"They got that part right, but I don't think it was Roy unless it was intended to be a murder-suicide."

Asha wasn't the intended target. She was collateral damage. The Whitehawk boys wouldn't cut the brake lines with their mother in the car, too risky. What about Buck? Not likely. If he'd accidentally killed Asha, he'd be even more messed up than he is now. It had to be Seth. What was his motive? The ranch?

We stopped for lunch on the way back and talked through everything we knew about both deaths and our list of suspects. We liked Seth for Asha's death, assuming that Roy was the intended target. We didn't have any evidence to connect him with the crime, but we decided to put a pin in it for now and concentrate on Roy's death. I had a feeling they were connected.

"We're not going to get very far until we know the real cause of death," I said.

"You read my mind. I'd like to see the coroner's report when we get back."

"Higgins admitted it was bogus."

"Yes, the cause of death may be in question, but I'd like to see the toxicology report."

***

Coop and I sat in the guest bedroom. I watched him study the report from the coroner. After fifteen minutes, I had to interrupt.

"What the hell are you doin'?"

He looked up from the papers. "I thought you wanted me to go over these."

"It probably took less time to write them than it's taking you to read them."

"He had a bad liver."

"We know that."

"You're sure they used Roy's blood for these tests?"

"Who else's would they use?"

"Someone a little less... male," he said. "Unless Roy was on birth control."

"What?"

"Everything looks normal for someone with a bad liver, except for elevated estrogen and progesterone levels."

"How is that possible?"

"I was hoping *you* could tell *me*."

I frowned. "How do you know all this medical stuff?"

"I started working right after high school while I took some pre-med courses at night." He smiled. "Thought I might be a doctor when I grew up."

"What happened?"

"Katey Jo." His eyes drifted momentarily before they locked on mine. "You would have known that if you'd stuck around after high school."

"I needed to leave for my sanity."

Coop smiled. "How's that working out for you?"

I left the room to retrieve the two pill bottles I'd stashed in my bedroom dresser drawer—the ones I'd found in Roy's desk. I had trouble pronouncing the names printed on the labels. Coop said he thought one was a cancer medication, but admitted he'd never heard of the other.

He opened the first bottle and spilled a few pills into his hand. He shook his head as he held one up for me to see. "What does that say?"

I squinted to read the little numbers on the pill. "2... 3... 9."

"That's a birth control pill."

"How do you know that?"

"Same ones Jo takes."

"Somebody switched his pills. But why birth control?"

He opened the second bottle. Again, he shook his head.

"What are those?"

"I'm pretty sure these are high-dose acetaminophen."

"Tylenol?"

Coop nodded. "Generic form." He typed something into his phone and studied the screen. "That combination can cause severe liver damage or drug-induced hepatitis."

"So, Roy was taking medication that was making his liver condition worse instead of better."

"Certainly looks that way."

"Someone must have switched the pills to make it look like something else." I picked up one of the bottles. "We need to talk to this Doctor... Richards."

"He's not going to tell us anything because of HIPAA laws."

"Maybe I can get Ziggy to do it for us. He can say it's part of a murder investigation."

Jenn poked her head in the door and looked at me. "Coming to bed, or y'all planning on sleeping in here tonight?"

"I'll be there in a minute."

I waited until she left. "Let's keep this between you and me until we know a little more."

CHAPTER THIRTY-TWO

Sunday morning after breakfast, Jenn suggested we all go on a trail ride. She made some sandwiches and packed them in a cooler. We saddled up four horses and headed for Fletcher's Pond and a trip around the north end of the ranch. The north pasture and the area around the pond were mostly flat, but we would see some hilly territory before the day was done.

Jenn took the lead, with Alex riding alongside. Coop knew which end of the horse was which and handled himself better than I did when I first got here. We hung back a little. I wanted to spend some time with Coop where we weren't playing detective.

We stopped at Fletcher's Pond to walk around a bit. The water was up a couple of feet from the day we went fishing, and Alex turned and gave me a big wink. I'm sure he felt he had something to do with the rising water level. The pipe was no longer visible, so I didn't mention it.

The temperature hit sixty-five, which was a little above average for early November. Hopefully, the first snowfall was at least a month away. Living in Texas, I'd never seen more than a few inches at a time. I wondered if Alex had ever seen any.

The aspen trees that had been ablaze with color had lost most of their leaves. Jenn had brought Alex and me leaf-peeping, which I guess is a thing in these parts, about a month ago. I reckon Alex thought he was on another planet. I'd noticed that he never got to experience many things that I took for granted growing up. That bothered me.

We mounted up and continued our ride, skirting the western edge of the property. RMA's fields had been picked clean and their operation moved inside to the huge greenhouses for the winter. I hadn't known them to be bad neighbors. The deal they made with Seth wasn't a problem; it was the way Seth handled it that put a bad taste in my mouth.

The trail steepened, and the terrain became more heavily wooded as we wound our way up into the foothills. The horses didn't seem to mind. I had noticed how much thinner the air felt compared to Texas. I wouldn't want to attempt this trip without Chance under saddle.

We reached a clearing about the size of the one up on the ridge where I'd discovered the graves. We weren't as high up, but the view was no less breathtaking. From here, we had a nice view of the house and barn. A strategic view.

We were surprised to see one of the horses from the ranch grazing at the edge of the clearing when we arrived. He wore a saddle but had no rider. I shot a questioning glance at Jenn. She responded with a shrug.

Frank came strolling out of the trees a couple minutes later like he hadn't heard us coming. He smiled when he saw the four of us. "Great day for a ride, isn't it?"

"What are you doing up here?" Jenn asked.

"Seth showed me this place a while back, and I've been coming up here when I have some time off."

A while back? He'd only been here for a month. I glanced at Jenn, then back to Frank. What was he doing in the woods?

"I reckon it's a nice place to relax." I lifted my hat and ran a hand back through my hair. "And the view's not so bad either."

"A great place to recharge the soul after a long work week."

I used to give people the benefit of the doubt, but life has a way of slapping you down and making you question just about everything. Frank was hiding something, and I needed to find out what before it was too late.

I dismounted and walked past Frank's horse to get a better view. A rifle and a pair of field glasses hung from his saddlebag. I had a rifle with me, as well, on the off chance we might run into a bear. He also had a satellite phone sticking out of his bag. I pulled out my cell phone and held it in the air. No signal up here. As I moved it from side to side, I secretly snapped a picture of Frank.

Keep your friends close, and your enemies closer. That's what I had told Jenn. I needed to take my own advice. I looked out over the ranch below. "Kinda looks like a picture postcard, doesn't it?"

"Sure does." Frank glanced around at everyone. "You all have a pleasant ride. I'm gonna mosey on back to the ranch."

Everyone gave him a polite send-off as I studied the scene below. We were close to a half click from the house. With the right weapon, someone like Jenn might make a shot from here. But I'm talking some badass sniper equipment and a well-trained soldier. Frank wasn't ex-military as far as I could tell. You also had a clear shot at the trail leading up here. This clearing would be easy to defend.

Something else bothered me. Why did a ranch hand have a sat phone? Who would he call? Frank's engine was running, but somebody else was driving. I had an idea who that might be.

Coop said this looked like a great place to stop for lunch, so we threw down a couple of blankets and had a real picnic.

We spent a good hour laughing and talking about everything except Roy's death and our investigation.

The rest of our ride proved uneventful. Coop commented on the beautiful countryside. I hoped maybe someday he'd consider moving his family here. We returned home near dinnertime, and I offered to take care of the horses with Coop while Jenn whipped up something to eat.

Ziggy called while we were brushing the horses. He'd found a Doctor Richards in Colorado Springs, the only one in a hundred-mile radius. The doctor refused to confirm or deny treating Roy without a signed release from the next of kin. I told him I'd get Jenn to sign whatever he needed and accompany him if he'd be willing to take a ride over there.

***

Colorado Springs lies approximately fifteen minutes east of Redfield as the crow flies. However, there is rarely a direct route to anywhere in the state, and this was no exception. Coop and I rode with Ziggy in his cruiser on the forty-five-minute trip that took us north to Woodland Park, then around Pikes Peak down to Colorado Springs.

Doctor Malcolm Richards was younger than I'd expected. He appeared to tip the scales at about 250, and his round spectacles matched the shape of his face. He greeted us in the reception area and held the release papers in his sausage fingers as he read. A quick nod told us we'd cleared the first hurdle, and he led us down a narrow hall toward the back of the building.

"So, what can I do for you today?" he said when we were all seated in his office.

Ziggy took the lead. He introduced all of us and explained to the doctor that he was working on the investigation of a crime that took place in Teller County.

"How is it you think I can help?"

"Have you ever treated a man named Roy McDonald from Redfield?"

Richards frowned. "The name doesn't ring a bell. Let me check with my office manager."

He picked up his phone, spoke briefly, and waited.

I looked at Coop, who appeared to be thinking the same as me. How many patients could this guy have? We weren't sitting in the office wing of a big-city hospital. This was an old brick home that had been converted to a doctor's office. And Roy's last name wasn't Smith or Jones or some other dime-a-dozen name.

"What did this Mr. McDonald do?" Richards asked as he waited.

This was moving too slowly. "He died," I said.

Richards recoiled. "I hope you don't think I had anything to do with his death."

Ziggy shot me a sideways glance, then said, "No, sir. He was sick, and we just want to speak with the doctor who was treating him."

"Okay. Thank you," he said into the phone. "I'm afraid I can't help you. Mr. McDonald was not one of my patients."

"He had a couple of pill bottles with your name on them."

"That's impossible. What kind of pills?"

Ziggy must have sensed me sitting on the edge of my chair like a tag team wrestler just outside the ropes, waiting to jump in. He nodded in my direction.

I pulled up a picture on my phone. I didn't want to bring the bottles for fear he might keep them once he got his hands on them. He took the phone from me and studied it.

"One of these is for cancer patients. I wouldn't have prescribed it."

"Why is your name on the bottle?"

"I don't know."

"Maybe someone stole a prescription pad," Coop offered.

"No. Everything is electronic now. I—" He stopped, and his eyes drifted.

My foot tapped the floor. "You what?"

"About nine months ago, someone broke into the office and stole two of our computers."

"Would that allow them to write prescriptions in your name?"

"Theoretically, but as soon as we found out what they had taken, we shut down the old account and set up a new one."

"How did you write prescriptions in the meantime?"

"We keep some pads for emergencies. Usually, there's a pad in my drawer and the rest are in storage downstairs." He opened a drawer and held up a small pad.

Coop's eyes widened, and he straightened in his chair. "What if they weren't after the computers? They probably expected you to cut them off. The computers were a diversion, so you wouldn't go looking any further."

Richards picked up the phone again. "Can you do me a favor and check how many prescription pads we have in storage?" He paused. "I'll wait."

I knew what he was going to say next.

His fingers drummed the desk as he looked at us. "Thank you." He fired off a few rapid blinks. "She said they're all gone."

CHAPTER THIRTY-THREE

Shortly before I left Afghanistan, our Humvee took a hit from an RPG, no doubt because I'd held our convoy up rescuing a seven-year-old boy from a bombed-out room where he sat with his dead parents. I covered the boy as best I could when the RPG hit. The explosion ripped off my boot and took a couple of toes with it. Some people's joints ache before it rains. My damaged foot tingles when something bad is about to happen.

I'd only felt it a few times since arriving in Colorado. Each time it got a little worse. Today was no exception. We were slowly building a case against Seth, but there were still too many missing pieces. I feared we were giving him too much time to cover his tracks or to launch a preemptive strike.

Something else bothered me. Who would we present our evidence to? The sheriff appeared to play for Seth's team. I needed to go over his head to someone higher up the law-enforcement ladder, but at the moment I didn't know who that might be.

I hadn't checked in on Buck for a while, so I asked Coop if he wanted to take a ride to Hattie's place and meet the crusty old cowboy he'd heard so much about.

"Nice digs," Coop said when we turned the corner of Hattie's house and spotted the RV.

Buck did not answer the first knock, just as I'd instructed him. I knocked again to test him. No answer.

"It's Dillon," I called.

The door opened. I introduced Coop, and we all found a seat.

"How you holdin' up?"

"I could use a hooker and another bottle a bourbon."

I glanced at Coop and smiled. "I'll see what I can do about the bourbon."

"Hattie's been real nice, cookin' me meals from time to time." He let out a ragged cough, got up from his seat, and spit in the sink. "What have you boys been up to?"

"You know anything about the medication Roy was taking?"

"All I know is he was in a lotta pain. His doctor said he had liver cancer and prescribed somethin' for it." He dragged the back of his hand across his mouth and sat. "Roy said it was bad. Only had a few months left."

"The doctor told him that?"

Buck stared at me for a moment. "No, the tooth fairy left a note under his pillow."

"Okay," I said, shaking my head. "I guess I deserved that."

Coop chuckled.

"What if I told you one of the pills he was taking was for birth control?"

"I'd say you been smokin' some a Hattie's wacky tobacky."

"The other was a form of Tylenol," Coop said. "Together, they can do a number on your liver."

Buck couldn't hide his confusion as he looked at Coop, then back to me. "The pills were makin' him worse? What kinda doctor gives pills to make you worse?"

"That's what we'd like to know," Coop replied.

"So, you didn't know anything about that?"

"Hell, no. We've had our differences in the past, but I didn't care to see a man suffer. Now you're tellin' me it was the doctor's fault?"

"We can't find his doctor."

"I told him he should go see one a them big-city doctors in Denver or Colorado Springs, but they don't make house calls, 'specially out here in God's country. Roy didn't like leavin' the ranch, so Seth found him a country doctor from around here somewhere. His name was Richards. He came out to the ranch every so often an' doctored him."

I glanced at Coop and gave him a quick head shake, in case he was thinking about mentioning our visit with the real Doctor Richards.

"Well, Buck, we should probably get going. You sure you gonna be okay?"

He paused for a moment. "Don't you boys tell anybody, but I miss that ranch."

I'd never seen Buck cry, and I'm sure I never will, but I could've sworn his eyes got a little misty. "Believe me, Buck, the ranch misses you, too."

A smile flickered on his face before his expression fell. "How's that new foreman workin' out?"

"I don't like him. His name's Frank Snyder. You ever hear of him?"

He shook his head. "Can't say that I have. What's he look like?"

"I can show you," I said as I grabbed my phone. I pulled up the picture of Frank I took on our trail ride and held it up.

Buck studied the screen. His bushy eyebrows nearly touched as he narrowed his eyes. "That ain't no foreman." He paused and his mustache twitched. "That's Doctor Richards."

***

Coop and I discussed this latest development on the way home. The last time Doctor Death showed up at the ranch, Roy took a dirt nap. It bothered me that he might be back for round two. Buck had told me he overheard Seth say he'd take care of us one way or another. Who was he talking to? What did *take care of us* mean? Send us back to Texas, or maybe plant us up on the ridge next to Roy and Asha. Is that what brought Doctor Death back?

"We need to understand the connection between Seth and Frank."

Coop looked at me from the passenger seat. "Didn't he tell you Frank was an old friend from Kansas City?"

"Yeah, and what a lucky coincidence that he bumped into him out here in the middle of nowhere the day he fired Buck."

"When we get back, I'll see what I can find online. Maybe they were both in the military together."

"I doubt it. I can usually tell a soldier when I meet him. Seth maybe, but I'd bet money that Frank never wore a uniform."

"What about me? I might have done a tour while you were away."

I laughed. "No offense, Coop."

He smiled. "None taken."

"We need to be on high alert from now on. Maybe you should tell Jo and the girls to stay in Texas. You might want to catch the next flight home, yourself. I wouldn't want you to get shot again on my account."

"I'm a little insulted that you would even suggest that. Did Sundance bail on Butch, or Hutch on Starsky?"

"Jenn says we're more like Dumb and Dumber."

Coop smiled. "Maybe so, but they stuck together."

"We need to circle the wagons and make sure Jenn is aware of any potential threats. She can take care of herself, but we need to keep her in the loop." I paused. "I don't need to tell you I'd be lost without her. The day I walked into that second-hand store in Dallas, and she smiled at me from behind the counter…" I sighed. "That was the best day of my life."

"I know it was, Bish. Me and Jo, we can tell every time we see you two together."

I crossed the cattle guard and pulled up in front of the house.

"I think the three of us need to have a strategy session tonight," Coop said. "Write some of this stuff down on a big evidence board, you know, like the detectives do on TV."

"Good idea, but we'll need to hide it. Seth still comes over for dinner sometimes."

"That's gotta stop."

"What happened to *business as usual* and *keep your enemies closer*?"

"I think that ship has sailed."

***

After dinner, Coop fired up the laptop while Jenn and I spent some time with Alex. We all watched an episode of *CSI* before we put Alex to bed. Coop explained all the technical stuff so us rookies could follow along.

When Jenn returned from getting Alex settled, we moved to the kitchen table.

Coop flipped open the laptop. "Here's what I've found so far. Seth was indeed living in the Kansas City area, stationed at Fort Leavenworth. It turns out Doctor Death—"

Jenn interrupted "Please don't call him that."

"Sorry. Frank spent some time there, too. More precisely, three to five. He did a stint in Leavenworth prison for armed robbery back in 2010. There was a little overlap in their time there, but it's unlikely that they knew each other given their respective situations."

"In the five years after his release," he continued. "Frank got pinched three times for violent crimes. Once in Kansas and twice in Colorado."

"I knew he was trouble," I said.

"Wait. It gets better. All three times he was represented by Forsythe and McLarin, and all three times the jury acquitted."

Jenn frowned. "How does a low-life like Frank afford to hire such hotshot attorneys?"

"He may have had some help. I looked up Forsythe and McLarin and found that they are very good and very expensive, with an impressive client list."

"I'm getting a bad feeling in my boot about this."

"Until last year, Rocky Mountain Agriculture was their biggest client."

"What happened last year?"

"RMA bought them and brought them in-house."

Jenn got up and retrieved three beers from the fridge. "So, they've got so much money that they can afford to have their own high-powered legal team?"

"They're in a lucrative line of work."

I didn't want to say it out loud, but somebody had to. "So, Frank Snyder, a.k.a. Doctor Death, is RMA's fixer."

"It appears that way."

The color disappeared from Jenn's face. "I never should have come out here. And now I've dragged you and Alex along with me." She looked at Coop. "I'm sorry you got involved, as well."

Coop hooked a thumb toward me. "It wouldn't be the first time, and it's probably not the last."

Jenn looked like she was about to throw up.

"What is it?"

"This is all my fault. I saw this coming, but I didn't want to believe it."

I had to get up and walk around. My foot felt like a barroom dartboard at happy hour. "Believe what?"

Jenn looked at me with the saddest eyes. "Please don't be mad at me."

"Tell me what's going on, and then I'll decide."

"I got a call from Uncle Roy about a year ago. We hadn't spoken in a long time, but it felt like yesterday. He asked me to come out to the ranch to help him with something. He'd always treated me like his daughter, so I was happy to oblige."

She paused for a moment as she chugged the last third of her bottle. She set it down and stared at it as she turned it in her hands. "I spent a week out here. He was sick, you know? Uncle Roy never married, but he had a love affair with alcohol. He went downhill after Asha died, and his liver went from bad to worse. They diagnosed him with liver cancer, and he wanted me to help him get his affairs in order."

Coop cleared his throat. "Where was Seth at the time?"

"He was here, helping out with the ranch. That was the problem."

"Why was that a problem?" I sat back down.

"After Seth had talked Uncle Roy into leaving him the ranch, he started pushing him to ditch the horses and switch to growing marijuana. A lot of money was just waitin' to be made, and Seth wanted in."

"Wait. I thought both of you were in the will."

"Not at that point. Just Seth."

"How did you feel about that?" Coop asked.

She shrugged. "I guess I never really thought about it. While I was there, Roy told me he planned to add me to the will, but he wanted to keep it our little secret."

"So, when Roy died, Seth thought he was getting everything?"

"I guess so."

I remembered Buck saying how mad Seth had been when he returned from the lawyer's office. Surprise! His inheritance had decreased by half. I wondered if he still would have killed him if he'd known.

Coop cleared his throat. "Why did he want to cut Seth out?"

"He told me he didn't trust him anymore."

"Sounds like Roy wanted you to advocate for him after he was gone."

She nodded. "When Seth continued to push him about the pot farm, he told him, *over my dead body*."

"In hindsight," Coop said. "That was a poor choice of words."

I shot Coop a sideways glare, then turned to Jenn. I stopped pacing and let out a long breath as I ran my hands back through my hair. "I wish you would have told me all this sooner." That's what I said. What I wanted to say was, *What the hell, Jenn. You're just telling me this now? It would have been nice to know what I was getting myself into. And what about Alex? You brought him out here knowing you were going to have a fight on your hands.*

"I'm sorry, Dillon."

I walked over to the fridge and grabbed three more beers. "Okay. Now, what are we going to do about it?"

Chapter Thirty-Four

Jenn frowned. "I'm worried about Alex."

"What if you send him to Bradley?" Coop offered. "He can stay with Jo and the girls. If we think it's safe again, they can bring him back for Thanksgiving."

Jenn shook her head. "I couldn't impose like that."

"Jenn, it's not a bad idea," I said. "Alex is an easy target. They can get to you through him, and they know it."

"I'll call Jo right now." Coop pulled out his phone and stepped into the next room.

Jenn placed her hand on her chest. "I'll miss him so bad."

"I know. But you'd never forgive yourself if something happened to him."

"This sucks. Why can't we call the sheriff and have both of them arrested?"

"I wish it was that easy. We don't have enough evidence, and besides, Sheriff Pecker is probably working with them."

Coop returned. "It's all set whenever you're ready."

"The sooner, the better," I said. "Why don't you book him a flight right now?"

She wrinkled her nose. "Do you think he should fly alone?"

"We don't have much of a choice."

"He'll be fine," Coop said. "The flight attendants will help him, and Jo will be waiting for him at the gate."

"I guess." She sighed. "I'd go with him, but I'll be damned if I'm going to run away from this. We need to settle this thing."

"I know, Babe. I would take him, but I'm not leaving you here."

"There's strength in numbers," Coop said, making his case to stay.

Jenn picked up the laptop from the table and sat on the couch. She found him a flight out of Colorado Springs the next afternoon.

"Perfect," I said. "You can get him packed in the morning. Coop and I are going to look for Roy's journals. I think we should have another go at his office, too."

Coop frowned. "How are we going to do that with Seth around?"

"We need to distract him." I patted Coop on the back. "You up for a little night mission?"

***

After breakfast, Jenn called the school and told them Alex wouldn't be back until after Thanksgiving. The school administrator gave her a hard time, even after she offered to pick up his assignments so he wouldn't fall behind. After a rough night, Jenn's fuse was shorter than usual. I took the phone before everything exploded.

I gave Hattie a call after I hung up. Her daughter, Raven, was Alex's teacher. I explained the situation and asked if she'd intercede with her daughter on our behalf.

Missing two weeks of school didn't seem to bother Alex too much. Going to Texas and living with strangers was a different story. I thought he'd be used to the drill by now, but he'd grown fond of Jenn, and I imagine leaving her brought up some pretty painful memories. He'd also been through enough shit to know that we were all in some kind of danger.

Raven texted a half hour later to say she would drop off Alex's work on her lunch hour. I thanked her and told Jenn as she pulled a load of Alex's clothes out of the dryer.

She brushed past me. "I need to get his things packed."

"Jenn."

She stopped and turned, her arms full of warm clothes.

"Slow down. His flight isn't until four. We don't have to leave until two."

She blew a few strands of hair that had fallen across her forehead, then took a deep breath and nodded.

"Seth and Frank are on their way up to the pasture to fix the fence we cut last night, so Coop and I are going to go through Roy's office again."

"Be careful," was all she said.

I grabbed the keyring, and we headed off to the stable. I figured we had at least an hour. We got in the door a little easier this time, and I locked it behind us. Coop put his finger to his lips, then motioned for me to stay put by the door. He scanned the layout of the room before concentrating his efforts on the wall opposite the desk. He scrutinized a glass-front case filled with medical supplies and a six-foot metal storage locker. I watched him gently lift the lid from one of the boxes on top of the locker.

"Clear," he said after he reached inside.

"What's that?"

He held up a small video camera.

"Day-um!"

Coop examined the device. "Motion-activated. It sends video wirelessly to a control unit where it gets recorded."

"Won't they know you disabled it?"

He set it on the case. "With any luck, we didn't move around enough to activate it. Before we leave, I'll turn it back on. If we're careful, it will be like we were never here."

"Great. Let's get to work." I sat at the desk and opened the first drawer. "This is where I found the pill bottles."

"We'll have to assume you were caught on tape."

"Shit." I held up the pistol. "I guess we can also assume they know that I saw this." I opened the chamber, loaded the bullets that I'd emptied last time, and shoved the gun into my belt.

"What are we looking for?" Coop asked as he rifled through one of the file cabinets.

"I don't know, but I'm hoping we'll know when we see it."

Coop opened another drawer. "Do you think his journals are out here?"

"No. Too personal. He probably kept them at the house where Seth or Buck or any of the hands wouldn't have access. Jenn said he wrote in them every night."

"Stupid question... Did you check his bedroom?"

"Nothing."

"I think we should check again." Coop pulled on the bottom drawer handle. "One of those keys fit this?"

"No, Jenn and I tried them all."

Coop motioned for me to get out of the chair, pulled a drawer completely out of the desk, and set it on top. He stuck his hand in the opening and felt around the underside of the desktop, then examined the back of the drawer. He replaced the drawer and tried another. The third drawer was the charm. Coop removed a key that he found taped to the outside back wall of the drawer. He smiled a triumphant smile as he turned it in the lock and pulled open the reluctant file cabinet drawer.

I checked the time on my phone. We still had a good half hour.

"Cooper Hill does it again." I patted him on the back. "You think you can do the same thing with that locker over there?"

A two-foot cardboard tube sat diagonally on top of some papers and a couple of boxes of ammo inside the drawer. I set the ammo on the desk and popped off one of the end caps from the tube. I dumped the papers onto the desk and unrolled them.

Coop ran his hand up and down the back corners of the locker. "Found the key."

"Hold that thought," I said. "Check this out."

Coop looked over my shoulder at architectural plans for the Asha Whitehawk Therapeutic Riding Center.

"Doesn't look like a pot farm to me," Coop said.

"It looks like another reason to kill Roy." I turned to Coop. "What's in the locker?"

He opened the doors and we went through the contents. Mostly medicine, chemicals, syringes, and other veterinary implements. Buck was right about keeping Alex away.

We put everything back the way we found it except for the gun, ammo, and blueprints. Coop replaced the camera to its original spot, carefully turned it on, and we left quietly like we were never there.

My phone rang as we were locking up.

"Hey, Zig. What's up?"

"You need to delete this call from your phone when we're through."

"Sure. What's the matter?"

"Sheriff's on his way over with an arrest warrant for Jenn."

***

"We got trouble. The sheriff is coming for Jenn." I handed the ammo and the plans to Coop. "Stash this stuff in the house."

We ran the length of the stable and out the door. A sheriff's car had just skidded to a stop in front of the house and another sped up the driveway.

"Use the back door," I said.

Coop nodded.

I took a couple of steps and then stopped. "Wait. Take this, too." I handed him the gun.

Sheriff Pecker stood outside his car and watched me approach. I stepped in front of him to block his path. Jenn opened the front door and stepped outside.

"What's going on here?" I asked.

"Get out of my way." Pecker gave a push as he walked past.

I don't like being pushed.

Ziggy exited the second vehicle and gave me a *don't-do-any-thing-stupid* look.

"Deputy," Pecker called out without looking back. "If anyone causes any more trouble, I want you to cuff 'em and take 'em into custody."

Ziggy stood toe-to-toe with me while Sheriff Pecker climbed the front steps. "Stand down, soldier," he whispered. "Now is not the time."

Alex appeared beside Jenn. "Mama?"

"Back inside, honey."

He made a hasty retreat as the sheriff stopped in front of Jenn.

"Jennifer Myles, you're under arrest for the murder of Roy McDonald."

"You can't be serious."

I pushed Ziggy, and he pushed back.

He locked eyes with mine. "Neither of us wants to see you in handcuffs." He lowered his voice. "You won't be able to help her if you're both locked up."

Pecker turned Jenn around and pulled out his cuffs.

I called out. "Is that really necessary?"

He turned to me with a glare that would make an attack dog turn and run, then snapped the cuffs around Jenn's wrists.

Jenn struggled as he led her by the arm down the steps.

"This is bullshit, Jenn. Don't worry. We'll be right behind you."

She looked at me, her eyes a mix of fear and confusion. "You don't have time. I didn't finish with Alex. You need to leave in a couple hours so he doesn't miss his appointment."

Smart girl. No mention of packing or airports. We couldn't be too careful. "Don't talk to anyone. I'll find a good lawyer as soon as I get back."

Ziggy held his ground in front of me while Pecker pushed Jenn into the back seat.

Pecker closed the door and turned to me. He raised a hand and pointed two fingers at his eyes, then turned them toward me before he climbed into the front seat and sped off.

CHAPTER THIRTY-FIVE

I walked into the house to find Alex at the window. He looked as nervous as a long-tail cat in a room full of rocking chairs. "Where's Mama?" he asked.

"She had to go into town to straighten something out."

He wrinkled his nose. "How come the policeman tied up her hands? Did she do something bad?"

"No. It's just a misunderstanding."

"What does that mean?"

"It means that someone told some lies about Mama and now she has to go down to the police station and tell them the truth."

"When will she be home?"

"I'm afraid it might be a while, so I'm going to have to drive you to the airport."

He folded his arms across his chest. "No. I don't want to go."

"C'mon, little man. You need to stay strong for your mama. In Texas, you'll see Memaw and meet your Aunt Jo. They'll take good care of you."

He unfolded his arms and hung his head.

I walked over to him and dropped to one knee. "It's what Mama would want you to do."

"Will I ever see her again?"

My heart dropped below my stomach. "Of course you will. We'll all be together for Thanksgiving. Remember what I told you about Thanksgiving? We get to eat all kinds of good food and lots of great desserts."

"And presents?"

"That's Christmas... but you never know."

"What about Christmas?" Coop said from the bottom of the stairs.

"I was telling Alex that we were all going to be together again for Thanksgiving."

"You know what my favorite part of Thanksgiving is?"

Alex looked at Coop and shook his head.

"Aunt Jo's pumpkin pie. She has a secret ingredient."

"What is it?"

Coop smiled. "I don't know. She wouldn't tell me."

"C'mon. What is it?"

"When you get to Texas, you'll have to ask her. Maybe she'll tell *you*."

The doorbell rang, and we all froze for a moment. I ordered Alex to move away from the window. I moved the curtain on the front door an inch to get a look outside. A woman with long black hair stood on the top step, her back toward me as she surveyed the paddock where Chance and a couple of the other rescues were horsing around.

Nicole? What the hell is she doing here? How did she even find me?

I panicked. Images of boiled bunnies and restraining orders flashed before my eyes. I glanced at Coop.

"Who is it?" he asked.

Words eluded me. After a deep breath, I opened the door. The woman turned and smiled. Her green eyes drew me in. She bore a striking resemblance to Nicole, but that's as far as it went.

I exhaled sharply, unaware that I'd been holding my breath. She tilted her head. "Are you okay?"

I hesitated, then nodded. "I'm sorry. How can I help you?"

"Actually, I'm here to see Alex. Is he home?"

"Alex?"

She held her hand out, palm down, just below her chest. "Young boy about yea high, short black hair, dark skin, likes to play video games..."

I smiled. "Oh, *that* Alex."

"Are you Dillon?"

"I am."

"I'm Raven Scott, Alex's teacher." She held up a satchel that I hadn't noticed her carrying. "I texted you earlier that I would be stopping by with Alex's assignments."

"Yes. Please come in." I held open the door and she stepped inside. "I knew you were coming, it's just that you caught me off guard."

Alex ran toward her. Raven bent down when she saw him coming. He threw his arms around her neck.

"Miss Scott."

"Hi, Alex."

He clung to her like a drowning boy clings to a life raft.

She looked up at me and fired off a few rapid blinks. "He's not usually this... affectionate."

I nodded like I knew. "He's missing his mama."

"Yeah, Mom told me that there's been some trouble here. It must be hard on all of you."

"You have no idea."

Alex finally released her, and she stood. He stayed by her side.

I watched her glance at Coop. "I'm sorry," I said. "This is my friend Cooper Hill. Coop, this is Raven Scott, Hattie's daughter."

"You know my mom?"

Coop smiled. "Doesn't everybody?"

She laughed and nodded. "Right?"

I took the satchel from her.

"Everything we'll be working on for the next two weeks is in there. I included plenty of instructions."

"We're grateful for you taking the time to deliver this. It's been a rough morning."

"You're welcome. Alex is a great kid." She tousled his hair. "If there's anything else I can do..."

"Thanks. I'll let you know."

Alex watched her leave from the porch. "Bye, Miss Scott."

I turned to Cooper, who wore a shit-eatin' grin. "What?"

"She remind you of anyone, Bish?"

"Maybe a little."

***

Coop offered to drive us in his rental car so the three of us wouldn't have to squeeze into my truck and throw Alex's luggage in the truck bed. We finished packing Alex's things, grabbed a quick lunch, and hit the road.

The drop-off at the airport went as well as can be expected. Alex cried. Coop found a helpful ticket agent who paged a flight attendant to get Alex seated on the flight. She assured us that someone would keep a close eye on him all the way to Texas and stay with him until Jo picked him up.

We discussed our options for handling Jenn's predicament in the car on the way home.

"You know how all this legal stuff works," I said. "What happens next?"

"First, they hold an arraignment, usually within forty-eight hours."

"So she's stuck in jail for the next two days?"

"Afraid so. The judge will read the charges and entertain a plea." He paused, presumably to let me catch up. "Depending on how she pleads at the arraignment—"

"What do you mean *how she pleads?*"

"Sorry. When she pleads innocent, they'll set bail and schedule a preliminary hearing where the prosecution will call witnesses and introduce evidence, and the defense can cross-examine witnesses."

"That sounds like a trial."

"Yes, but at this point, the prosecutor must show that enough evidence exists to charge the defendant and move to a trial."

"I don't see how they could have enough evidence. She didn't do anything."

"I guess we'll have to wait and see what they've got."

"How long do you think?"

"Usually, the preliminary hearing takes place within two weeks."

"What? Two weeks?"

"In the meantime, the prosecutor and the defense attorney exchange evidence in what's called discovery. So, we won't have to wait for the hearing to see what they've got."

I closed my eyes and squeezed the bridge of my nose. "She wasn't even there when he died."

"Let's say he was murdered. Do they know how? Do they have a murder weapon? Kinda hard to convict someone without that."

"Maybe it's a preemptive strike," I said. "Seth discovers we're coming after him, so he draws first blood and creates reasonable doubt by offering up another suspect."

"It's not a bad strategy, but he needs some plausible evidence, even if it is only circumstantial."

I shook my head. "We need to go down there right now and talk to her and find out what they might have told her. If I know Jenn, she's not going to go down quietly."

"Okay, but after that, we need to find her a good lawyer."

I pulled out my phone and dialed Mort's number. Mort had been the family lawyer since before I was born. At the moment, he was dating Mama and on the guest list for Thanksgiving.

He told me Mama was busy running the company and asked about Jenn.

"That's the reason I'm calling. She's been arrested for her uncle's murder."

"Roy was murdered?"

"It appears that way. I have an idea who did it but don't have enough proof. I believe he's trying to pin it on Jenn to create reasonable doubt."

"Where is she now?"

"County Jail, I imagine. Coop says she'll have to stay there at least until the arraignment."

"He's right. Did they schedule an arraignment?"

"I don't know. I'm on my way down there right now."

"Okay. Let me know what you find out." He paused. "Dillon, I'll help out as much as I can, but I'm not licensed in Colorado, so I can't represent her."

"Do you know anyone out this way?"

He paused. "I'm afraid I don't."

"Okay. Thanks, Mort. I'll keep you posted."

I looked at Coop. "I need to find an attorney."

***

We stopped at the Sheriff's Department, which sits across the street from the Teller County Jail in Divide, about a fifteen-minute ride up Route 67. No one there knew where Jenn was or when I could see her.

"If they brought her here, she'd be processed, then sent across the street to the jail."

"Did they bring her here?"

"I wouldn't know."

Had she been ordered to stonewall us, or was she just incompetent? I looked around at the empty office. "You must get so many people coming through here in a day that it's impossible to remember any of them."

She glared at me. I asked to speak to Sheriff Decker or Deputy Scott, but both were conveniently unavailable.

The clock on the wall behind her showed nearly six o'clock. She appeared to be packing it in for the night, and I imagined she was as hungry as I was.

"How late is this place open?"

"Someone's here 24/7."

"Thank you. Have a good day, Ma'am." I tipped my hat and walked out.

Coop leaned against his car with his arms folded. "Well?"

"Apparently, they lost her. I'm going to call Ziggy."

When Ziggy didn't answer, I called Hattie. I told her I needed a lawyer.

"Why? What did you do?"

"It's for Jenn, and he needs to be good. The sheriff is circling the wagons."

"I'm on it. I have a couple of connections."

Before I hung up, I asked her to have Ziggy call me. I wasn't leaving until I spoke to Jenn.

My stomach sounded like a cement mixer, and I wasn't sure if it was hunger or stress. Coop could probably use something to eat, as well. We grabbed a burger at a nearby restaurant and waited for Ziggy's call.

The call came in on our way back to the jail. Bad news. We wouldn't get to see her tonight. She'd been processed and moved to the jail. Visiting hours ended at six o'clock, and Ziggy didn't have enough juice for them to make an exception.

"What about her phone call? Doesn't she get a phone call?"

"She does. I'll check on that and get back to you."

I told Coop what he said, and we decided we had no reason to stick around.

Ziggy called back as we parked the car in front of the house. He said to expect a call from Jenn within a half hour. We went inside, cracked a couple cold ones, and waited for her call.

I appreciated Coop being there. Easier to go through something like this with a trusted friend. The empty house had lost the joyful noise of a young boy and a loving friend and mother. I didn't realize how much I needed that until it was gone.

I kept my phone close and pounced when it rang. Jenn's voice lacked its usual confidence and enthusiasm, but it was damn good to hear it. She didn't know much, other than her arraignment wouldn't be until Monday. I had a feeling Sheriff Pecker had something to do with the schedule. I told her I was working on hiring an attorney so she didn't have to rely on a public defender who was probably a drinking buddy of the sheriff or Seth, or both.

I told her I'd visit her in the morning after I had a few words with Seth. She suggested I bring Coop with me when I talked to him. As much as she wanted to spend time with me, she didn't want to do it in adjoining cells.

CHAPTER THIRTY-SIX

After a quick breakfast, we caught up with Seth in the barn.

Every muscle in my body tightened when I saw him. Coop must have noticed my hands clench into fists, and he placed his hand on my shoulder. I shook it off and marched over to where Seth was loading bales of hay onto the conveyor belt that ran through a plexiglass tube to the stable. He probably shouldn't have mentioned his claustrophobia the first time he showed me the system.

Seth didn't hear me coming over the hum of the conveyor motor. In one smooth motion, I grabbed him by the arm, turned him around, and pushed him up against the conveyor. He had no leverage. I could easily boost him up onto the belt and send him down the tunnel.

"Why are you doing this to Jenn?"

I pushed a little harder. His eyes filled with terror as they darted back and forth between the tunnel and me.

"You better call off the dogs and get her out of there." I glanced down the tunnel as the motor continued to whine.

He held up his hands. "I can explain."

Coop tugged me from behind. I loosened my grip, and Seth scrambled to his feet.

I got up in his grille. "You better start explaining right now."

He put both hands on my chest and pushed me back a step. I let it slide to hear what he had to say. Coop turned off the conveyor.

Seth had a bit more courage with the conveyor off. "You think you know everything, don't you?"

Not a good way to start. I let it slide again.

"You've been here... what... a month?"

"Long enough to know Jenn didn't kill her uncle."

"Really? What if I told you he wasn't her uncle?"

"I'd say you better be able to back it up."

"What do you really know about her?"

I didn't like his tone. "How is Roy not Jenn's uncle?"

"It might have something to do with the fact that she was adopted."

I flinched, and he saw it.

"Sounds like she forgot to mention that little fact." His voice reeked of sarcasm.

I needed to make a quick recovery. "Most people don't like to talk about things like that."

"Well, let me fill you in." The terror in his eyes moments ago had been replaced by arrogance. "Little Jenny Lee Jones was plucked from a foster home at age ten by Roy's sister, Peggy Myles. She had three sons, and desperately wanted a daughter." A smirk snaked its way across his lips. "I thought you two were close. I'm surprised she didn't tell you any of this."

I clenched my fists. He was getting dangerously close to a ride on the conveyor. I felt Coop's hand on my shoulder again, and I took a deep breath.

"Why would that have anything to do with her wanting to kill him?"

"That's not why she killed him. That's why you shouldn't believe everything she says."

"Are you calling her a liar?"

"Did she tell you she convinced Roy to leave her the ranch?"

"She told me that Roy didn't trust you, so he added her to the will."

"That part may be true, but did she tell you about the third will? One with only her name on it? Apparently, half the ranch wasn't enough for her."

Jenn never mentioned any of this. "Where were you when Roy died?"

"You should ask your girlfriend that question."

"I'm asking you."

"You don't get to ask questions. You don't belong here."

"No alibi. I didn't think so."

"I was at home... with an overnight guest."

"Really? What was his name?"

Seth's back stiffened, and his eyes became little slits. "I think it's time you packed up your shit and went back to where you came from."

"That ain't gonna happen."

Seth cleared his throat. "Now, if you boys will excuse me, I have work to do."

Smug bastard. "Wait a minute. If the farm belongs to Jenn, what are you still doing here?"

"Fortunately for me, Roy never got to sign that bogus will."

"Bish." Coop tugged at my arm. "We need to go."

I looked at Coop. His eyes pleaded with me to let it go for now. I shot a *this-isn't-over* glare at Seth. "You better get Jenn out of there."

Coop grabbed my arm, and I followed him out.

The conveyor motor whined again when we'd reached a safe distance.

***

I told Coop I would go to the jail alone. They only allowed one visitor at a time, so I figured he'd be more comfortable hanging out at the house than sitting in my truck in the prison parking lot.

On the drive up to Divide, I thought about what to say to her, but more importantly, what she might say back. I didn't want to believe anything Seth said earlier, but the fact that Jenn had never mentioned any of it gave me pause.

I left everything in my truck except my ID and entered the Teller County Jail for what I hoped would be the first and last time. I wanted to believe she'd be out on bail and home before we knew it. That reminded me we still didn't have a lawyer.

I watched Jenn sit down on the other side of a sheet of plexiglass. Her eyes lacked their usual sparkle. Otherwise, she looked as good as can be expected wearing a DOC jumpsuit.

I had questions I needed answered, but I didn't want to jump in with both feet.

"Y'all sure are a sight for sore eyes," she said.

"You, too, Babe. I miss you."

"Not as much as I miss you. How's Alex?"

"He made it to Texas without a hitch. He's with Jo and the girls now."

She wiped a tear as she nodded.

"Are they treating you all right in here?"

"One of the guards is a little creepy, but otherwise I can't complain. I just hate not being able to see you guys or to come and go as I please."

A silence descended between us. I took a deep breath, and we locked eyes. "How come you never told me you were adopted?"

Her mouth fell open before she made a quick recovery. "Who told you that?"

"The same person who told me you convinced Roy to change his will."

Her eyes darted back and forth. "Can we not do this here?"

"Where do you suggest we do it?" I held up my hands in frustration. "Coop and I found a pretty good burger place down the road. Maybe they'll let me take you out to lunch."

"Don't be a jackass."

I sighed. "I'm sorry, but I feel like you've been keeping things from me. Important things."

"Everything I've ever told you has been true." She paused. "I may have just left out a few details."

"Well, they're front-page news now, and I gotta tell you, they're not helping your case."

"I didn't kill Uncle Roy."

Unsure how to respond, I said nothing. Probably not the smartest approach.

"Dillon?"

"Do I believe you're capable of killing someone over money? No. But maybe you thought you were saving him from a slow, painful death. Your words."

A glare was her only reply.

"I'm sorry, but I have a lot to process here. Why did I have to hear all this personal stuff about you from Seth?"

"I hoped you would stand by me like I did for you when *you* were arrested for murder. They had at least as much circumstantial evidence against you as they do against me. Why can't you just believe me?"

I remained silent again, studying her eyes. Blue fires burned making it hard to get a read on what was really going on behind them.

She spoke into the silence. "Did you find a lawyer?"

"I'm still working on it." The fact was, I'd forgotten all about it until I walked into the jail. Who could blame me, after finding out my girlfriend, who was in jail at that moment, might have actually killed someone?

She hung her head.

"Stay strong. I'll get you out of here one way or another."

***

I told myself on the way home there was no way Jenn killed Roy McDonald. It bothered me that it felt too much like I was trying to convince myself. Seth had gotten under my skin. That's exactly what he wanted to do. What made it worse was I let him.

Hattie called to say she'd found a lawyer in Colorado Springs to take Jenn's case. Barry Whitaker, a seasoned defense attorney, was a longtime friend of her husband. She texted me his contact info when we hung up. Pop or Luke or somebody upstairs must be looking out for me and sent Hattie my way. She had a heart of gold, and I don't know how I would have gotten by out here without her.

I called Whitaker, who told me he planned to visit Jenn that afternoon. He had a call in to the prosecutor's office to see what they had in the way of evidence against her. We planned to meet at the courthouse before the arraignment on Monday to discuss strategy.

Coop was on the phone with his wife when I got home. I asked about Alex, and he handed me the phone. Talking with Alex again brought a smile to my otherwise tired face. He sounded in good spirits. He asked about Jenn a couple times, but he seemed to be preoccupied with his new friends Katey Jo and Carrie Beth. They were ten and eight, respectively, and a pleasant distraction. I felt relieved that he wasn't moping around down there.

"I hope you don't mind," Coop said when I hung up the phone. "I did a little snooping while you were out."

"Depends on where this snooping took place."

"After I went through yours and Jenn's stuff..." He paused for effect. "Seriously, I went over Roy's room with a fine-tooth comb."

"And?"

"Remember that bookshelf your daddy made you with the secret compartment under the bottom shelf? You know, where you hid all the stuff you didn't want me to walk off with?"

"You knew about that?"

He held his arms out at his sides. "It's me. Remember?"

I smiled and nodded. "Seriously, what did you find?"

"A little fireproof safe."

"Good job, Coop."

"Next to a stack of journals."

Chapter Thirty-Seven

My eyes widened. "You found the journals?"

We looked at each other for a second, then without a word, raced up the stairs. The safe and the journals sat on the bed.

"Did you find the key?"

Coop held out his arms again.

"Yeah, yeah, I know. It's you." I paused. "Are you going to open it?"

He pulled a key from his pocket and turned it in the lock, then stepped back and gestured for me to do the honors. I felt bad invading Roy's private space without Jenn there, but we didn't have time to waste. I lifted the lid and dumped out a few legal papers and two-thousand dollars in strapped twenty-dollar bills.

"Bail money," Coop said.

I picked up one of the papers. "This looks like the first will, dated 2015 and naming Seth as the only heir to the estate." I picked up the second paper. This one had Jenn and Seth listed together. The second had been signed around the time Jenn said she visited.

At the moment, I was more interested in the journals. I picked one up and thumbed through it while Coop examined another.

"Looks like he skipped penmanship class in school," Coop said.

The more I studied it, however, the quicker I deciphered his scribbles. We scooped up the seven books and took them downstairs.

We skimmed a lot of personal stuff in the first four books that didn't interest us. The fifth started around the time Seth appeared without notice, looking for work. Roy liked his work ethic and gave him increasingly more responsibility.

Within a year, Roy's health declined, and he turned over the day-to-day operation of the ranch to Seth. But Seth and Roy had differing opinions on how to run the ranch. Roy had always raised horses and had worked mostly with rescues. There wasn't a lot of money coming in, but Roy didn't care.

Seth, on the other hand, had bigger plans. Marijuana had been legalized in Colorado, which created a climate reminiscent of the gold rush back in the state's glory days. This time, Seth wanted a piece of the action. He urged Roy to sell off the horses and plant the new cash crop, or lease the land to a large grower like RMA.

Roy had no intention of getting involved in this new *green rush*. Seth backed off.

I looked up at Coop. "Seth gave up too easily. I think he switched tactics."

"I agree. Roy signed his own death warrant." Coop stood. "I think I'm gonna die, too, if I don't get something to eat."

I glanced at the clock on the wall. Seven-thirty. "Yeah. Let's grab a sandwich and keep going."

Ten minutes later, we were reading Roy's chicken scratch writing between bites of ham and cheese sandwiches washed down with a couple of Coors.

"Here's his new tactic," I said. "He brings in Doctor Richards, a.k.a. Frank Snyder. Poor Roy thinks Seth's trying to help, but he's trying to put him in the ground."

"He probably brought in a lawyer to write that first will, too."

"Seth sets himself up to inherit the ranch while he's slowly killing Roy."

"His mama must be proud."

"Roy's liver condition continues to decline," I continue. "In the meantime, Seth shoots himself in the foot when Roy gets wind of a deal he's trying to make for the ranch. Roy second-guesses his decision to leave the ranch to Seth. When he gets the cancer diagnosis from Richards, he has the plans for Asha's Riding Center drawn up. He decides to sell off more land to finance the deal so he can see it through before he dies."

"Seth can't let that happen," Coop says. "He calls an audible. His plan isn't working fast enough, so he has to take matters into his own hands."

I frown. "Roy died of a heart attack."

"That's easy enough to fake."

"Really?"

"Potassium chloride is what I'd use," Coop said. "It'll mimic a heart attack and leave no chemicals behind that would show up on a tox screen. It metabolizes to byproducts that are ordinarily found in the body."

"So it's untraceable?"

"Pretty much. A blood test will show elevated potassium levels, but whenever any muscle tissue is damaged, large amounts of potassium are released into the bloodstream. So, a coroner would likely list the cause of death as a fatal heart attack."

"Good thing bruises are traceable, or he might have gotten away with it."

"Yeah, you need a crooked sheriff when you leave bruises."

I went back to reading. "The next entry talks about Roy rewriting the will to add Jenn." I read some more. "He brought her out here to tell her and to show her his plans for the ranch and get her to honor his wishes after he died. He made her promise not to tell Seth about the new will."

"And she never mentioned this?"

I shook my head. "Makes me wonder what else she's hiding."

"Poor Jenn. Roy put her in a tough spot."

"And she put the rest of us right there beside her."

Coop met my gaze. "Are you second-guessing coming out here?"

"No. I love Jenn and want to be with her. Now I want to help her. I just wish I knew all this shit ahead of time."

"Maybe she figured if she told you, you wouldn't come."

"That could be, but I deserved to know all the facts before I made such a big decision."

I guess I didn't blame her. I'd like to think that if the roles were reversed, I would have told her, but I didn't know for sure.

"Can you hand me another book?"

Coop shrugged. "There aren't any more."

"What?" I moved the books around, looking for one that I hadn't read. "This can't be all of them. He lived for another month, and it seemed like he'd been writing more. He wouldn't have just stopped."

"We don't know what his last days were like. Maybe he got too sick."

"To write?"

Coop thought for a moment. "Roy kept these books hidden in a secret compartment. What if these were the archive, and he kept the current book handy on the nightstand?"

"That's where it would have been when he died. Whoever boxed up his stuff and moved it to the attic must have seen it."

"My money's on Seth. How else would he have known about the third will?"

***

I needed to find out how much Buck knew about what went on at the ranch during that final month. Coop and I took a ride to see him the next morning.

I knocked on the RV's door. While I waited, I glanced at the pond where I pictured Jim Scott sitting on the dock in his shorts with a fishing pole in his hand.

"Open up, Buck. It's Dillon."

I got worried when he didn't answer after the third knock. Coop followed me as I walked around the trailer. I noticed movement in the trees behind the garage. I had only walked a few feet past the tree line when I saw it.

"Mornin' boys," Buck said, pants around his ankles, squatting at the base of a large tree.

"Really, Buck?" I turned around too late. I couldn't unsee that.

"What's the matter? You never seen a Buck shittin' in the woods?" He laughed.

I grabbed Coop. "We'll wait inside."

Buck joined us a few minutes later. His movements were a little off, and I suspected he'd had a few drinks before breakfast.

"You know, there's a nice bathroom in the back," I said.

"I don't like to shit where I sleep. Besides, there's no hookup. Unless one a you boys wants to come by every couple days an' empty the tank."

"Hard pass," Coop said, holding up his hands.

"Did you hear Jenn's in jail?"

"Hattie told me." He shook his head. "That was a dirty trick. No way that sweet girl killed her uncle."

Coop nodded. "We feel the same."

"We found Roy's journals, but the writing stopped about a month before he died. We don't know if something made him stop, or if we're missing one or more of them."

"We were wondering," Coop said. "If you could shed some light on what was going on at the ranch just before he died."

He looked from me to Coop, then back to me. "Roy kept to himself a lot near the end. Spent his time between the house and his office. He died there, ya know?"

"That's what I heard."

"That fake doctor was there more than usual." His expression fell for just a moment. "Then Jenny came to visit."

"When was that?"

"Just a few days before he died. She invited me over for dinner one night. She's a helluva cook, that one. You got yourself a keeper."

"A few days? Don't you mean a month?"

"If I meant a month, I woulda said a month."

"She was there twice leading up to his death?"

He hesitated. "Maybe. I don't recall." He stood and walked the few steps to the kitchen. "You boys wanna join me for a bit a whiskey?"

We shook our heads. "Maybe you've had enough this morning," I said. We needed him to have a clear head, but that ship might have already sailed. "C'mon, Buck. Think. Was Jenn there again before he died?"

He glared at me as he poured himself a shot. He raised it to his lips and stopped. "Now that you mention it," he said, circling back to a previous conversation. "I did see a writin' book on the table by his bed."

"What were you doing in his bedroom?"

He emptied the glass and poured himself another. "I recall we all set a spell after dinner until Roy said he was tired. He went to bed while me and your missus had another drink and some conversation. Before I left, I went in to say goodnight."

"What did you and Jenn talk about?"

"Anything and everything, I guess." He paused and his eyes drifted. "Roy was gettin' worse, and I was worried about my job if somethin' bad happened to him."

"You mean if the cancer took him?"

He looked at me like I had three heads. "No, I mean if a tree fell on him." He paused. "I didn't think someone was gonna kill the poor bastard if that's what you mean."

This seemed like a good enough reason to pour myself a shot and throw it back. I waited for him to continue. When he didn't, I asked, "Did Jenn say anything about your job?"

He pulled a rag from his pocket and wiped his nose. "She told me not to worry. Said she'd take over and keep things runnin' the way they was."

"What about Seth? Did you know he had other plans?"

"She told me not to worry about Seth, like she would take care a that."

"When did she tell you that?"

"After Roy went to bed."

"No, I mean what day?"

"I don't know. What day did he die? It was the night before that."

I glanced at Coop and then back to Buck. "So, she was here again. Did you see Jenn the next day?"

"She spent some time with Roy in his office."

"Did either of them seem upset?"

"Not to my knowledge."

"Did you see her at all after Roy died?"

"Everything went sideways after that. I don't believe I saw Jenn no more."

Why would Seth risk killing Roy when Jenn was there unless he planned to pin it on her from the get-go? And if he did, why wait until now?

"Who found him?"

"I did." Buck cleared his throat. "He was laid out like road-kill on the turnpike. I called 911, but it was too late."

"Where was Jenn?"

"Don't know. Musta left town, 'cause I didn't see her again until she showed up a few months later."

***

Jenn's arraignment couldn't have gone worse. Her lawyer, Barry Whitaker, did a decent job, but the judge shut him down and denied bail. The preliminary hearing was scheduled for the first week of December. This, of course, was unacceptable. I felt the vein in my forehead twitch like it was about to pop.

"You've got to do something," I said to Whitaker.

"The only thing we can do now is prepare a good defense." He sighed. "But that won't be easy."

"I don't care how this looks. Jenn didn't kill anyone."

"That may be true, but we have to prove it."

"This can't go to trial. Not here. The sheriff is in on this. No doubt there'll be dirty water in the jury pool, as well."

"There are two ways to keep that from happening. Either I prove she's innocent, or you find the son of a bitch that killed Roy McDonald."

I nodded. "Then we better get to work. I've lost too many people in my life. I'm not going to lose another one."

I'd met with Whitaker before the arraignment. He told me up front that her chances didn't look good. I didn't want to believe it, but after he went over the evidence the prosecution had, getting her out of jail seemed like a tall order.

I had already heard most of it from Seth, but a new piece of evidence bothered me more than any of the others. The prosecution claimed to have the murder weapon—a syringe containing traces of potassium chloride—with Jenn's fingerprints all over it.

CHAPTER THIRTY-EIGHT

I'm sure there's an explanation for the evidence against Jenn, but I'm having a hard time believing that a jury would feel the same way.

"It's ten days to Thanksgiving," Coop said. "Maybe I should call Jo and have her cancel her plans."

"I told Jenn I'd have her out of there one way or another, and that's what I'm gonna do."

"Her preliminary hearing isn't until December. How do you figure—"

"We're going to find the real killer."

Coop's eyes told me he wanted to believe me.

I waved a dismissing hand. "Now, make yourself useful and go gas up my truck. I've got some calls to make."

Coop gave me a confused look.

"There's a pump behind the barn."

I called Sam Higgins and asked him to meet us at his office to have another chat. He reluctantly agreed, but we would have to wait until after lunch. Next, I dialed Mort's number.

Mort had offered his help with any legal questions I might have regarding Jenn's case. I didn't know a wherefore from a whereas, so I asked if he would review Roy's will if I faxed him a copy. He agreed. When I told him about the syringe, their so-called smoking gun, he suggested we challenge the chain of custody. If it was a plant, they might not have the required documentation. If the chain was broken, it might be inadmissible in court.

I asked about Mama, and he went on for five minutes about how well she was doing at work, and how happy the two of them were. He was clearly smitten.

When Coop returned with my truck, I told him we were taking a ride to the coroner's office in Cripple Creek to meet with Sam Higgins.

His eyes lit up. "We have to stop at the Colorado Grande Hotel. It's haunted. I saw a show about it during one of those ghost hunter marathons."

"I've heard of it. Buck says the hotel's restaurant, Maggie's, has the best ribs he's ever eaten."

If Coop was a dog, his tail would be waggin' to beat the band. "That's the ghost's name. Maggie."

I checked the time. "If we leave now, we can get lunch there before we meet with Higgins."

The twenty-minute ride put us in Cripple Creek around noon. We had plenty of time for lunch. We didn't see any ghosts, just a lot of history and some great food. Buck might not know much, but he knows his ribs. Coop ordered a big steak when I told him I was buying. We walked the half mile to the coroner's office when we finished.

Higgins wasted no time ushering us into his small office and closing the door. He knew there could only be one reason for our visit. He moved some things around on his desk and motioned for us to sit.

"I hope you didn't come down here to stir up more trouble."

"No more than we already have, I reckon." I offered a smile to cut some of the tension. Higgins did not reciprocate.

"Okay, I'll cut to the chase. When did you find out about this smoking gun the prosecutor has?"

"If you're talking about the syringe, I only heard recently, after they reopened the case."

"Is that why they reopened it?"

"I believe it is."

That and them not wanting me to see the police report or any other records.

"Where has it been all this time?" Coop asked.

"Like I said, it's the first I heard of it."

"I think it's bogus." I stood and leaned over his desk. "It didn't come up in the first investigation because it didn't exist."

"No one did a proper investigation at the time."

"That's the problem." I straightened up and shook my head in disgust.

"Look, I just do what I'm told. That's a police matter. Maybe you should talk to them."

"You mean Sheriff Pecker?"

"Believe me, I understand your frustration."

"Oh, so your girlfriend is also in jail for something she didn't do?"

Coop put a hand on my shoulder, and I sat.

"Let's take a breath," he said. "We came down here to ask a few questions, not to debate police protocol or the validity of the physical evidence."

Higgins leaned back in his chair, and I followed suit.

"I thought we were on the same side here," I said.

"You need to understand, this is my livelihood."

"Well, this is my girlfriend's life." We locked eyes for a moment.

He turned to Coop. "You have some questions?"

"Assuming Jenn is, in fact, innocent, could someone have picked up her prints off an object like a drinking glass and transferred them to the syringe?"

"It's possible."

"How would *you* do it?"

Higgins smiled for the first time. "You think I do this kind of thing?"

Coop held up his hands. "No. Of course not. All I know is what I see on TV. I thought maybe you might come across this kind of thing from time to time."

"I'm happy to report that there aren't many murders around here."

Higgins appeared more comfortable talking with Coop, so I backed off.

"I would use a piece of clear tape," Coop offered.

Higgins nodded. "My choice as well. However, such a transfer probably wouldn't hold up under microscopic evaluation, but we're not equipped for that."

"Okay. So we've established her prints could have been planted. Let's talk about potassium chloride."

"Yes. The weapon of choice for getting away with murder. That and perhaps succinylcholine. They're virtually undetectable."

"So, the prosecutor needs to prove Roy died from potassium chloride, given Jenn's fingerprints on the syringe."

"Yes."

"But you said it was undetectable."

"I said it was *virtually* undetectable. Nothing I know of is undetectable."

I jumped in. "Logically then, if the defense can prove he died of something else, their smoking gun is no longer smoking."

"Of course."

"I watched an episode of *Hawaii Five-0*," Coop said, "where they were having trouble determining the cause of death. It turned out to be aconite. It's so rare that nobody ever looks for it."

"Aconitum napellus or monkshood," Higgins said. "I'm familiar with it, but I've never come across it in nearly forty years on this job. It comes from a plant that grows wild in this part of the country. Very potent. A single drop could kill you."

"A drop?" I frowned. "I thought it was a plant."

"To use it in a situation like this, you would distill it and inject it into the body."

"How do you test for it?"

"Liquid chromatography with tandem mass spectrometry is the only way I know to test for aconite, but that's not anything that can be done locally."

"Where would they do it?"

"You don't seriously think that—"

"Where?" I cut him off.

"Denver is the closest, but the test is expensive."

"I'll pay for it." I moved to the edge of my seat. "You told me you saved blood and tissue samples. Isn't this why you do something like that? They got it wrong the first time and you know it. Maybe you can fix it."

He paused for a moment. He didn't want to admit I was right. I'm sure part of him wanted us to walk out of there quietly and let him ride out his pension. I hoped the other part, the part that lived to see justice done, the part that had been trampled on by the likes of Sheriff Pecker, would rise up and seize the day.

"I'll make some calls," he said after a long silence. "Everything we've said here today doesn't leave this room. Am I clear?"

I nodded.

"You boys need to be extra careful. If you touch the plant or get a single drop on your skin, it could be fatal."

We left quietly after I thanked him for doing the right thing.

I turned to Coop when we got outside. "*Hawaii Five-0?*"

He smiled and shrugged. "What can I say? I'm a TV junkie."

"I gotta admit, sometimes that's not such a bad thing."

We rode in silence for the first ten minutes. If the test for aconite came back positive, it could blow their case out of the water. Even if Higgins got a sample tested, it would most likely take days to learn the result. Admittedly, it was a Hail Mary, but I wasn't ready to bet Jenn's life on one play with plenty of time left on the clock.

I broke the silence. "We need to steal a play from their playbook."

"Whose book and what play?"

"Maybe we should give Jimmy a call and see if he can get us some equipment similar to what Seth installed in Roy's office. Something is going on between Seth and Frank, and I'd love to be a fly on the wall when they talk about it."

Jimmy Arroyo had been the third of our *Three Amigos* at Bradley High. We'd done everything together, then gone our separate ways. Jimmy was the brains of our trio, a real computer nerd, so it was no surprise he'd landed a job with a big tech firm in Arlington as a security systems product manager. He'd hooked us up earlier this year when we needed a similar favor.

"I like it." Coop smiled. "I'll take care of the installation."

"How many cameras and where you fixin' to install them?"

"They spend a lot of time in the barn. We'll need two cameras with good microphones." He paused. "I'm gonna need a couple of hours to install all that. How do we distract them?"

"We'll figure something out. Just get the equipment here ASAP."

"I'm on it."

We stopped at Hattie's store on the way home to use her fax machine, then swung by Hattie's house to check on Buck.

I knocked on his door and was relieved to find him inside with his pants on.

"How's Jenny?" he asked when we walked in.

"Not too happy right now. She's stuck in jail for at least the next two weeks."

He pulled out a bottle of bourbon from the cupboard and held it up in our direction.

We waved him off.

"Suit yourselves."

"Buck, you know what aconite is?" Coop asked.

He emptied his glass and set it on the counter. "Sure do. Use it sometimes to calm the horses when they're travelin'."

"Really? Don't you mean *kill* them?"

"Oh, if they ate the flowers, it would kill 'em, alright. The pills just calm 'em down."

"Like Valium for horses," Coop said.

I turned to Buck. "You think somebody gave some of those flowers to our horses?"

"I don't think *somebody* did it, I think *them Whitehawks* did it."

"Stop it with the Whitehawks, already. They didn't kill Roy or poison the horses."

"Says you."

"The Whitehawks have a pretty solid alibi. They were in prison when Roy died."

He waved a dismissing hand. "Aaaah."

"Did Roy keep any aconite at the ranch?"

"There's probably a bottle in his office under lock and key." He looked at me. "You best keep your boy away from there."

"Copy that. So, the pills wouldn't kill you?"

"I reckon if you ate enough of 'em."

"The coroner says it can be injected. Do you think the fake doctor brought it with him?"

Buck shrugged.

"When this doctor visited the ranch, did you ever see him talking to Seth?"

"From time to time." He closed one eye and tilted his head. "They nearly came to blows one day. Seth had a burr in his saddle 'bout somethin' or other. They stood toe-to-toe, hollerin' at each other for a spell before the doctor left in a hurry. That was the last I seen of him."

"When was this?"

"Just after Roy passed."

He poured round two and knocked it back. "When you reckon I might get my job back?"

"I'm workin' on it."

As we walked back to the truck, Buck stuck his head out of the RV's door. "You tell little Jenny that Buck says hey."

Chapter Thirty-Nine

I started the truck in Hattie's driveway, but before I shifted into reverse, a sheriff's car pulled in behind us and Sheriff Pecker climbed out.

"I received a complaint from a neighbor that a couple of strangers was walkin' around out here while Hattie wasn't home. You wouldn't know anything about that, would you?"

"I might. We stopped in to see her, but she wasn't there."

He glanced at the RV. "That's a fine-looking piece of camping equipment back there. I hope you boys aren't thinking about stealing her."

"No. Hadn't thought about it. Like I said, we came by to see Hattie."

"That's right." He looked at Coop, then back at me. "You boys sit tight while I have a look around."

I checked the rearview while Pecker walked toward the RV. He had us blocked in. I prayed for Buck to remember our security protocol and not answer the door if Pecker knocked.

He walked around the RV, then knocked on the door. No answer.

"Sheriff's Department. Open the door."

No answer. He knocked again before walking back to my truck. I blew out the breath I'd been holding.

"What were you doing down in Cripple Creek?"

He caught me off guard. How did he know that? Higgins wouldn't have told him. Was he having us followed?

Coop leaned forward. "It's my fault. I'm something of a ghost hunter and I wanted to see the Colorado Grande while I was here."

Pecker looked from Coop to me. "Who's your friend?"

"His name's Cooper. He's an old friend here to visit for a spell. Is that frowned on around here, too?"

"No." He glared at me. "We just don't like people sticking their nose where it don't belong."

"The only place I stuck my nose today was in a big plate of ribs at Maggie's Restaurant."

"Listen Mr. Smartass, you best stay in your lane or you and I are going to have a problem."

"Roger that." I met his steely glare. "Can we go now?"

He walked back to his car without another word and sped off.

Coop looked at me with a smirk. "Nice to see you've been making friends out here."

"Did you see anyone tailing us?"

Before he answered, we locked eyes, and we both said, "GPS tracker." We jumped out of the car and felt around inside the wheel wells. Nothing in the front. When we got to the back wheels, Coop said, "Got it."

The same thing had happened a few months ago when a crooked cop in Bradley attached a tracker to my car. I found it with the help of a scanning device that Jimmy had provided. I planned to dispose of this one in a similar fashion.

We arrived home around five o'clock, too late to visit Jenn. I would drive up there in the morning. Mort called after dinner with news about the will. He told me it contained a no-contest clause that stated if an heir challenges the will and loses, they get nothing. Probably why Seth didn't challenge the second will after being blindsided.

Another clause, this one less common, provided that if one beneficiary is convicted of wrongdoing in connection with the deceased, he or she will get nothing. Jenn's arrest suddenly made sense. Seth didn't want to take a chance on contesting the will and possibly losing everything, so he manufactured a case against Jenn. Maybe in his twisted mind, sending her to jail was more humane than killing her. More importantly, if she was somehow convicted, the ranch would be all his.

I thanked Mort and explained what I'd learned to Coop.

What we'd learned was potentially useful. The prosecution's case appeared strong. They had means, motive, and, according to Buck, opportunity. It appeared Jenn was at the ranch the day Roy died. That crippled our original defense. The only thing left was to discredit the so-called murder weapon.

***

Jenn sat across from me, and I studied her through the plexiglass. I wanted to get her out of this place and take her home. She looked a little better than the last time I saw her, but I knew it was an act for my benefit.

I put my hand up to the glass, and she did the same. It wasn't skin on skin, but I swear I felt her energy through that piece of glass. After a bit of small talk, I told her what Mort said about the will and my theory for why she'd been arrested.

She shook her head. "I don't understand how they could have a syringe with my fingerprints."

"We figure they transferred your prints to the syringe from something else you touched."

"They can do that?"

"Coop says it's not that difficult." I took a deep breath and asked about something that had been bothering me. "Buck told me you came out to the ranch a second time… right before Roy died."

"I should have told you." She shifted uncomfortably in her chair. "But I knew how bad it looked."

"Not as bad as it looks if you were still here when he died."

A few seconds passed with no response.

"Please tell me you left before he died."

She closed her eyes. "I wish I could."

"Jeezus, Jenn." I stood, no longer able to sit. "This is bad. You're not being there when he died was our defense. Lack of opportunity was all we had."

Jenn hung her head as I paced in a tight pattern.

"I'm sorry, Dillon."

"I know."

"I didn't kill him."

"I know that, too."

I stopped pacing and studied her sitting there in that damn jumpsuit. I'd never seen her so vulnerable. All I wanted to do at that moment was hold her and tell her everything would be all right.

"I need to know everything this time."

The guard gave me the stink eye, and I sat. "What happened while you were here the second time?"

She took a deep breath and nodded. "Uncle Roy called and wanted to see me again. Said it was important. When I arrived, he spent two days showing me everything about the ranch and how to run it, like he was fixin' to hand it over right then and there."

"How was Seth while you were there?"

"We didn't talk much, which I thought was a little strange. He was nice enough when we did, but I got a bad vibe from him, like he didn't want me there."

"Buck said you had dinner the night before Roy died. What happened the next day?"

"More of the same in the morning. In the afternoon, he took me to his office in the stable and showed me plans he had drawn up for the Therapeutic Riding Center he wanted to build in Asha's name. I told him I thought it was a great idea. Then he showed me the will he'd had drawn up, leaving the entire ranch to me."

All conveniently caught on camera. "What did you think about that?"

"It made me nervous. I figured Seth would pitch a fit when he found out. But Uncle Roy didn't trust that he'd honor his wishes. Seth was more interested in growing marijuana."

"What happened to that will? I mean, Seth owns half the ranch."

"I don't know. Uncle Roy told me he planned to have it witnessed and filed the following day."

"He told you this in the office?"

"Yes." She tilted her head and looked at me with squinted eyes. "Why is that so important?"

"Because you were being watched."

"What? By who?"

"I'm not sure, but my money is on Seth."

"You weren't there. How do you know someone was watching."

"Coop found a wireless video camera in Roy's office. Someone was watching or maybe recording Roy whenever he was in there."

"And you think it was Seth?"

"If Seth thought Roy was about to cut him out of the will, that's a pretty strong motive, but he wouldn't know that unless he saw the video."

"Roy died later that day in his office. Do you think the camera recorded the murder?"

"It's likely, but if Seth didn't turn the camera off before he killed him, he surely destroyed the video after the fact."

"What if Seth didn't kill him? He might have a video of the actual killer. We need to find out."

"Seth won't tell us anything. Either way, he's gonna want to keep that information to himself. If he killed him, he'd be saving his own ass. If it was someone else on that video, I'm sorry, but he's not going to come forward and save you. He wants you to go down for this, so he gets the ranch."

"Go ahead, say it."

"Say what?"

"I told you so." She sighed. "You never trusted him. I should have listened to you."

"That kind of talk isn't going to help."

Neither of us said anything for a few moments. In the silence, I had time to think. The video of their conversation, if it still existed, could help us. Jenn wouldn't have motive to kill him until after the new will was notarized. Seth, however, would want to make sure the will never got signed.

I hesitated for a moment. "You found Roy, didn't you?"

She nodded. Tears flowed, and she brushed them away.

"What did you do?"

"I went and got Buck. He called 911. He told me to go back to Texas and not to let anyone see me leave."

Buck had lied. He was covering for her. I needed time to think. Someone had a video of Jenn in the room with Roy's body. Time stamps can be altered. I'd seen it done before. That evidence was enough for a jury to convict.

"Say something."

I shook my head to clear it. "We need to find the real killer."

CHAPTER FORTY

After meeting with Jenn at the jail, I stopped at the restaurant where Coop and I had lunch the other day. I searched the parking lot for a car with out-of-state plates. An SUV full of camping gear with Arizona plates caught my eye. I stuck Sheriff Pecker's GPS tracker inside the rear wheel well and headed back to Redfield.

I called Higgins on the way to see if he'd sent a sample out to be tested. The call went straight to voicemail. I didn't leave a message. I stopped at the hardware store to check in with Hattie.

Hattie leaned against the counter, chewing on a fingernail when I walked in. She motioned toward the back of the store, and I followed her. She closed the door and took both my hands in hers.

"What's wrong?"

"Sam Higgins," she said with a shaky voice. "He's dead."

I took a step back. "When?"

"They found him this morning. Nothing official on the cause of death. Ziggy said it looked like a heart attack."

"It's never what it looks like around here."

"Sam was a good man." Tears flowed. "A month ago, he was standing right where we are now. Yesterday, we talked in the office. He was a little pale and not himself. I should have said something."

"He wasn't sick, he was scared. Poor bastard must have seen it coming. It's my fault for dragging him into this."

"I set up the meeting." She rubbed her eyes with her fists. "But let's not go down that road."

"He was working on something important for me."

"Do you think that's why he died?"

"You said you saw him yesterday in the office. Your office, in Woodland Park?"

She nodded.

"What was he doing there?"

"He was on his way to Denver and stopped in to say hello." The tears flowed again.

I took a step toward her, and she cried into my chest. I held her for a few moments in silence.

Hattie raised her head enough to see the wet spot her tears had left on my shirt. She pulled back just enough to wipe it with her hand, as if that might remove it. "I'm sorry."

"Don't be." I met her gaze. "Maybe you can help me."

"How?"

"I think he was going to a lab in Denver because of me. I asked him to do some additional testing to see if we can determine what killed Roy. Sounds like he delivered it himself, but I don't know where he might have taken it."

"I wouldn't know anything about it."

"Maybe you or Ziggy can find out."

"That's a big ask. That test probably cost him his life. And it could cost me mine if I go sticking my nose into his business."

"I don't think it's the only reason he's dead, but the fact is, he stuck his neck out to help us. I'd hate to think he died for no reason."

"Dillon," she sighed. "I want to help, I do, but—"

"It could prove Jenn's innocence."

She hesitated before nodding slowly. "I'll talk to Zig."

"I just need a copy of the test results. If there's anything I can do, I'll be happy to help."

"Zig might know what lab they use up there. What kind of test was it?"

"I'd never heard of it." I reached into my back pocket and handed her the paper. "I wrote it down."

Hattie studied it, then slipped it in her pocket. "Oh, I almost forgot. There's a rodeo at the fairgrounds tomorrow night. I usually give Buck a couple tickets, but I thought you and your friend Cooper might need a break from all this detective business. They're yours if you want them."

"I appreciate the offer, but I think I'm gonna have to pass. Maybe next time."

"Suit yourself."

I pulled her back in for a hug. "Thank you. I know Sam was a friend, and I'm sorry for your loss. Please let me know as soon as you hear from Ziggy."

***

I found Coop working on the surveillance equipment when I got home. The package arrived while I was out, and he'd wasted no time getting everything unpacked, assembled, and tested.

I told him about Higgins.

"Jeezus, Bish. We're gonna have to watch our backs."

"I think he might have dropped off the test sample in Denver, but I don't know where. I asked Hattie if Ziggy could intercept the results."

"Let's hope so, or we might be back to square one."

I pointed to the pile of equipment and manuals on the floor. "How does all this stuff work?"

He picked up one of the devices. "We have two of these cameras that we'll install in the barn out of sight. I've got an idea of where we can put them to get the best coverage. They use motion detection and will send the video to my iPad, where it will be recorded. Now, all we need is an opportunity to distract Seth and Frank for a couple of hours."

I pulled out my phone and dialed Hattie's number.

"What are you doing?"

"I have an idea."

I held up my hand to Coop as Hattie answered. "Do you still have those tickets?"

"Sure do. I'm glad you changed your mind."

"I was hoping you might do me a favor and sweet-talk Seth into taking them. We need to get Seth and Frank off the ranch for a couple hours."

"I think I can handle that." I felt her smile over the phone.

"You're the best."

"That's what I've been tryin' to tell you."

I ended the call and looked at Coop. "With any luck, Seth and Frank will be at the rodeo tomorrow evening."

"I'm not even going to ask." He nodded. "I'll be ready."

With that settled, I suggested we discuss everything we knew so far about Roy's case and make some notes. The information we'd been gathering was piling up, and we needed to organize it.

A triumphant smile flashed across Coop's face. "I thought you'd never ask. Come with me."

He led me upstairs and into one of the spare rooms. He opened the closet door and wheeled out a large whiteboard with several pictures taped to it and notes written everywhere. I didn't know what to say.

"It's an evidence board."

"I gathered that. Where did it come from?"

"I ordered it along with the cameras."

"It's brilliant."

He tilted his head and lifted an eyebrow. "*It?*"

"I mean *you're* brilliant."

"That's what I've been tryin' to tell you."

"OK, back to the board. We've got a couple things to add."

He needed to sit down when I told him that Jenn was the one who found Roy. The fact that it had been captured on video wasn't lost on him.

"We need to run through everything we've got and come up with a game plan."

Coop was right. We needed a plan. Seth had the luxury of sitting back and waiting for Jenn to be convicted. His plan was in place. Time was on his side, not ours.

I studied the board. "Hattie? Really, Coop? Maybe if Roy died from smoking too much weed."

"These are the people we know and their connections to each other. Hattie has a close connection with Buck, who, in case you forgot, was a prime suspect for a while. I'd bet money he's got some skeletons in his closet."

"Buck is a crusty old pain in the ass, but I believe he's harmless." I covered my face with my hands, then ran them up through my hair. "Let's start at the beginning with what we know."

"Okay. Roy's journal says that Seth showed up about three years ago looking for work."

"Seth told me Roy asked him to come here and help out while he was sick. He said Roy had some kind of treatments that kept him from doing the work himself."

"Didn't Buck say Seth was the one who brought in the fake doctor and the bogus medication that made his condition worse?"

"That was two years ago. Seth had already been here for a year. He's lying to cover up why he really came out here. He wasn't looking for a job, he had his eye on a big payday. Recreational marijuana was legal in Colorado and Seth probably figured Roy was wasting all this land on a bunch of stray horses."

Coop paused to write on the board. "So, he plays the long game, settles in and works hard to get into Roy's good graces and somehow talks him into leaving him the ranch."

"Then along comes Asha, and Seth is afraid Roy's gonna change the will. So, he blows the brake lines and kills her before that happens. But he couldn't have known that only she would die. I think he was after Roy, and Asha was collateral damage."

More writing. "So, Seth lays low and tries to convince Roy to grow marijuana instead of raising horses, but Roy turns him down."

"Asha's death wasn't a total loss, because her sons blamed Roy and wanted revenge. They get blamed for burning down the barn, but I think Seth was trying to bankrupt Roy's horse business, so he'd have to try something else."

"Like growing weed."

I nodded. "Yeah, but sending the Whitehawks to prison may not have been such a good idea. They might have been able to save Seth the trouble of killing Roy. More importantly, it gave the Whitehawks the perfect alibi. They were both in prison when Roy died."

"Sounds like Seth got impatient and brought in Doctor Death."

Something didn't fit. Too much of a coincidence that Seth just happened to know RMA's hatchet man. At this point, RMA may have gotten impatient with Seth's failed attempts. "What if Seth didn't bring him in?"

"What do you mean?"

"Remember the water pipe I found? Seth made a deal with RMA behind Jenn's back. Maybe he did the same thing to Roy."

"Okay." Coop paused to think, probably searching through the archive of detective shows stored in his brain. "So, he makes a deal for the land thinking it will all be his soon. But it's not soon enough for RMA, so they send in Doctor Death to speed things up."

"Roy wrote that he didn't trust Seth and his doctor. He suspected the treatment was making him worse instead of better."

"If Seth found out, he would have to go to Plan B." Coop dragged an index finger across his neck.

"Seth or Frank. Either one could have gotten impatient. Maybe one held him down while the other gave him the lethal injection. Either way, Seth gets the ranch and the deal can proceed."

"So they thought. They even had a crooked sheriff to falsify the coroner's report and squash the autopsy."

"I'd pay money to have seen Seth's face when they read the will." It was the first time I'd smiled in days.

"Yeah. That created a whole new set of problems."

"Now it's Jenn who's in the way, and Doctor Death conveniently returns as the new foreman." The last part bothered me.

A knock on the front door interrupted our conversation. Our eyes locked briefly before we scrambled to put everything away. Coop pushed the board into the closet while I ran downstairs.

I opened the door to find Sheriff Pecker standing on the front porch with a thumb tucked into his belt and the other hand on his service revolver.

"How can I help you, Sheriff?"

"There's been some trouble down at the jail."

Chapter Forty-One

The sheriff paused, and my stomach did a slow somersault. "Is Jenn all right?"

"She's gotten herself into a bit of trouble."

"What kind of trouble?"

"She started a fight with another inmate. I had to move her to solitary confinement."

"You sure Jenn started the fight?"

He nodded.

"How long will she be in there?"

"Hard to say, but she won't be able to have any visitors."

How convenient for him. "You didn't have to come all the way out here to tell me."

"Just a courtesy. With you being new here and all, I wanted to make sure you understood how things work around these parts."

He let his words hang in the air for a few moments.

I forced a smile. "Well, I sure do appreciate the hospitality I've received since I got here. I'll be sure to tell all my friends in Texas they should think about moving to Redfield."

He forced a smile. "I'm sure Texas is a nice place, too."

I didn't wait around for him to say anything else. I closed the door as Coop came down the stairs.

"What was that about?"

"Sheriff is using Jenn to get to me. Said he had to throw her in solitary after she started a fight. No more visitors."

"Is she okay?"

"He didn't say she was hurt, but I bet she's madder than a wet hen."

Jenn's got a temper, and you don't want to cross her, but this reeked of a plan by the sheriff or his co-conspirators to keep me away from her. Divide and conquer. One down, one to go. I believed the sheriff, Seth, and Frank were working together, so an attack could come from any direction. I was glad we'd sent Alex away. This was about to get messy.

The sheriff had become a bigger problem than I'd first imagined. Initially, he was nothing more than a nuisance, tossing around veiled threats and flexing his small-town, small-minded muscle. But I'd since recognized that the deck was stacked against us. If we were ever going to get any justice in this county, it would have to be from outside sources. I'd have to go over his head. Sadly, I had no idea how far up this cancer had spread.

Ziggy was a friend, and he appeared to be cancer-free, but he was a deputy, he reported to the sheriff. I wasn't sure who Pecker reported to, or who might have jurisdiction over his little domain.

I knew someone who might be able to help. Hattie's husband had been a state trooper; perhaps she still kept in touch with his old partner or other friends on the job who might be able to help. I called her and she gave me a name. Lieutenant Dave Brickman had been her husband's partner and a trusted friend. He worked out of Troop 2B in Colorado Springs. She said she'd reach out to him and tell him to expect my call.

Coop hooked a thumb toward the stairs. "Let's get back to work."

"You hungry?" I asked.

"Always."

My appetite has been AWOL lately, but it was getting late and we should probably eat something. "I'll order a pizza."

Coop pulled the board from the closet while we waited for our dinner to arrive.

"So, can we assume that Frank is back to clean up Seth's mess again?" he asked.

It made sense, but I still had my sights set on Seth. "You think Frank killed Roy?"

"I'm on the fence. That might be the way it plays out on TV, but Seth has the most to gain. RMA's got too much to lose if they get caught killing the landowners who get in their way. That's really bad PR."

I agreed. "Okay, let's say Frank showed up for moral, or in this case immoral, support. He posed as a doctor to convince Roy that he's dying."

"We don't know if the first will had been drawn up yet. If not, that could have been their objective."

"Assuming that was the plan and Roy puts him in the will, he can't kill him too soon without it looking suspicious. He needs to wait a reasonable amount of time."

Coop shook his head. "Frank doesn't strike me as a reasonable kind of guy."

"So, Frank takes matters into his own hands."

"Does he? RMA might have Frank on a short leash after all the trouble he's caused them in the past. Maybe he strong-arms Seth into moving ahead with their plans."

"I can't believe I'm saying this, but what if Seth had second thoughts about killing his uncle?"

That would mean Seth had a conscience. From my perspective, that was a stretch, but I didn't know him all that well. The question was, should I give him the benefit of the doubt?

Coop raised an eyebrow. "Are you jumping off the *Seth-did-it* bandwagon?"

"No. I'm just putting it out there. Feel free to rip it to pieces."

It was true that I wanted Seth to go down for this. He rubbed me the wrong way from the first day we met and it went downhill from there. Truth be told, he reminded me a little of an ass-hat named Josh Wilkerson from back home in Bradley, Texas.

Josh married my high school sweetheart, Nicole Garcia, while I was in Afghanistan. Admittedly, I dropped that ball when I ran off and enlisted right after graduation, but the small-town walls were closing in after my younger brother Luke's disappearance became a cold case. If that was all he'd done, I probably wouldn't have even made the connection.

I returned to Bradley after ten years, when my father died. Something didn't smell right with the circumstances surrounding his death, so I started asking questions and discovered a link to Luke's disappearance. Josh's father, the Bradley police chief who was as crooked as a dog's hind leg, dispatched his son, Officer Josh Wilkerson, to make it all go away.

Josh couldn't scare me off, so he arrested me on trumped-up murder charges. When that didn't stick, he tried to blow me up along with his soon-to-be ex-wife—a nice package deal had it worked. I reckon that's why I made the connection with Seth. That, and their arrogant eyes.

I shook my head to clear it and hoped my disdain for Seth and what he represented wouldn't cloud my judgment.

Coop worked on the board, probably unaware that my mind had drifted.

A knock on the front door interrupted our session again.

"That would be dinner," I said.

I walked the warm box into the kitchen, where Coop already had two cold beers on the table. I breathed in the smell of warm crust, hot pepperoni, and a hint of burnt cheese.

Coop opened the box and let out a nervous laugh. "Looks like the pizza guy left *you a* tip."

"What?"

He turned the box around. A piece of paper had been taped to the inside of the lid. I read it and lost my appetite.

The handwritten note said, "*Stand down or you're next.*"

CHAPTER FORTY-TWO

Coop shook his head. "Day-um, Bish, you're not winning any popularity contests out here, are you?"

I sat and took a long draw on the bottle of Coors that Coop handed me.

He set his plate down. "Who do you think did this?"

"Same person who killed Sam Higgins, I reckon." I nodded. "We're getting close."

"What are you going to do?"

"I'm not going to let anybody or anything stop me from getting Jenn back."

We'd stumbled into dangerous territory again, but this was the first time I'd felt like I had a target on my back since I'd left Bradley. After seven years in Afghanistan, Seth McDonald or Frank Snyder didn't scare me. That's not to say that I wouldn't mind trading the Silverado for a Humvee right about now.

Coop pulled out a slice and took a bite.

"Jenn is the primary objective," I said. "Solving Roy's murder is secondary."

"You're not a lawyer, Bish." Coop shook his head. "Why don't you let Whitaker do what he does best? Granted, we're not detectives either, but we've done this before. Nobody else is working this case."

He was right. As far as ever finding the real killer, we were all she had.

"Finding Roy's killer might be the only way to get Jenn out." His words hung in the air for a few moments.

"Can you keep a secret?" I asked.

"I'll put it in the vault."

"What?"

"*Seinfeld?* The vault?" He looked at me like I should have known this, then waved a dismissing hand. "You're hopeless."

"Can you keep it or not?"

"Sure, I can keep a secret."

I left the room and returned a few moments later. I set a small box on the table in front of him.

He smiled. "For me?"

"Just open it."

He flipped open the lid and shook his head. "I can't accept this. You know I'm already married."

"You think she'll like it?"

"The ring she'll like, it's you I'm not so sure about."

"It's Mama's. She gave it to me before she left. I think she knew I'd need it soon."

"That's great, Bish. I'm happy for you."

"It's not just about me anymore. Alex needs a proper family."

"When you gonna pop the question, *Pop*?"

"I plan to do it when everyone is here for Thanksgiving."

"Then we'd better get moving."

My appetite was back. I tossed a couple of slices on my plate, grabbed my beer, and we headed upstairs to pick up where we'd left off.

I studied the board. "Where were we?"

He tapped the picture of Frank that I had taken on our trail ride, the one Buck had identified as Doctor Richards. "We were debating whether Seth pulled the proverbial trigger, or Frank got impatient and stepped in."

"The surveillance video holds the answer."

"Seth might not be the sharpest knife in the drawer, but if it was him on that video, he probably destroyed it."

"Assuming that Seth was the one who had it. What if Frank set up the camera?"

Coop wrote a question mark next to the word camera on the board, then drew two lines—one to Seth and one to Frank.

"That video might be a get-out-of-jail-free card for either one of them," I said. "If it still exists, it's exactly what we need to identify the real killer and get Jenn out."

"We should be able to tell who took the video by identifying the other end of the wireless connection."

"How do we do that?"

"Well, without Jimmy here, we do it the old-fashioned way. It's called breaking and entering. There has to be a laptop or an iPad on the other end. We might even find some interesting movies to watch."

"I'll bring the popcorn."

"Why don't you call Hattie and see if she got Seth to bite on the rodeo tickets. We can do this tomorrow night."

"Roger that."

Hattie had good news. Seth was all over the tickets and it looked like Frank was going with him. We'd have the ranch to ourselves for a few hours tomorrow night. We planned to install the cameras, then pay a visit to Seth's cabin down by the river. I wanted to ask Jenn if she had a spare key someplace, but regrettably, she was unavailable. We would need to grab that big ring of keys that Roy left and try every damn one of them.

My phone rang and a number I didn't recognize appeared on the screen. Dave Brickman, with the Colorado State Patrol, introduced himself and asked how he could help. He'd reached out to me rather than wait for my call because Hattie had given him the impression that I was in trouble. I gave him a rundown of what had been happening at the ranch. He'd heard of Sam Higgins' passing and was particularly interested in the two different coroner's reports.

We shared a disdain for the reigning sheriff of Teller County, so he understood my apprehension. I explained my theories about Roy's and Sam's deaths, as well as Jenn's incarceration. I told him I needed someone to turn to when I unearthed enough evidence to back up my allegations.

Brickman assured me he was that guy. I asked him to keep my name out of anything that might get back to Sheriff Decker. I mentioned the pizza box threat and my fear that the sheriff might have gone into the pizza delivery business. He said we didn't need any more deaths in Teller County and suggested I do as the note said.

He offered to dispatch additional manpower for the Redfield area until this case had been resolved. In the meantime, he would request the case files and police reports, and he instructed me to turn over any new evidence directly to him.

Before we hung up, I told him about the test samples that Higgins had presumably delivered to a lab in Denver before he died. Brickman said he knew the lab that the coroner used and would intercept the results for me.

This was a huge relief. However, I wasn't about to stand down. I'm not saying I didn't appreciate the additional support, but the investigation needed boots on the ground right here at the ranch.

After ending the call, I let out a breath that I felt like I'd been holding for a month. I filled Coop in and shared Brickman's contact information with him, in case I wasn't able to make the call later.

***

We kept an eye on our suspects all day. When they crossed the cattle guard in Seth's truck on the way to the fairgrounds, we grabbed our gear and headed for the barn.

I didn't like the fact that walking into the barn reminded me of stepping into enemy territory. The ranch had felt like home until Frank Snyder showed up and all hell broke loose. We were alone in the barn, but I had the feeling that Seth or Frank watched from the shadows. I wanted to put all this behind me and move on with my plans.

Coop decided on two good spots to set up the cameras and got right to work. He had done the technical stuff ahead of time, so this mission was about placing the devices and final testing. I didn't have much to do, but I guess I was there for moral support and maybe muscle if someone found us.

With the first camera in place in the front of the barn, we moved to Buck's workshop. I couldn't bring myself to call it anything else. Truth is, I missed the old fart.

I rifled through the shop while Coop worked on the second camera, hoping to find a clue or some additional evidence. I didn't find anything.

"I'm going to head over to Seth's and see if I can get in."

Coop gave me a thumbs-up. "I'll be done here in about ten minutes."

I walked down to Seth's cabin and pulled out the key ring. A light burned in the window, but it didn't appear anyone was home. I had watched Seth drive off the ranch a half hour ago, so it wouldn't be him.

I tried key after key with no luck. There must have been forty keys on the giant ring, and I wondered what they all opened. Key number twenty-two was a winner. I stepped inside and closed the door.

A lamp blazed on the end table near the couch. The place looked rustic but surprisingly homey, and I understood why Seth might have stayed there rather than move into the big house. Nothing seemed out of place, like he had a maid clean up after him. I'm not sure what I suspected, but it wasn't this. I guess I expected more of an early dorm room style, which would have made my snooping easier. I wouldn't have to be so careful about disturbing anything.

I wasn't exactly sure what I was looking for. Coop had mentioned a laptop or iPad, so that's where I started. All this wireless technology made finding things more difficult. Call me old-school, but back in the day, you could follow the wires.

Coop let himself in as I headed to the bedroom. A laptop computer sat on a small desk in the corner of the room. I called for Coop. He opened it up, and we waited.

"Damn it!" I said when the lock screen asked for a password.

"No worries. I expected this." He pulled a little gadget that resembled a flash drive from his pocket and plugged it into the side of the computer.

"Will that get us in?"

He tapped a couple of keys, and the screen changed. "Let's hope so."

Leave it to Coop. A million tiny letters and numbers marched across the screen. They filled it up from top to bottom and kept moving.

"Now we wait."

"How long?" I asked. "We don't have all night."

After about five minutes, the parade ended and numbers began dropping off the screen. I walked over to the window and looked outside. Seth wouldn't be back for at least a couple of hours. I knew that, but I looked anyway. I didn't have the stomach for this line of work.

"How we doin'?" I called from the window.

"Almost there."

By the time I rejoined Coop, a single word, well maybe not an actual word, was all that was left of the digit parade. It sat above a red *Submit* button.

"That's the password?"

Coop smiled. "Let's find out."

With one tap, we were in. He removed the gadget and slipped it into his pocket.

"I don't suppose you can go down to your local Walmart and pick up one of those bad boys."

"A friend of a friend. That's all I can say." He continued navigating his way around various screens. "Here it is."

Some sort of digital dashboard appeared on the screen. A couple more clicks and we were looking at Roy's office. We now knew Seth was the man behind the camera. Finding the video from the night of the murder was probably a long shot, but I asked Coop to look anyway.

He found several video files and began opening them one at a time. The first few showed Roy at his desk or moving about his office. Jenn and I starred in the next one. We rifled through the office looking for Roy's journals, unaware that we were on camera. The next video starred Jenn and Roy on the day of the murder. They talked about ranch stuff and the plans for the Riding Center.

Then he said it. He told her about the new will. Jen looked like her seat had caught fire. She expressed concern about how Seth might take it, but Roy calmed her down. The will was bulletproof. I worried that Jenn wasn't. He assured her Seth would leave in search of another get-rich-quick scheme. All Roy asked of her was to see his plans through.

He showed her the will and told her he needed to have it signed and notarized, which he planned to do the following day. I closed my eyes and thanked whoever up there was looking out for us. Any jury could see that Jenn wouldn't kill him until after the will was signed.

I needed to get a copy of this video to Brickman. Fortunately, Coop was like a Boy Scout, always prepared. He pulled out a flash drive and copied the file.

The video from the night of the murder was not among the files on the computer, but the mission wasn't a total loss. We didn't have a smoking gun, but we had the next best thing. Motive.

CHAPTER FORTY-THREE

I called Brickman the following morning to tell him about the video. His excitement was tempered by the fact that we obtained it illegally. It would be inadmissible in court.

"We took a copy," I said. "The original is still there. What if you got a warrant to search his place?"

"We need probable cause."

I realized that Seth's laptop might be a double-edged sword. We hadn't watched every video. He might have one of Jenn with the dead body, proving she was there when he died.

"I thought I told you to stand down. We don't need any more dead bodies."

I hesitated. "Roger that."

"I have some good news. We found Frank's home base in Pueblo. It's a high-end condo owned by RMA. We're looking into his relationship with the company."

Coop's iPad pinged. I ended the call and joined him at the dining room table. The screen lit up to show Frank entering the barn. He poked around in the office for a while before making a phone call. He left the barn a few minutes later, and the screen went dark.

Coop walked into the kitchen, and I followed him. I'm not sure why. Neither of us spoke. I watched him pour a glass of orange juice.

"You're hovering," he said.

"I'm sorry. I don't know what to do with myself. I hate the thought of Jenn sitting in jail and me out here doing nothing."

"You're not doing nothing."

The iPad pinged again, and we hurried into the dining room. Frank returned to the barn with Seth. They stood together looking at something on Seth's phone.

Seth pointed at the screen. "That's the night he died. I caught her red-handed."

"She doesn't know?"

"Hidden camera."

"Why didn't you turn this over to the prosecutor?"

"I didn't think I needed to. Everyone thought it was a heart attack until Walker Texas Ranger, stuck his nose where it didn't belong."

Frank smiled. "You're just mad because he kicked your ass."

Seth glared. "I've got to go make a phone call."

My stomach moved up to the back of my throat. I swallowed hard. "What just happened?"

Coop shrugged.

How could we be so wrong about this? Who was he going to call? I had to sit. After a couple of deep breaths, I shook my head. No. I wouldn't let myself go there. Jenn didn't kill Roy. Seth was lying. They both were lying. They had to be. So, what were they watching?

My phone rang. Brickman calling.

"I got the test results. The sample tested positive for aconite."

I gave Coop the thumbs-up sign. He nodded triumphantly.

"How did you guys know to test for something so rare?"

I wasn't sure if he was impressed or thought maybe we had something to do with it. "We need to test Higgins for the same thing, ASAP. Can you do that?"

"Sure."

"How soon can you have Higgins' results?"

"I'll put a rush on it. I should have something for you tomorrow."

"What does this do for Jenn's case?"

"It certainly doesn't hurt it."

I asked him to send a copy of the results to Barry Whitaker before I ended the call.

"I'd bet my left nut that Jenn doesn't even know what aconite is, let alone how to kill someone with it."

Coop nodded. "I reckon so. You just need to convince a jury."

I watched the video feed over Coop's shoulder. Frank, now alone, tossed bales of hay onto the conveyor belt.

"Back it up," I said. "I want to see Seth and Frank again."

We studied the clip more closely, which was easier to do after some of the initial shock had worn off.

"It looks scripted," I said.

"Yeah, no Academy Awards here."

"I think we're being played." I nudged Coop. "Maybe I should've stuck around and helped you hide the cameras better."

Coop pushed back. "There's no way they found those cameras that quickly."

A thought came to me as I watched Coop sit there and scratch his head. "What if they had their own cameras and watched us hide ours?"

"That makes more sense." He met my gaze. "They could have cameras in the house for all we know. Bugs, too."

"I wish Jimmy was here to sanitize the place."

A smile flickered on Coop's face. "They might be watching us watching them watching us."

I had to shake my head to clear it after that.

"I didn't see anything on Seth's computer for the barn. Do you think Frank planted the cameras there?"

"We probably should have checked Frank's place when we had the chance."

"It's okay," Coop said. "They want you to believe they've got an open-and-shut case against Jenn. They probably figure if you believed she was guilty, you'd give up and go home."

"Let's see if there is some way we can play them back."

"Yeah, without her you're nobody."

"I wouldn't have put it like that, but—"

"What I mean is, if Jenn's gone you have no standing at the ranch, no reason to be living here."

"Right. What if I tell Seth I'm fixin' to pull up stakes and move on? He might believe it, given my situation."

"They'll no longer have any reason to kill you."

I liked the sound of that. "We won't be able to stall for long. We'll need to move quickly to mount an offensive."

"They'll think they've won and drop their guard. They won't know what hit 'em."

***

Just to be on the safe side, Coop and I searched the house for cameras and listening devices but found nothing. We should have done this as soon as we discovered the camera in Roy's office. I'd hate to think what a disadvantage we'd have been at if they'd been listening to our conversation this morning, let alone over the past couple of weeks.

I called Whitaker to fill him in and suggest a new strategy. Jenn's lack-of-opportunity defense wouldn't hold up if the prosecutor got his hands on that video. She needed to admit she was here, and she found Roy's body. Sam Higgins, God rest his soul, provided us with a better defense when he delivered those test samples to Denver.

The prosecution's case rested on one piece of physical evidence, their smoking gun. Jenn's fingerprints on the alleged murder weapon could have put her away, but the killer screwed up. The evidence was a plant. We knew that for certain now because, rather than leave traces of aconite on the syringe, they went with the more common potassium chloride. Aconite detection requires special testing and could easily be overlooked. We would have missed it had it not been for Coop's obsession with TV crime shows.

High levels of potassium, which are common with heart failure, were found in Roy's body, according to the coroner's report. The killer most likely didn't want to risk handling aconite any more than he had to or tipping his hand to the actual cause of death, so he opted for potassium chloride on the bogus syringe. Without a murder weapon, Jenn's chances had improved considerably.

Reasonable doubt was now a viable option, but the safer play would be to identify the real killer. I'd whittled the list down to two suspects, Seth and Frank. I could make a case for either one, but nothing that would stand up in court without physical evidence.

"One more thing," I said. "Can you sit on the test results for a while?"

"Not a problem. I haven't received a discovery request yet."

"Good. I'm sure Seth thinks the trial is a slam dunk. I want to keep it that way as long as possible. And I'm also having a sample from Sam Higgins tested. My guess is the results will be the same. Higgins died while Jenn was in jail."

"I'll let you know when I get the request."

As long as the legal proceedings were moving forward as planned, Seth or Frank wouldn't feel the need to move to Plan B. I had a bad feeling about what that might be.

***

I opened the hood of my truck and waited for Seth to take the bait. He watched from just inside the barn door as I tinkered around. Frank joined him for a moment before he disappeared back inside. Seth lit a cigarette and continued to watch.

C'mon Seth. Channel your inner control freak and mosey on over here to find out what's going on. You know you want to.

Seth took a long drag then crushed the cigarette under his boot before walking my way. I pulled the dipstick to check the oil as Seth came to a stop a few feet from the front fender.

"Whatcha doin'?"

"Makin' sure she's roadworthy," I said without looking up.

"Going somewhere?"

I pushed the dipstick back in and straightened up. "Isn't that what you wanted?"

He said nothing.

"You won. I'm goin' back to Texas, *where I belong.*" I said the last part with some attitude.

"Where's the boy?"

"Alex. He's there already."

Seth nodded.

"I reckon with Jenn out of the picture, there's nothing for me here."

"I'm sure it's for the best."

I wanted to drop him like a bag of rocks, but I had to stick to the plan.

"You're probably not going to keep the horses. Make sure you find them a good home."

He nodded. "I'll see what I can do."

I offered a sigh of resignation.

"When do you plan on leaving?"

"Got some packing to do. Should be ready to go in a couple days."

"You need any help with the truck?"

What a guy! "Thanks, but I got it covered."

"OK, then."

I saw an opportunity to get some more information before I let him go. "By the way... I think I know what killed those horses."

"You do?"

"Yeah. Aconite."

Seth met my gaze with a confused look. "What's that?"

He didn't even flinch.

"It comes from a poisonous flower called monkshood."

"How do you know that's what killed them?"

"Just a hunch."

He hesitated for a moment, then turned and walked away.

Seth didn't kill Roy. I'm sure he wanted to, but someone beat him to it. Someone with a job to do. Someone with access to knowledge and resources... and satellite phones.

CHAPTER FORTY-FOUR

Coop had watched the exchange from inside the house. He agreed that Seth's reaction appeared genuine. Frank had to be our guy, but he was slippery.

We could spend a lot of time trying to make a case against Frank, but without that critical piece of evidence, and given his high-priced legal team, we might never make it stick. In the meantime, Jenn would be stuck in jail, or worse, convicted on circumstantial evidence by a tainted jury.

We knew Seth had recorded the murder, but we didn't know if the video still existed... until now. If Frank killed Roy, which was the consensus, that video represented a get-out-of-jail-free card for Seth. He had it somewhere. All we had to do was flush it out.

So, the logical thing to do would be to go after Seth. He was no doubt looking at a conspiracy charge and might use the video as a bargaining chip.

My thoughts went back to my last conversation with Brickman. He needed probable cause to get a warrant. Coop and I had probable cause when we broke into Seth's place, didn't we? Whoever was on the other end of the camera in the office might have a video of the murder. A judge should understand that.

Or how about this? Seth is a person of interest in a case where the victim was killed with aconite. It made sense to search his place for the murder weapon, or at least traces of the poison. Either of those scenarios sounded like probable cause to me.

I called Brickman to see what he thought. He agreed to contact the judge about a warrant and told me he'd let me know as soon as he had something.

Waiting had never been my strong suit. I told myself that Frank wasn't going anywhere yet. He'd been assigned to neutralize the Jenn situation. I think he'd planned to kill her until Seth got his friend Sheriff Pecker to arrest her on trumped-up charges. A conviction would remove her from the will without the mess.

Either way, Frank was stuck. Jenn wasn't dead, and she wasn't convicted. The sheriff may have tripped him up when he put her in solitary to keep me from talking to her. Frank may have been able to get to her in the general population. At any rate, he had to see this through. His dilemma offered little solace, other than him staying around long enough for us to grab him up.

A police raid at the ranch might spook Frank, so I called Brickman back and asked him to get two warrants that he could execute simultaneously. The second would hopefully turn up traces of aconite at Frank's condo. He agreed and told me to sit tight until morning.

***

I had a feeling it would be a long night. I paced around the living room after dark, as nervous as a turkey in November.

"Relax," Coop said. "Where's he gonna go?"

I stopped and parted the curtain a couple of inches. I couldn't see Frank's place, but I could see his truck. "If RMA has one of Brickman's guys on the payroll, Frank might be in there packin' his shit right now."

"If it was me and I knew they were coming, I'd go back to the condo and destroy any evidence that might be there."

I turned. "Thanks, Coop. That helps me relax."

"Instead of wearing a hole in the floor, why don't you go pack a go-bag in case he leaves? We'll jump in the truck and follow him."

I nodded. "Good idea." I patted his shoulder and walked toward the stairs. "Keep an eye on his truck."

I threw a duffel on the bed and tucked Pop's .45 caliber pistol, a box of ammo, and a pair of field glasses inside. Some cash and a couple pairs of warm socks went in next. Downstairs, I added some candy and protein bars. I dropped the bag by the door and checked the window.

"I was hoping that would take longer," Coop said.

I shrugged.

"It's cold out there. He's probably watching TV by the fire, which is what we should do. You need a distraction."

"Maybe you're right." I took a deep breath. "I'll get some wood. You find something to watch."

When I stepped outside, I heard something that made me stop and listen. An engine idled in the distance. No lights down by Frank's place. Then something moved in the dark. Frank's truck rolled slowly down the drive with its lights out. I ducked behind the woodpile and watched it roll by on its way to the front gate.

I waited for it to pass the house before I ran inside.

"Grab your jacket. Frank just drove by."

"What? I didn't hear anything."

"I saw him." I grabbed the go-bag. "Hurry. We can't let him get away."

I fired up the truck and tore through the front gate. By the time we reached the main road, there was no sign of him. He had no reason to go south. I turned north and gunned the engine.

A half mile down the road we spotted taillights ahead, and I slowed down. It appeared to be Frank's truck. We followed it to a closed diner on the edge of town. He pulled into the parking lot and waited. We parked and watched from about fifty yards up the road. I pulled out the field glasses and identified the truck as Frank's.

A few minutes later, a sheriff's car pulled in next to him. I held my breath as the driver's door opened. If Ziggy stepped out, we were screwed.

I exhaled sharply when Sheriff Pecker climbed out and placed his hat on his head. Frank exited his vehicle and flipped the glowing end of a cigarette toward the road. They spoke briefly, shook hands, and returned to their vehicles.

I turned to Coop. "I don't like this."

"It looks like they're saying goodbye."

"If he's headed back to Pueblo, I'm calling Brickman."

"The back of his truck is empty. Where's all his stuff?"

"No time to pack. I'm sure he needs to travel light in his line of work, anyway."

Pecker left first. We slid down in our seats as he drove by. Frank pulled out and headed back toward the ranch. He couldn't get to Pueblo that way. Nothing south of here on this route but Cripple Creek and some winding mountain roads, so we gave him some space. I wanted to make sure he was inside before we crossed the cattle guard.

Coop and I made it into the house undetected. Sleep would not come easy tonight, so I asked Coop if he wanted to take shifts watching Frank's place. He told me to shit in my hat.

"What do you think that was with the sheriff tonight?" I said.

"Nothing that can't wait 'till morning."

My mind spun with possible scenarios. "What if Pecker is releasing Jenn back into the general population, or worse, he's planning to move her and he's telling Frank where the best time and place is to get to her?"

"Look, man, I know you're worried. I am, too. But we need to trust Brickman. He'll be here in the morning, and with any luck, Frank will be in custody before he can leave the ranch."

I let out a long breath. "Yeah, you're probably right."

"We've got a big day tomorrow. We need to get some rest."

Good luck with that.

CHAPTER FORTY-FIVE

I awoke to my phone ringing on the nightstand. Sunlight filled the room, and I rubbed the sleep from my eyes as I picked up the phone.

"We're on our way," Brickman said. "I got both warrants. I plan to execute them simultaneously."

I jumped out of bed and hurried to the window. "I'm looking at Frank's truck right now, so he should still be on the property."

"Good. If we find what we're looking for, we'll grab him up on the spot."

"Can you post someone at the gate in case he tries to run?"

"Will do."

I told him about the meeting with Sheriff Pecker and my fear that Frank might be getting ready to bounce, or that something was about to go down with Jenn. He offered to send someone to the jail to keep an eye on things.

"What can I do to help?"

"Stay out of the way."

I didn't make any promises.

Brickman's ETA was twenty minutes. I threw on some clothes and ran downstairs to find Coop pouring two large cups of coffee.

"You're gonna make someone a good wife someday," I said.

"You look like you had a rough night. What time did you get to sleep?"

I shrugged. "Not sure, three maybe."

"When did you last see Frank's truck?"

I attempted a smile. "Not sure, three maybe."

He handed me a cup. "I heard your phone a few minutes ago. Brickman?"

"Yep. Should be here in about fifteen."

"Not much we can do but wait."

"He told me to stay out of his way."

Coop nodded. "Good advice."

I walked over to the front window and sipped the hot coffee as I looked outside. "Have you seen Frank at all this morning?"

"No. I saw Seth earlier, but I think he's back inside for breakfast."

"Let's hope he stays there so Brickman can take him by surprise. I'd like to avoid a shootout at the O.K. Corral."

"What if Frank sees the cops and tries to run?"

"Brickman is planning to seal off the gate."

Ten minutes later, two police cruisers pulled up in front of the house. Coop and I hurried out to the porch where Brickman introduced himself and asked about Seth's location. I told him I'd show him.

Brickman looked at the two of us. "I only have one vest."

I turned to Coop. "Sorry, buddy. I can't have you getting shot again on my account. Stay here and keep an eye out for Frank."

Coop looked like the cheese just fell off his cracker. "Yeah. Will do."

I slipped into the black police vest and opened the passenger door.

Brickman gave me a look across the top of the car. "You're in the back."

I glanced at Coop, who did little to conceal his amusement. I shrugged and climbed into the back seat.

I pointed the way to Seth's cabin. Brickman told me they planned to arrest Seth immediately, cuff him, and try to scare him into giving up the video to save himself. He told me to stay in the car.

I watched from the back seat as Seth met the three officers at the door before they all went inside. Five minutes seemed like an hour. When they finally emerged from the building, Seth wore cuffs, and Brickman flashed a thumbs-up sign.

I got out of the car as two officers pushed Seth into the back seat of the other cruiser and drove off.

Brickman smiled. "He gave up the video."

"Starring Frank Snyder?"

"Wasn't his best performance."

My neck and shoulders released some of their tension. "And Jenn?"

"She'll be free to go as soon as we can do some paperwork."

"Thank you."

"You deserve some of the credit, but we still need to get Frank." He paused. "They found aconite at his condo, so that's two strikes against him."

"Did they find any det chord?"

My phone rang. Coop calling. I looked from the phone to Brickman. "What about the det chord?"

He nodded.

"What's up, Coop?"

"Frank's on the run. I saw him take off from behind the barn."

"Is he headed for his truck?"

"No. The ATVs."

I turned and ran.

"Dillon."

"Frank's running," I yelled over my shoulder.

"Wait!"

I didn't. No one here knew this land better than me. I kicked up a cloud of dust as I ran for the ATVs. An engine whined, and Frank hauled ass toward the upper pasture on Alex's new Kodiak. *How many times have I told that boy not to leave the key in it?*

I jumped on the other ATV. I wasn't so lucky. No key.

"Dillon," Coop yelled, running toward me from the back of the barn. "Key!"

He wound up and threw a strike to my waiting hand.

"Thanks, pardner." I fired it up. "Call Jacob Whitehawk and tell him I have a package for him at the north end of the ranch. Tell him to hurry."

I took off after Frank. He had the better vehicle and a head start. The Kodiak has a top speed of 70 mph. Fortunately, I'd had a limiter installed for Alex's safety that capped the speed at 45. I wasn't sure how fast this one could go, but it was at least 45. I gunned it.

My engine noise drowned out his. I lost him and might have been racing off in the wrong direction. The shortest route off the property was near the pond, where the ranch bordered RMA's fields.

The speed limiter wasn't the only safety feature I'd added to Alex's ATV. I'd equipped it with a GPS tracker. I slammed on my brakes and pulled my phone from my pocket to open the app. *Got 'em!* He didn't appear to be headed to the pond, but higher up. Maybe the clearing where we found him two weeks ago. But why?

I made a quick call to Ziggy and asked him to provide chopper support. I told him to look for the circle of rocks I'd found in the upper clearing, then a half klick southeast for a smaller clearing. He told me the sheriff was in custody, so the chopper could be airborne in under five minutes with an ETA of approximately fifteen.

If I let Frank get far enough ahead to set up a defensive position in the clearing, it could be all over by then... and not in a good way. I wasn't sure what kind of firepower he had with him or if he might have a weapons cache hidden up there in the woods.

I zipped along at nearly 60 mph. Brambles and branches tore the sleeves of the jacket that I wore under the Kevlar vest. My speed diminished considerably when I reached the steeper terrain ahead. I checked my phone. Ziggy should be in the air by now.

A chopper appeared in the distance. Too soon to be Ziggy. *Damn it!* The clearing was an extraction point. I'd bet money that the chopper had an RMA logo on the tail. I needed to get to Frank before that bird landed.

Frank's tail lights flashed through the trees. He sat on the vehicle in the clearing with his back toward me. Probably just got there. Fifty feet was all that separated us. At twenty feet, he turned. No time to stop and dismount. I gunned the engine and jumped as he drew his gun.

I slammed into his body, my hand pushing the gun away as it discharged. We hit the ground hard enough to knock the gun from his hand and the air from his lungs. I gained my feet first and kicked the gun away, but Frank was up quickly.

The popping sound of the chopper's rotor grew louder, and I glanced up to get a fix on its location. Frank took advantage of my momentary distraction. He coiled his body like a snake, then spun his leg around in a wide arc toward my head. I pulled back a fraction of a second late. His foot landed a glancing blow. I shook it off.

Frank had skills. He also had a tell. His eyes moved in the direction of the spin a split second before the rest of his body.

This might be a fair fight after all, but I wouldn't let that happen again.

As we circled each other like two animals in a death match, he pulled a dagger from his belt. I wasn't fooled by its small size. With a little knowledge of anatomy, he could make the four-inch blade as lethal as a shotgun blast.

He lunged at my chest below the ribcage. He knew what he was doing. I stepped back, and the blade missed its mark. He lunged again. This time, I grabbed his wrist. It gave a loud crack as I wrenched it 180 degrees and used his momentum to bury the blade in his side. He let out a yelp that could have been for the stab wound or the hand dangling grotesquely from the end of his arm.

Frank removed the blade with his good hand and tossed it aside as the chopper closed in on our position. The noise from the rotor pounded in my ears. A man with a sniper rifle leaned out of the open helicopter door. I knew how difficult it was to shoot while hanging out of a helicopter in flight. I kept moving.

We continued our circular dance as we exchanged a couple of quick jabs. I noticed his eyes move to the left. A kick followed. I ducked and swept his leg. He went down.

I pounced, but somehow he slipped from my grasp. I jumped to my feet. Frank ran toward the chopper as it descended. Thirty feet. Twenty feet. I ran after him, but the downdraft made it feel like running into a hurricane. I caught up to him before the chopper landed. The sniper slid over to our side to line up a shot, but we were underneath him.

Frank hooked his good arm around one of the skids and yelled for the pilot to take off. I grabbed him by the waist as his feet left the ground. I wasn't about to let him get away with murder. With my feet still on the ground, I used them to push up and then let my dead weight drag Frank down. He lost his grip, and we both fell ten feet to the ground.

A second chopper appeared over the ridge. The cavalry had arrived. Frank's ride hesitated for a moment, then banked sharply and retreated in a hurry. I pinned Frank facedown on the ground, my forearm on the back of his neck, and his good arm wrenched behind his back.

The sheriff's helicopter touched down about thirty feet away and Ziggy jumped out. He ran over to my position and pulled out his cuffs. He had a little trouble cuffing Frank's broken wrist and glanced at me with a raised brow.

I smiled and shrugged. "He started it."

Jacob and Jeremiah Whitehawk pulled into the clearing. They parked their Gator and jumped out.

I asked Ziggy to give us a minute, then walked toward the boys.

"Thanks for coming so quickly." I paused as they frowned in confusion. "I told you I'd find your mama's killer."

Jacob pointed at Frank. "That's him? You sure?"

"One hundred percent."

I noticed Jeremiah's hand twitch, and I stepped in front of him. I shook my head. "You don't want to do that."

He glared for a moment, then pulled a pistol from his belt and slapped it in my waiting hand.

I nodded and smiled. "I can only give you boys a couple of minutes with him, so make the best of it."

Jacob gestured toward Ziggy. "What about him?"

"Let me worry about him. Just stay put until I give the signal."

"What was that about?" Ziggy asked when I returned.

"C'mon, I want to show you something," I said, turning him around.

I put one arm around Ziggy's shoulders and gave a thumbs-up behind my back with the other. The Whitehawks didn't waste any time opening a can of whoop-ass as we walked in the opposite direction. It wasn't a fair fight, but Frank had it coming.

Ziggy tried to turn around, but I squeezed tighter. We stopped and looked out over the ranch below.

"Beautiful view from up here, don't you think?"

Ziggy frowned. "What are you doing?"

"Making good on a promise."

"You know I'm going to have to break this up."

"Yeah, I know. Frank killed their mama. I think they deserve another minute or two."

CHAPTER FORTY-SIX

I waited for Jenn outside the jail. I had to hold back happy tears when she walked through that door in her street clothes. We ran to each other like the end of some sappy movie. She jumped up and wrapped her legs around my waist. We kissed for, well, a mite longer than we should have in such a public place.

"I sure did miss that," she said when we came up for air.

"Roger that."

She smiled. "Did y'all miss me?"

"Like a squirrel misses his nuts."

She gave my shoulder a playful slap. I carried her all the way to my truck, eager to leave this place in the rearview.

"Can we stop at that burger place down the road? I can't wait to get some real beef in me."

I raised an eyebrow. "Are we still talkin' about burgers?"

She flashed that smile that I'd surely been missing. "Keep it in your holster, cowboy. You'll get your turn."

Jenn called Jo from the restaurant and talked to Alex. The world was right again.

***

We had plenty to be thankful for, so Jenn and I agreed to put on a big Thanksgiving dinner and invite everyone who'd helped us through these difficult times. The big day was just around the corner, so we made a few calls. But we knew a crusty old cowboy who didn't believe in phones. He required a personal invitation.

We drove to Hattie's house. Jenn stood next to me as I knocked on the RV's door.

"It's Dillon and Jenn."

The door opened, and Buck greeted us with the biggest smile I'd ever seen cross his weathered face. He invited us in and threw a big hug around Jenn. I settled for a vigorous handshake.

We sat and explained how everything went down.

"With Frank in jail, I'm gonna need a new foreman," Jenn said. "Y'all know anybody who might be interested?"

"Damn straight. When can I start?"

"The sooner the better. Those horses aren't gonna feed themselves."

I witnessed a second smile, this one bigger than the first.

"And we're saving a seat for you at the table for Thanksgiving."

His eyes filled up, and he blinked back a tear. "You don't have to do that."

"We want to," I said.

Jenn smiled. "You're part of the family."

He couldn't blink back the tears any longer and dragged the back of his hand across his face. "I'd be honored."

"Great," I said. "You can bring the turkey."

Buck frowned so hard his bushy eyebrows nearly touched. He glanced at Jenn who shook her head to let him off the hook.

He waived a dismissing hand. "Aaaah."

***

We had to wait until Tuesday for Alex and the rest of our friends and family to arrive from Texas. We kept ourselves busy preparing for our first Thanksgiving together. The guest list included Mama and Mort, Coop and his family, Hattie, Ziggy, Raven, and Buck.

On the way to the airport, Jenn was as happy as a puppy with two tails. I guess I was pretty excited, too. Coop said this was the longest he'd ever been away from Jo and the girls.

After a tearful reunion at the airport, we loaded the baggage and headed home. Mama and Mort followed us in a rental car. Alex and the girls took turns telling stories about their big adventure the entire ride.

Buck waved as we pulled into the drive. He met us and helped unload the luggage. Alex ran to him.

"Uncle Buck," he said as he wrapped his arms around Buck's waist.

I glanced at Jenn. She shrugged.

Buck looked like a fish out of water. He eventually smiled and patted Alex on the back.

Alex showed the girls the empty guest room, and I helped Mama and Mort settle into one of the cabins down by the river.

***

The day before Thanksgiving was a flurry of activity. After the gang had been fed a hearty breakfast, Jenn sent me into town to pick up a few last-minute items at the market. Coop offered to ride shotgun.

"It sure is good to have the family back," Coop said.

"Looks like Alex and your girls hit it off."

"You noticed that, too?"

"I reckon he's got a little crush on one or both of them."

Coop raised an eyebrow. "Maybe you guys should move back to Texas."

I smiled. "I was thinking the same thing, just the other way around."

As we pulled into the parking lot, it appeared everyone in town had the same idea. On the way into the store, a man coming out bumped into me. It felt deliberate. He never said a word, and I watched him walk away like nothing happened.

Ordinarily, I'd have gotten up in his grille and maybe shoved him backward, inquiring about his *problem*. But not today. Today was a good day and tomorrow looked even better. For the first time in a long time, everything seemed right with the world. I let it slide.

Coop put a hand on my shoulder just in case. I told him everything was cool.

I thought about taking Coop to the Wet Whistle for a quick one on the way home, but home is where I needed to be today. I dropped a twelve-pack into the basket, figuring the Red Valley Ranch was as good a place as any to throw back a couple with good friends.

***

Jenn and Mama spent the rest of the day in the kitchen. Hattie had offered to bring the desserts. Ziggy told me that she made the best pumpkin pie in the county. He should know, on account of him being the new Teller County sheriff, and all.

After they arrested Sheriff Pecker for conspiring with Frank and Seth, Ziggy became the acting sheriff until the next election. He needed a new deputy and suggested that the job was mine if I wanted it. The offer took me by surprise. I needed a little time to think about it.

When the big day finally arrived, the house smelled like a five-star restaurant. But surrounded by everyone I knew and loved, it felt like home. I noticed Jenn watching Raven horse around with the kids in the living room. She shot me a sideways glance, her expression unreadable.

I joined her. "What?"

"She remind you of anybody?"

"Who, Raven?"

She snorted. "It's a little scary."

I shifted my weight. "Imagine what I thought when I first laid eyes on her."

Jenn smiled. "I'd rather not."

She left me standing there as she joined the other women in the kitchen to take care of some last-minute details.

I watched the game with the men.

During a commercial break, Coop tapped my shoulder and gestured toward the front door. I followed him outside.

"You gonna do it today?"

"Do what?"

"Don't bullshit a bullshitter."

"After dinner."

"You got the ring?"

I patted the left pocket of my jeans.

"I'm happy for you, man."

"Thanks. I'm realizing there's a fine line between happy and scared to death."

"Why are you scared? She's gonna say yes."

"Maybe that's what scares me."

Mama stuck her head out of the door. "You boys better get inside or you're gonna miss dinner."

Neither of us wanted that to happen.

Before we ate, we took turns mentioning what we were thankful for. I stole a sideways glance at Jenn. Our eyes met, and we had a moment. I could have sworn the same thing happened between Hattie and Buck.

I had trouble sitting still after dinner. The Dallas Cowboys played their annual holiday game on TV, but I had trouble concentrating. I couldn't keep my eyes off Jenn while the girls finished cleaning up in the kitchen. They joined us, and Coop nudged me.

I wiped my sweaty palms on my jeans. "I need a minute," I whispered.

A minute turned into ten, then twenty. I'd been thinking that I wanted to do this in private, then make the big announcement to everyone there. I had to get Jenn away from the crowd.

Ziggy took a seat next to me before I could make my move. "I meant what I said about the job."

"You want me to be your deputy?"

"You'd be a good one. Probably better than I was." He turned sideways to face me. "You solved Roy's murder when no one else could."

I glanced at Coop then back to Ziggy. "I had help."

"We make a great team."

"I don't disagree, but—"

Someone knocked at the front door. Everyone turned to me like I should know who was there. I shrugged and walked to the door, a little relieved by the distraction.

I opened the door to find the man I'd bumped into in town yesterday. I suddenly had the feeling that our earlier meeting was no accident.

"I hope I'm not too late for dinner," he said.

My foot tingled as I sized up the stranger. Something bad was about to happen. "You must be lost."

"I don't think so," he said, looking past me.

Jenn approached and stopped about eight feet off my right shoulder. I glanced at her and didn't like what I saw on her face.

My adrenaline spiked, and I took a defensive stance. "Who the hell are you?"

The man stood still, tall and thin with a nasty scar above one of his beady little eyes. My hands instinctively closed into fists as his eyes shifted from me to Jenn then back.

"Whoa, big guy," he said, holding up his hands. He looked at Jenn. "Honey, tell John Wayne here who I am."

Jenn's wide eyes held a mixture of fear and surprise. She knew him. She gave a tight shake of her head.

I turned to the stranger. "I think you best leave before—"

"My name is Finn Rafferty." He held out his hand for me to shake it.

I did no such thing.

He pointed at Jenn. "That girl, Jenny Rafferty, is my wife."

I looked at Jenn. She stood frozen like a deer caught in his headlights. The others in the room looked away like they wished they were anywhere else.

My temperature rose. I didn't know what his game was, but I wasn't interested in playing. "You best get on your way to wherever you came from and never look back."

He glared at me for a moment, then wisely chose not to be a hero. "Sure. I can see you've got company. We'll talk another time." He smiled and blew a kiss in Jenn's direction.

I thought I'd been doing a good job of anger management, but I still had a short fuse, and this jackass just lit it. "What was that?"

He flashed a smug smile, and I resisted the urge to punch it off his face. I pushed his chest, and he stumbled backward.

Jenn called out from somewhere behind me. "Dillon!"

He recovered his footing and shook his head. "I was hoping that you and I might get along, but I can see—"

"Go on, get outta here."

I had a clear physical advantage, and he knew it.

I watched him climb into his rental car and kick up dust as he drove off. I had an uneasy feeling we hadn't seen the last of Finn Rafferty.

Rain fell as Jenn joined me on the porch. I should have been celebrating as I watched the thirsty ground drink up the water as fast as it fell. It hadn't rained for weeks and folks around here feared that a wayward spark might light up the whole county.

Jenn stood behind me with her arms wrapped around my waist. "Dillon?"

"Yes, Mrs. Rafferty?"

"That's not funny."

I turned around. "You're damn right it's not." I took a deep breath. "What was that about?"

"It's not true."

"You know him. I saw it in your eyes."

"Yes, but it's... it's a misunderstanding."

"You best clear it up quick."

My first instinct was to protect myself. Who was this interloper who turned up out of nowhere with a claim that could shatter one more attempt at mending my ramshackle heart? I'd already had more than my share of folks who'd shown up to steal away the people I loved. I would not be adding Finn Rafferty's name to that list.

Jenn forced a smile and patted my chest. "Why don't y'all come back inside?"

"I need a minute."

After a few seconds of hesitation, she returned to our guests. I felt a little guilty for sending her back in there alone, but I didn't want to say something I might regret later.

The door opened again behind me as I stared out into the rain. She'd best be coming out here with an explanation. A good one.

"Look," Alex said.

I turned.

His eyes were the widest I'd seen them. "It's raining."

It was raining alright, in a way he couldn't understand.

"I did it. I made it rain."

I watched as the skies opened up. "You did that?"

He nodded and held out his fist. I forced a smile and bumped it.

"Just like you taught me." He jumped from one foot to the other, swinging his arms around and chanting.

If it had been any other time, I would have joined him.

"We best get back inside." I picked Alex up and slung him over my shoulder. I turned and stared down the empty drive.

If Finn Rafferty ever came back through that gate, he'd have one helluva fight on his hands.

***

WHAT'S NEXT FOR DILLON AND JENN?

Peace doesn't come knocking. Trouble does.

An unexpected knock on your door when you live in the middle of nowhere is never a good thing. When the man at the door claims to be the husband of the woman you are about to propose to, it becomes a nightmare.

The stranger isn't just after Jenny. He wants the horse ranch she inherited from her uncle. And when threats turn into blackmail, kidnapping, and attempted murder, Dillon swears to protect the family he's building no matter the cost.

But when the stranger is found dead, the tables turn. Suddenly, Dillon is the prime suspect in a killing he didn't commit. To clear his name, he must dig for the truth and uncover the secrets someone will kill to protect. Yet every clue forces him into choices where black and white blur to gray, and one wrong move could destroy everything he loves.

Fire and Rain is the satisfying final installment in the Rain Mystery Trilogy. Pick up your copy today.

A Note from the Author

Thank you for investing your valuable time in reading my novel. I hope you enjoyed the story.

Please visit **www.davidhomick.com** for more information about me and my books and to sign up for my mailing list using the button at the top of the page. You can write to me through the site if you're so inclined. I'd love to hear from you.

Word of mouth is the most powerful promotion any book can receive. If you enjoyed this book, please tell your friends. A shout-out on your favorite social media sites would be cool, too.

I want you, the reader, to know that your review is very important to me and to others that may be considering buying this book. You can leave an honest review on Amazon. It doesn't have to be long, just a sentence or two. Your comments are greatly appreciated, but a simple star review is also appreciated.

Thank you, and I wish you all the best.

Available on Amazon
Time Traveler's Playlist: A Classic Rock Time Travel
Adventure
From Time to Time: A Time Travel Romantic Thriller
Karma Dog: Unleashing Redemption
Changing the Station: How One Stray Dog Found Its Purpose
Don't Curse the Rain (Rain Mystery Trilogy Book 1)
Rain Dance (Rain Mystery Trilogy Book 2)
Fire and Rain (Rain Mystery Trilogy Book 3)
Broken Angels
Reason to Live